ELLE GRAY

BLAKE WILDER

THE
CHOSEN
GIRLS

❀ Created with Vellum

PROLOGUE

THE SHRILL BLEATING of her cellphone jerked Paula Kennedy out of the deep grip of sleep. Still groggy, she rolled over and flipped on the lamp atop her nightstand, then put on her glasses. Paula picked up her phone and pulled out the charger, then looked at the screen. The call was coming from a number she didn't recognize.

Twin currents of annoyance and dread rippled through her. In her experience, when getting a call at two-thirty in the morning, it was either somebody drunk with a wrong number, or somebody with terrible news. Paula took a deep breath and let it out slowly as she connected the call, silently praying for the former.

"Yes?" she asked.

"Is this Paula Kennedy?"

The voice was firm and official-sounding. And they knew her name, which dashed her hopes that it was some drunken idiot. That realization wrapped her heart in a fist of ice and squeezed so tight, she felt like she couldn't breathe.

"Y—yes," she replied, wishing she could be anybody else in that moment.

"Ma'am, this is Detective DeLeon with Seattle PD," he said, his voice reluctant. "I know it's late and I apologize, but would it be possible for you to come down to the station?"

"I—I don't understand. Why would you need me to come down to the station?"

There was a pause on the line, and in that silence, Paula heard her own heart shattering. Every fear a mother has rose in her mind, and she felt herself trembling. Her stomach roiled and she tasted bile in the back of her throat.

"I've already taken the liberty of sending a car to pick you up," said the man on the other end of the line. "They're outside your house already. If you can get dressed and let those officers bring you to the station—"

Paula moved quickly to the window in her bedroom that faced the street outside. Her heart dropped into her stomach when she saw a police car parked in front of her house. A pair of officers leaned against the car, waiting. For her. She shook her head, covering her mouth with a hand, and squeezed her eyes shut.

"Ms. Kennedy?"

Wanting to deny that any of her fears could be proven true, Paula felt herself slipping into outrage. Indignation. It was as if Paula thought if she got angry enough, then none of the terrible thoughts that were rattling through her mind could be true. It was as if she felt that if she could just control the situation, her fears would prove unfounded.

"I don't understand. What is this about?" she asked, her tone icy cold.

"Ms. Kennedy, it would be better if we spoke face to face. So please, I'd appreciate it if you got dressed and went with the officers—"

"I'm not going anywhere until you tell me what this is all about," she hissed.

There was another brief pause on the line and Paula felt her anxiety swelling like a balloon. It grew bigger and bigger until it was so large, it felt ready to burst.

"Ms. Kennedy, I'm truly sorry," DeLeon said. "But we need you to come down to make an identification."

"An iden—identification?"

"Yes, ma'am. I'm sorry, there's no easy way to say this..."

Paula closed her eyes, silently willing him to stop speaking. To not say the next words, she feared would come out of his mouth.

"Ms. Kennedy, I'm sorry to say that we have a body here we believe is... that we believe is your daughter. That we believe is Summer."

A long, keening wail filled her ears, and it took her a moment to realize the sound was coming from her. She gripped the phone tightly, her teeth clenched.

"H—how? How did it happen."

There was a long pause on the other end of the line and Paula's mind immediately jumped to a million different scenarios, each one more horrendous than the last.

"It would be better if we didn't get into the particulars on the phone," Detective Deleon said at last. "Please, just come down so we can talk about it."

Paula opened her mouth to speak, but couldn't force the words out. She shook her head and closed her mouth, silently wishing this would turn out to be nothing but a vivid nightmare. Silently wishing he would tell her this was nothing but some sick, terrible joke.

"I'm sorry, Ms. Kennedy. But I'm going to need you to come down to make the identification and answer a few questions," DeLeon said, his voice sounding almost mournful.

"I—I can't," she whispered.

"I know this is difficult, and I'm so sorry," Deleon responded. "But I'm going to need you to go with the officers I sent over."

Paula felt weightless; like her heart stopped dead in her chest. A cold chill swept through her and she trembled wildly. Tears spilled down her cheeks.

When Paula opened her eyes again, she saw the ground rushing up to meet her.

ONE

I NVESTIGATORS ARE NOW SAYING *the homicide at the Cascades Campground is linked to a series of robberies that run from California to the Canadian border, though this is the first reported homicide. The victim, now known to be retired high school teacher Steven Corden, is said to have been on a cross-country road trip...*

"What a bunch of crap," I mutter.

I turn the TV off and toss the remote onto my desk, disgusted by the news coverage of Mr. Corden's murder. It's been a few weeks since Paxton, Astra, and I found his body in the small lake at the RV park, and then were shot at by some unseen gunman hiding in the woods. The gunman took off on a motorcycle before we could gather ourselves enough to hit back at him. I can still hear the whining engine of the motorcycle echoing through the woods, taking the gunman and all the answers I was seeking along with him out into the night.

"Robbery gone wrong, huh?" Astra asks, her voice wry as she pokes her head into my office.

"Apparently so."

She drops down into the chair across from me and crosses her legs. She looks at me with a small smile curling a corner of her mouth upward.

"Funny. I seem to recall it differently," she says.

"You and me both," I reply. "This robbery-gone-wrong story is totally shades of what happened with my parents all over again."

She obviously hadn't drawn the same comparison, and the smile fades from her face. Astra clears her throat and sits up in her chair.

"Sorry," she says.

"Nothing for you to be sorry about," I reply, giving her a small smile. "I don't expect you to know what I'm thinking all the time."

She takes a beat to gather herself, then points to the stack of files on my desk. "What's all that?"

"All of this," I explain, "is me trying to figure out what Mr. Corden wanted to talk to me about. What it was that got him murdered."

"Any idea yet?"

I shake my head. "Nothing. Not a clue."

Astra leans forward and plucks a file off my desk. Sitting back in her seat, she flips through it, a frown on her face. The file is thin, so it only takes her a moment to finish, and when she does, Astra looks up at me.

"What's with the dossiers on the Supreme Court Justices?" she asks.

"I haven't the foggiest just yet. The only thing those three have in common is that they're all dead," I say. "Justice Sharp died most recently—heart attack. About eighteen months ago,

Justice Boone had a stroke. And a year before that, Justice Kettering died in a car accident."

Astra nods. "Yeah, I seem to remember all of that at the time it happened," she says. "But what does that have to do with anything—least of all with your parents?"

"That's an excellent question. And one I've got no answers for."

I pick a small notebook up off my desk and hold it up for her to see.

"What's that?" she asks.

"Corden's notebook. But all his notes are in his shorthand. I haven't been able to figure it out yet," I say. "The only thing I've been able to figure out is something called 'The Thirteen'. It shows up in his notebook a few times."

She cocks her head. "The Thirteen? What in the hell is that?"

"Because I can't make heads or tails out of Mr. Corden's shorthand, I don't know if it's a who, or what," I tell her. "And because we've been so busy lately, I haven't had a whole lot of time to devote to cracking his code."

"You gotten anything from the locals about the shooter?"

"Nothing. I'm keeping an eye on the investigation, but I'm not feeling really optimistic about it bearing any fruit," I sigh. "I think my best avenue to figuring anything out is following the leads from Mr. Corden. The trouble with that is, if he really was a CIA spook, I know he wouldn't have put everything down in writing. He would have kept some of it in his head— and now it's gone along with him."

"We'll crack the code. We'll figure all of this out," Astra states with more confidence than I feel at the moment.

"I hope so."

My cellphone rings and when I glance at the display, I see it's a call from Marcy Bryant—the local crime blogger and podcaster who has really made a name for herself in the true crime genre, to go with her masterful investigative reporting. She's a smart, intuitive, and driven woman who's really got her finger on the pulse of the city.

She's also Brody Singer's girlfriend. From what I hear, it's even Facebook-official now. Between his technological wizardry and her tough-as-nails investigation skills, the two of them have proven incredibly valuable to both me in Paxton in solving all sorts of cases. They work for the PI firm Paxton founded after he was unceremoniously fired from the Seattle PD a few years back. My team with the BAU is pretty great, but it sure does help to have a link to some people not bound by some of the red tape we deal with within the Bureau.

I connect the call and press the phone to my ear. "Marcy, hey," I say for Astra's benefit. "How are you?"

"I'm keeping busy. I've got two production meetings, three deadlines, an editorial review, and an interview out all just today. Oh, and a tattoo touch-up appointment, too."

"Jesus, girl," I chuckle. "Take a day off to relax, for once."

I can almost hear her eyes rolling through the phone. "Because you're absolutely one to talk, Blake."

I laugh softly. "Touché," I say. "So, what's up?"

"Just wanted to give you a heads up. They found a body floating in the duck pond in McGeary Park," she tells me. "SPD's doing their best to put the clamps on information—total media blackout. Sounds to me like there's somethin' big brewin' out there."

"And I assume you're telling me with the hope that after we go out there and check it out that I'll give you the scoop?"

"Would I do that?" Marcy replies. "I just thought of it as a favor to a friend."

I laugh softly. "You sure know how to charm a lady."

"You're damn right," she chuckles. "Let no one say that I'm not resourceful."

"I would never," I tell her. "And besmirch the name of the best reporter in the Pacific Northwest?"

"All right, all right," Marcy replies. "Enough flattery."

"Hey, I know you've got eyes and ears everywhere," I say. "You happen to hear anything about that murder out at the Cascades RV Park?"

"I haven't. At least, nothing but the official story that it's a robbery gone wrong. You think there's more to it than that?"

"I know there is."

"Huh. Well, let me do some digging and see if I can turn anything up."

"I appreciate that. I also appreciate the heads up about the girl in the pond," I tell her. "I'll tell you what I can, when I can."

"Deal."

"Thanks, Marcy. Talk to you soon."

I click off the call and drop my phone onto my desk then look up at Astra. She flashes me a wide grin.

"That girl is a real go-getter," she says. "Honestly, Brody doesn't deserve her."

I laugh. "To his credit, he seems to know that," I reply. "So, feel like heading out to McGeary Park?"

"Beats sitting around in the bullpen all day," she shrugs. "Let's go."

TWO

McGeary Public Park, Downtown Seattle

THE DAY IS OVERCAST; a light drizzle is falling as we pull into the parking lot. The SPD has set up a perimeter around the park, keeping the press and the gawkers about a hundred yards away from the action. And as if they're trying to downplay what's going on in the park, there are only a couple of patrol cars, a white van marked with the Medical Examiner's logo emblazoned on the side, and a black SUV in the lot.

Astra and I get out of the car and head for the secondary tape line that's strung across the back end of the lot. It's a bit of a strange addition to me, since they've got the front end of the lot blocked off as well. I guess they're worried about people who slip through that first barrier.

"Seems like a bit of overkill to me," Astra notes.

"I guess they really want to make sure nobody gets through."

"Keeping everybody a mile away, then setting up a double barrier kind of defeats the purpose of trying to look low key about everything, doesn't it?" Astra says, gesturing to the scant police presence in the lot.

I laugh. "I'd think so. But hey, we know the SPD's stellar reputation for competence, don't we?"

We badge our way past the cop at the inner tape line and follow a long, winding concrete path from the parking lot that leads deeper into the park. Trees and bushes press close on either side. A hushed silence falls all around us. There isn't an insect or a bird to be heard anywhere. We emerge into a large, round clearing, and in the middle of it is a pond. A concrete footpath winds along the edge of the water with benches spaced evenly around it as well.

I look around at the space. Trees and bushes ring the pond, forming an effective screen, but footpaths lead in and out of the area at the four compass points. Large willows stand close to the pond in a few spots, their long, leafy branches dangling into the water. Patches of reeds and lily pads are scattered around the quiet pool, providing sanctuary for some of the wildlife. This is a popular spot for birdwatchers, as this park apparently attracts some rare and beautiful birds. At least, that's what it said online when I did a quick search after Marcy's call.

"Secluded. Quiet," I observe. "Especially in the middle of the night."

"Perfect place to dump a body," Astra notes.

"Our guy is going to have to be pretty fit to haul a body this far though."

She nods. Distance-wise, it's not a far trek from the parking lot to the pond. And the concrete footpath helps. Our guy wouldn't have had to traverse bumpy, uneven ground. But no matter how you slice it, carrying dead weight requires fitness and strength. It also requires a familiarity with this place. He would have had to have known about it, since McGeary isn't one of the more popular public green spaces in the city—which I'm sure suits the birdwatches just fine. That tells me our guy probably lives in or around Seattle.

Astra and I walk to the edge of the pond and watch as they pull the girl out of the water. She's laid on a stretched-out black body bag, her eyes open wide and staring at the sky. Her face is twisted and contorted, in an expression caught somewhere between agony and terror.

"It never gets easier to see these things," Astra says softly.

I shake my head. "I doubt it ever will."

We make our way over to the body and squat down near the edge of the body bag. The girl was no more than twenty. She has blonde hair that falls to the middle of her back and cornflower blue eyes. She's thin but has full breasts and hips, and cool, pale skin that looks almost waxy in death.

"Jesus," Astra whispers. "Whoever did this really worked her over."

I nod. "Yeah."

The young woman's body is covered in cuts and punctures. Her skin is bruised and mottled in places, and I count at least twenty strange markings on her breasts and stomach. Deep purple bruises form a ring around her neck.

"Her eyes show petechiae," Astra says, peering closely at the girl's face. "Combine that with those bruises around her neck and I'd say we've got a strangler on our hands."

"And judging by the amount of damage he did to her body, I'd say we're dealing with a sadist as well," I say, pointing to the points of puckered flesh on her chest and neck. "What do you think those are? Cigarette burns, maybe?"

Astra nods. "That'd be my guess. Sadistic bastard."

A man I'd guess to be in his mid-thirties takes a knee next to us. He's got smooth, dark skin, dark hair that's cut almost military short, and warm, caramel-colored eyes. He's wearing the blue coveralls of the medical examiner's office and has a friendly smile on his face.

"Eric Young," he introduces himself, his voice carrying a slight Southern twang to it. "Crime scene tech extraordinaire."

I give him a grin. "Blake Wilder and Astra Russo, FBI."

"Feds, huh? And what's so interestin' that it brought the big, bad Feds out to our humble little crime scene?"

"Maybe we just enjoy looking at bodies," Astra replies with a shrug.

Eric laughs and shakes his head. "Dark, Agent Russo. You got one dark sense of humor."

"You have to have an appreciation for gallows humor in our line of work," she points out.

"True enough," he replies. "True enough."

"Do you have an estimated time of death?" I ask.

He shrugs. "She's been in the water a while, and it was cold last night," he responds. "That's gonna play hob with the TOD."

I frown and nod, but I expected the answer. Exposing a body to the elements, not to mention putting it in water, makes getting an accurate reading on temperature and other indicators next to impossible. Not to mention the fact that putting a body in water is going to wash away any trace evidence.

"What are you thinking?" Astra asks me. "Forensic coun-termeasure?"

"Could be," I reply, then turn to Eric. "I know the water did a number on her, but I'm hoping you somehow got lucky as far as trace evidence goes?"

He shakes his head. "Oh-for-two. Hopin' to see if we can find anything back at the lab, but don't hold your breath on that."

I look down at the body and point to the abrasions and

bruising on her inner and outer thighs. "Looks like she might've been sexually assaulted."

"ME's going to have to determine that, but I'd go out on a limb and say you're right."

"Do we have an ID on her?"

Eric nods. "We found her purse tossed over there in the bushes. Name's Summer Kennedy. Nineteen years old and a student at U-Dub," he says. "And before you ask, we dusted it for prints and got nothing."

"So, our killer is meticulous," Astra says. "But why leave her bag in the bushes?"

"Because he didn't care," I reply. "He knew he didn't leave any prints and knew the water would wash away any trace. Our guy is good."

"Creepily good," Eric adds.

"Makes it seem like this isn't his first rodeo, don't you think?" Astra asks.

"Could be," I respond. "Could also be that he's watched a lot of crime TV. Cart before the horse."

"Yeah, yeah, yeah. I know," Astra replies with a smile. "I'll try to keep them in the right order."

"Agents Wilder and Russo."

I get to my feet as Detective TJ Lee walks over to us. He doesn't look hostile exactly, but he doesn't look exceptionally warm or friendly either. Astra gives me a sly smile and a wink, then she and Eric stand and walk off a little ways, engaging in a quiet conversation with him to give Lee and me a little privacy.

"Detective Lee. It's nice to see you again," I greet him.

"You too," he replies. "Though, I'm curious as to what you're doing on my crime scene."

"We got a tip that you had a body. We just wanted to come down and see what was happening. That's all."

"A tip, huh?"

I nod. "We do get those from time to time."

He frowns. "So, what is this? You have no faith in us lowly city cops? Feel like you have to come down and babysit us?"

I laugh softly and bite back the reply that's on the tip of my tongue. The truth is, I have plenty of faith in some of the cops that fill out the ranks of the SPD. Emphasis, some. In particular, what I don't have faith in is the SPD brass. They go out of their way to complicate things. To hide things—especially from the public. They obfuscate and misdirect rather than operate with any sort of transparency.

If the SPD brass put as much effort into working with the public and keeping them informed as they do into their own little Machiavellian schemes, I have little doubt Seattle would be one of the safest cities in the nation.

That has an unfortunate trickle-down effect on the men and woman on the front lines—people like Detective Lee. Personally, I think he's a first-rate detective. More than that, he cares about this city and the people in it. Lee is a guy who eats, sleeps, and breathes his oath. He does his job, and he does it well. But he's always been held back from doing even more because of the department's petty politics.

"It's no reflection on you, Detective Lee. I'd hope you'd know me well enough by now to know I have the utmost respect for you and the work you do," I say.

He purses his lips and nods, then looks down at the ground for a moment, seeming to be gathering himself. He raises his head again and his expression seems to be slightly less frosty.

"So, what are you really doing down here then?" he asks.

"My tipster said that the brass—meaning Deputy Chief Torres—was bending over backward to drop the curtain on this scene," I tell him. "And if Torres is going out of his way to hide something, that never fails to make me curious. Always makes me want to take a peek and see what's behind the curtain."

Lee chuckles to himself and runs a hand through his short black hair. "I suppose that's fair," he acknowledges. "But you have to know that word of you being here is going to get back to him."

I shrug. "Let it. I couldn't possibly care less about what Torres thinks. I don't play politics. My only interest is in finding out who killed this girl," I say. "And I'm pretty sure that's all you care about too."

He pauses for just a moment and then nods. "Yeah. That's true."

We stand together, staring down at the body of Summer Kennedy, the silence marked by the solemn weight of the moment pressing down on us. It's never easy to find the body of a murder victim. But it's even more difficult—at least for me— when that victim isn't really even an adult yet. When they're as young as this girl, with her whole life stretched out before her. Who knows what she could have done? Who she might have become? She could have been destined for great and world-changing things.

But now, her only destiny is a box in the dirt. Everything she could have done, everything she could have been—gone. Snuffed out. And for what? It's a tragedy. Such a waste of life and promise. Honestly, it infuriates me. Every case we take on upsets me. But the murder of a younger person who's only just beginning their life sends me into a deeper, darker rage.

"You know why Torres wants a gag on this?" I ask.

Lee shakes his head. "No idea. You know how the Deputy Chief is," he says. "He always wants to keep the bad stuff out of the news and portray the city as a safe, fantasy world where crime doesn't happen."

"Which of course, only ensures that more crime will happen."

"Exactly," Lee nods. "But he knows how to play the game.

Knows how to navigate those waters and keep himself clean. Torres knows how to insulate himself from any blowback."

"It's going to catch up with him someday. Don't lose heart. That wheel will come around," I tell him. "In the meantime, just keep doing your thing. It's guys like you who do the actual work to help make the city safe."

I have no doubt that Lee will keep doing his job until his dying breath. It's just who he is. Being good police is in his blood. But I can see the toll the job and dealing with people like Torres is having on him. Lee is looking a little more run-down than the last time I saw him. I hate to see it, because Lee is a passionate, talented investigator.

Seattle could use more of him and less of people like Torres. And I silently vow to do my part to shine a bright light on that fact.

THREE

King County Medical Examiner's Office; Seattle, WA

"So, what are we doing here this early in the morning?" Astra asks.

"I thought we'd have a chat with Rebekah before the powers that be get in."

"Ahhh. Subverting local law enforcement again, are we?"

"Seemed like a nice way to start the day."

She laughed softly. "I couldn't possibly agree more."

Astra and I are at the King County ME's office, the day after the police pulled Summer Kennedy out of the pond. Even though Detective Lee and I are playing nice with each other, I don't expect that he's going to share information with me. Which means I need to do the digging on my own. I check in at the front counter and ask the receptionist behind the bullet-proof window to page Dr. Shafer for me.

"You've got that dog with a bone look in your eye," Astra remarks.

"Do I?"

She nods. "You do. I've seen it enough to know what it looks like," she says. "But how do you know this wasn't just a one-off murder and is something we should be interested in?"

"Oh, are we not interested in catching murderers now?"

She laughs. "Of course, we are. But you usually only get that special gleam in your eye when you're thinking there's something big brewing."

"In my experience, sexual sadists rarely stop at one," I say. "It's like that potato chip commercial—you can't have just one, or something like that?"

"You did not just say that," she groans. "Now I will forever associate my favorite honey barbecue potato chip with murder. Thanks for that."

"You're welcome," I reply, flashing her a grin. "But on a serious note, the brazenness of the murder makes me think there are others out there. The fact that he didn't really take care to hide her personal effects and take forensic countermeasures makes me think this is something worth keeping an eye on."

"Careful. You're coming very close to putting the cart before the horse there yourself, boss."

"Just doing my due diligence."

The double doors that lead to the lab area open with a pneumatic hiss and my old college roommate and best friend steps out. Rebekah Shafer is a spritely five-foot-three with fair skin, brown eyes, and rust-colored hair done in a pixie cut. She's always been a fireball and a bottomless well of energy. Her smile is wide open, warm, and totally infectious. That's been her personality since our college days.

"How are you doin', babe?" she asks.

"Good. I'm good, thanks. And yourself?"

"Underpaid and overworked," she replies. "The usual."

"I hear that," I say. "You remember my partner, Astra?"

"Yeah, of course. Nice to see you again, Agent Russo."

"Just call me Astra."

"Will do," she chirps, then turns to me. "And I assume the fact that you're holding a cup from Starbucks and a bag of donuts from my favorite place that you're here to pump me for information that I'm not supposed to be sharing."

"And this is why I love you, Beks," I chuckle. "You actually are the brightest crayon in the box."

She laughs and nods to the receptionist who opens the doors for us. We walk through and follow Rebekah through the labyrinth of corridors, finally coming to her office, which seems to be a reflection of her personality. It's all done up in bright colors with a bookcase full of kitschy knick-knacks and photos of her and some of her friends in various places, all of them with wide smiles on their faces. It's not like the offices of some of the other ME's I've dealt with over the years. Most of them seem to embrace the dull, lifeless atmosphere of a morgue. Not Rebekah though. She's far too vivacious for all that.

Rebekah ushers us inside and I set the bag of donuts and coffee down on her desk. She drops down into her chair as Astra and I take the seats across from her. Rebekah takes a sip of her coffee, then opens the bag and peers inside, a wide smile crossing her face almost instantly.

"They're still warm," she says as she pulls an apple fritter out of the bag.

She takes a bite, and the groan of pleasure that escapes her is positively obscene. But then she wipes her mouth with a paper napkin and smiles.

"You know exactly how to butter a girl up," she says.

"We do our best."

"So, which body are you wanting to take a look at today?" she asks.

"Summer Kennedy," I reply.

"Of course, you are," she replies. "The one body the SPD put a gag order on. Just one of these times, I'd love it if you asked me to see a body that doesn't risk my job to show you."

"That doesn't sound like the Beks I know and love. Where's the fun and adventure in that?" I reply with a laugh.

"A gag order?" Astra asks.

She nods. "No information to any news outlet who comes calling," she tells us. "Or to anybody else, for that matter. I have to assume that's probably aimed at you."

"It wouldn't surprise me," I shrug.

"Can't take this one anywhere," Astra cracks.

"Don't I know it," Beks says with a laugh. "Well, come on then. I'm assuming you timed your visit so we didn't run into any of my bosses, so let's not waste the time."

We all get to our feet and Rebekah leads me out of her office and down a long corridor to the autopsy suites. She looks around furtively before opening the doors and letting us in. We follow Rebekah over to the bank of refrigerated trays, the stainless steel gleaming dully in the fluorescent lights overhead. She checks the tags on the doors and finds the one she was looking for and pops it open. Reaching inside, she grabs the handle on the tray and pulls it out.

The body is covered by a blue sheet that Rebekah pulls back to reveal the body of Summer Kennedy. She pulls it down to just above the breast line, revealing the top of the Y incision left behind by the autopsy. Her face is pale and her skin is waxy. In death, the bruises around her neck stand out even more than they did at the scene yesterday.

"I'm guessing the cause of death was manual strangulation," I start.

"A cookie for you," Rebekah replies.

"What else can you tell us?" Astra asks.

"I didn't actually do the autopsy, so give me just a sec," she says.

Rebekah goes over to the desk in the corner and flips through the charts hanging on the wall. As she does that, I look down at Summer's face and feel a pang of pity. She was just nineteen years old and had her entire life ahead of her. She was far too young to have had her life snuffed out.

Beks and I were her age when we first met. Some of those memories come flooding back as I stare down at Summer's face; they really don't seem so long ago.

"All right, it appears she was sexually assaulted and tortured. We found no fluids though, so our perp either used a condom or the water she was dumped in washed it away. We can't determine that at this point. And wow, this guy really gave her a beating," Rebekah mutters as she flips through her chart. "There are over two dozen cigarette burns. Multiple cuts and punctures. She had three cracked ribs and took a hell of a beating, though only on her body. Strangely enough, your unsub didn't hit her in the face."

"Wanted to keep her pretty," Astra notes. "Just like Gary Suban."

I nod. The similarity to a case we handled a few weeks ago, where a serial killer would assault and murder young women, then make up their face to preserve their beauty, isn't lost on me.

"Sadistic prick," Rebekah adds. "Anyway, abrasions on the wrists and ankles suggest she was restrained while she was getting worked over."

"Do we have the tox screen yet?" I ask.

Rebekah shakes her head. "Unfortunately, we aren't going to have those back for a while," she says. "The lab has a major backlog of cases they're trying to get through. Not even I can cut that line."

"That sucks," Astra sighs.

"Have any other cases come through recently that match this one?" I ask.

Rebekah shakes her head. "None that come to mind. But we're a pretty big office, so I don't know every case that comes through," she replies. "I can take a look through the files to see, if you'd like?"

I shake my head. "No, don't worry about it. But thanks," I tell her. "We can look into it."

"Blake is bored and needs a serial killer to chase," Astra quips.

"She does that sometimes, doesn't she?" Rebekah says with a grin.

Astra nods. "Yes, she does."

"You guys are hilarious," I remark dryly. "Like I said, I'm doing my due diligence. Sexual sadists—"

"You're not going to try to ruin my favorite chips again with that horrible metaphor, are you?" Astra responds.

"Well, not now."

"Chips?" Rebekah asks.

I shake my head and smile. "Forget it. It's just Astra being Astra."

"Guilty as charged," Astra says.

"Think you can slip us the tox screen results when you get them?" I ask.

Rebekah nods. "Yeah. I can manage that. Might cost you coffee and a couple more apple fritters though."

I laugh. "I think I can manage that."

"Deal," she grins. "Now, you two had better get out of here before my bosses get in."

"We're gone. And thanks, Beks," I say, then lead Astra out of the autopsy suite.

FOUR

Wilder Residence; The Emerald Pines Luxury Apartments, Downtown Seattle

ELLA FITZGERALD's smooth and sultry voice fills my apartment as I pour myself a glass of chardonnay, then carry it over to my desk and take a seat. As my laptop boots up, I take a drink of my wine and let the soft music wash over me, trying to clear my mind of the mental detritus accumulated over the afternoon. Ordinarily, I'd light some candles and take a long, hot bath, but I haven't been able to shake the situation with Mr. Corden's murder and trying to find the link to my parents.

It's been a long, long time since I've felt this spark of anticipation about their case. There just hasn't been any new information to get worked up about. But with everything that's happened with Mr. Corden, I feel like there's been some movement. I feel like I have a new lead to follow. But because I can't crack Mr. Corden's shorthand, it feels like a dead end. It's not. The answer is there, I just can't get to it. Not yet, anyway.

I open the file sitting next to my laptop and look at his

notes. His scrawled, chicken scratch handwriting is tough enough to decipher on its own, but his shorthand—his personal secret language or code—makes it almost impossible. The only thing I've been able to interpret so far is the name The Thirteen. I don't know what it is or what it means. I don't know if it's a person or a thing. And not being able to figure it out is driving me bananas.

When my computer comes up, I call up all the databases and search engines I can think of and start the hunt all over again. I've been running a search for this Thirteen, whatever it is, ever since I interpreted that in Mr. Corden's notes. But no matter how many times or different ways I've run a search, I've come up empty.

I take a sip of my wine and stare at the blinking cursor in the search box, trying to figure out a way to run the search that I haven't yet thought of. I try a couple of things, but the results don't change, and I let out a growl of frustration. As I sit before my computer cursing up a storm under my breath, I hear the front door open and a set of keys hit the small table in the entryway.

"I've got Thai," Mark calls as he closes the door behind him.

He walks in with a bag from the new Thai restaurant down the street from my place that we've been to a few times. Mark sweeps into the kitchen and sets the bag on the counter, then turns and walks over to me. He places a kiss on the crown of my head and then he stops. I feel his body tense up as he takes a step back.

"Are you working on your parents' file again?" he asks.

I nod curtly, already knowing exactly where this is headed. "I am."

I turn and see him frowning down at me and immediately feel myself growing irritated. This is a conversation—or rather, an argument—we've had before. But we've had it even more so since the night out at the RV park when Astra, Paxton, and I were shot at. Since that night, he's been insistent that I drop the case.

"I thought we talked about this," he says.

"No, it's more like you talked at me about it."

"Fine. But I thought we agreed that things were getting too hot and that maybe you needed to back off. At least for a little while."

I stand up and walk to the kitchen to refill my wine glass with Mark following close on my heels. Standing with my back to him, I pour the wine, doing my best to keep from exploding.

"Blake? Didn't we agree that—"

I take a mental five-count, then turn around as calmly as I can. "No, you said you thought I should back off. I never agreed to anything."

"Somebody shot at you," he replies, his voice growing tight with anger. "Doesn't that mean anything to you?"

"It means I'm getting close to something. It means somebody thought Mr. Corden had information and they didn't want me to have it," I growl.

"Okay, fine. Somebody didn't want you to have the information. I get it," he shoots back. "But is it really worth getting killed to solve something that happened almost twenty years ago? Is it really worth damaging our relationship, chasing some truth that isn't going to change anything anyway?"

I take a long swallow of my wine, mainly to keep from screaming at him. That he'd say something like that not only fuels the anger already burning in me but also hurts me deeply. It's like he heedlessly ripped the scab off an old wound. It's about the most thoughtless, most callous thing he's ever said to me.

"I'm sorry if my parents being murdered and my sister

being abducted is inconvenient for you," I snarl. "But maybe if you'd had somebody you loved brutally murdered, you'd understand what I'm going through."

He recoils like I'd just slapped him, with a stricken look on his face. But that expression quickly melts away, replaced by one of anger. His eyes narrow and his jaw clenches. Both of us fall silent for a long moment, the unspoken tension between us crackling like thunder.

"I didn't mean it like that, and you know it," he said. "I'm just worried about you, Blake. You're... obsessed. It's not healthy. I'm sorry if my concern bothers you so much."

"This isn't about you or how you feel, Mark," I spit. "This has nothing to do with you."

"Maybe not directly, but I have to deal with the fallout. Not only do I have to see what you put yourself through, I have to sit and wonder if you're coming home that night, or if I'm going to have to go the morgue to ID you," he shouts.

I manage to bite back the scathing reply that's sitting on the tip of my tongue. But just barely. His concern is sweet but it's also annoying at the same time. No, actually, it's infuriating. He's not only turning this around on me but is also somehow making it all about himself. But my main issue is that I feel like the fact that we're dating makes him think he's entitled to tell me what to do, or guilt trip me about how my career choice makes him feel. It's a bad habit I need to break him of. Either that or we're going to need to re-evaluate our relationship.

"You do realize I'm a federal agent, right?" I ask. "And that once in a while, I'm going to get shot at. It's an occupational hazard. I can't deal with you freaking out every time things get a little intense, Mark."

"A little intense? No. Arguments in a grocery store parking lot can get a little intense," he raises his voice even louder. "Getting shot at is something else entirely. It's insanity."

"It's my job!" I shout back.

"This isn't. Correct me if I'm wrong, but what happened to your parents is not an FBI case. It's your personal obsession," he fires back. "Look, I'm sorry about what happened to them. I really am. But you getting killed to avenge a twenty-year-old memory isn't going to bring them back. It's only going to get you as dead as they are."

I stare at him in a stunned and furious silence for a long moment. The fires of rage building inside of me burn out of control, scorching through my veins and leaving me to see red. His words not only infuriated me, they cut me to the quick.

"How dare you," I hiss. "How dare you say something like that to me."

Mark's eyes widen and his mouth falls open as if he's only just realized what he said. He runs a hand through his hair and shuffles his feet, seeming to be trying to find his footing again. He knows he screwed up. I can see him trying to find a way to mitigate the disaster this evening has become. But so far as I'm concerned, there's no coming back from something like that. His words were cruel and stung me deeply.

"I'm sorry, Blake. I didn't mean it that way," he attempts, his voice soft.

"Really? Because it certainly sounded like you meant it that way."

"Listen, I—"

"No, I think I've heard enough," I cut him off. "I think you need to leave."

"Blake—"

"No. Please leave. Now."

He sighs heavily and rubs his chin, the stubble on his face making a dry, scratchy sound. Mark frowns, a pained look etched upon his face.

"Can we talk about this?" he asks.

"I think you've said enough," I hiss. "Now leave. Go. Get out of my house."

He opens his mouth to object, but closes it again without saying anything. He stares at me for a long moment, pleading with his eyes for me to give him a reprieve. But I can't even stand the sight of him right now.

He frowns when I don't say anything or offer him another chance and nods to himself. He turns and walks out of the kitchen, and I stand there listening in my silent fury until I hear my front door close.

When I'm alone again, I down my glass of wine and pour another, fighting back the tears. Getting blindingly drunk seems like a good idea to me right about now.

FIVE

"YOU HAD A FIGHT WITH MARK, HUH?"

I look up at Astra, who saunters into my office and drops down into the chair across from me with me a smile of feigned innocence.

"What makes you say that?" I ask.

"Because when you've had a fight with him, your brow is usually furrowed, and you get that little crease between your eyes."

"I get that when I'm concentrating on something."

She shakes her head. "Actually, you don't," she replies. "You only get that little crease between your eyebrows when you've had an argument with Mark."

I laugh and drop my pen on my desk as I sit back in my chair. "You're so full of it."

"Sometimes," she admits. "But in this particular case, I'm simply a keen observer of people and the world around me."

"If you say so."

"I do," she replies. "So, what was the fight about?"

I roll my eyes and let out an exasperated breath. I've been doing my best to avoid thinking about it all morning. Not that I've had all that much success, but I've been trying. Astra is staring at me expectantly, legs crossed, hands folded in her lap —the epitome of patience. Or stubbornness. I'm not entirely sure which it is with her.

"Would it matter if I said I didn't want to talk about it?" I ask.

"Not even a little bit."

The memory of our argument scrolls through my mind like some horrible highlight reel and makes me wince. For a man supposedly so concerned about me, he certainly knows how to get under my skin, and not in a positive way. And judging by how steamed I still am some ten hours later, he's still under my skin.

"Out with it, Wilder," she presses. "Keeping all that angst and anger stuffed down inside will kill you. It's poison in your veins."

"I think it's more a case of you being nosy as hell."

She shrugs. "Yeah, it could be that too."

We share a laugh as I rub my temples. If there's anybody I'm going to talk to about this, it'll either be Astra or Maisey. I might as well purge now. If I emotionally vomit all over her and get it out of my system, maybe I'll be a functioning human being by the time we get to Paula Kennedy's house.

"Okay yeah, we had a fight last night," I finally admit.

"Duh. You say that like I didn't already know that."

I self-consciously rub that spot between my eyes where she says I carry a crease when I fight with Mark. I don't feel anything, but that doesn't necessarily mean she's wrong. Astra is one of the most observant people I know. Her ability to pick up on stuff like this is sometimes frightening. Other times, it's creepy as hell. The one thing that's certain is that Astra usually doesn't miss a thing.

So, I tell her all about my ever so fun evening. She settles back in her chair and her eyebrow rises a couple of times, but she says nothing as I tell her my story. And when I finish, I flop back in my seat like I just exerted myself. I'm already ready to go home and have a glass of wine or two. The fact that it's just after nine in the morning doesn't matter. It's got to be happy hour somewhere, right?

"Ho-lee crap," she whistles. "I imagine kicking him out didn't go over well."

I shrug. "Haven't spoken with him yet today."

"Yeah, he's probably still asleep on a park bench somewhere."

"Give me a break," I reply with a laugh. "It's not like he doesn't have his own place."

"Does he?" she asks, arching one of her perfectly detailed eyebrows. "I just figured he was living with you now."

"Yeah, that would be a big no. I'm not ready to share a space with somebody," I tell her. "Anyway, that's what the blowout was about."

"So, on one hand," she starts, "I understand that he was concerned about your safety."

"Seriously? That was your takeaway?" I sputter. "Did you like, not listen to anything I said?"

"Hold on there, firecracker," she holds a hand out to settle me down. "I'm not done. Look, on a certain level, he's right. Your job does put you in dangerous situations, and that can affect him. In a relationship like that, you have got to give him space to express himself. He's got to be allowed to share his concerns with you. The fact that you are sometimes put in life or death situations... he's going to have a feeling about that. And if you two are together, he's got a right to his feelings."

"But—"

"Oh my god, I said I'm not done," she interrupts.

I relent, giving her back the floor.

"I already know what you were gonna say, and I agree fully. Even with all that considered, he doesn't have a right to put his feelings on you the way he does. Nor do his feelings give him a right to try and make decisions about your life and career, and they *especially* don't give him a right to cross the line like that about your family."

"I seriously can't believe he went there," I sigh. "I've never seen that kind of cruel streak from Mark."

"I have."

"What?"

"Don't you remember? The last time you kicked him out. Back during the Suban case. It was pretty much about this same thing, right?"

"Sort of? It was more about privacy in relationships. Because I blew up on him about his phone, and he blew up on me about my therapist," I say. "I'd gotten the call from Mr. Corden about my parents and didn't want to tell him what it was about."

"Exactly. He didn't even know what was going on and he went out of his way to mock you. Pretty cruel, if you ask me. You deserve to feel heard in your relationship, not... dismissed."

I sigh. "It's just sensitive for me. It's like he wants me to put both my career and my parents' case aside to prioritize my relationship with him, when I'm not necessarily sure if that's a thing I can even do."

"Bingo," she says. "And do you want that? If you intend on being with him for the foreseeable future, this argument will never go away. It'll just be the thing you argue about. Both your parents' case and your general safety. Is that something you want to deal with?"

"I told him when we got together that my job will always come first," I tell her. "How am I supposed to do my job if I have to hear his voice in the back of my mind telling me not to do this or do that because Mark is afraid I might get hurt?"

"You were an FBI agent before you met him. Unless he's a total idiot about what it is we do here, he knew going into things with you that your job entailed some risk. Hell, the two of you met while we were recovering from gunshot wounds after that Briar Glen case. So, while he has his right to express his feelings, he needs to understand not to center himself in these discussions. It's you who's putting yourself in danger. It's your life and your family you're dealing with. Not his. It's not his place to prioritize himself over that."

I run my fingers through my hair and stare at her. I remember a time not all that long ago when Astra was taking random guys home from the bar and now, after a few months with Benjamin, she's dispensing relationship advice and wisdom like she's Oprah.

"Who are you?" I ask. "And what did you do with my best friend?"

She smiles. "I'm just a girl who feels heard in her relationship."

"I don't buy it. You're like a pod person or something."

"For what it's worth, I do think it's genuine. He cares about you. And he's scared for you," she says. "I don't know. Communication is hard in relationships. But you guys have some serious challenges you need to deal with."

I take a sip of my coffee then set the mug down. "You kind of sound like you're hedging your bets here. He either cruelly crossed the line, or he just can't communicate his feelings properly?"

"That's not hedging. That's just the truth. But I know you; you're not going to change. This is who you are and always have been," she responds. "So, what I'm saying is that Mark has some major life decisions to make. If he can't handle the fact that you've got a dangerous job, maybe you're not the right fit for him."

I drum my fingers on my desktop. "That's a thought I've been having more and more lately."

"Does he know this?"

I shake my head. "No, not yet," I reply. "I'm just trying to get my head on straight. I need to figure out what's going on in my brain."

"That's a good place to start," she nods. "I think these are all basically symptoms of the bigger picture. Your career, your parents' case, your safety—basically, it seems like the thread running through all of it is that you don't know if this relationship with Mark is worth putting all those aside for. And the first thing you need to do is figure out what you want. It almost sounds like Mark is going to reach a point where he makes you decide between him and your parents' case."

"Giving me an ultimatum is about the stupidest thing he could do."

"I'm not saying he will. I'm just saying he could. Or he could make the decision for you," she replies. "One way or the other, you're going to have to decide what's most important to you—a future with Mark, or you continuing to work on your parents' case."

I sigh. "I hope it doesn't come to that. I really don't think anybody would be happy."

"It's going to be difficult. I'm sure being with someone who takes the kinds of risks you do is nerve-wracking. But it's also not easy to be with someone who won't support you and embrace you for who you are."

"I don't take risks," I protest.

Astra rolls her eyes. "You have got to be kidding me. You are so full of crap right now."

"I don't take unnecessary risks," I amend my statement. "And you take the same risks I do."

"Yeah, but I'm with somebody who doesn't get all freaked out about it," she replies with a sly twinkle in her eye. "Benjamin thinks the idea of us kicking in doors is kind of hot."

We share a laugh, which is followed quickly by a thoughtful silence. She's made a lot of really good points and has given me a lot to think about. There's no question about that. And she's right, I need to figure out a lot of things on my own before the situation with Mark becomes more untenable than it already is.

"My two cents—"

"I think you've given me about fifty dollars' worth already," I cut her off.

"Shut up," she grins. "I think you two just need to have a long talk. Y'all both need a come-to-Jesus moment to see where this thing between you is going. Or if it's going anywhere at all."

She's not wrong. She's not wrong at all. I'm going to have to give some more thought to it. But right now, we've got work to do, so I get to my feet.

"We need to go talk to Summer Kennedy's mother," I tell her. "It's been long enough. The SPD should have already interviewed her, so it's our turn."

"Running a shadow investigation?"

"Unless you object."

"Oh, hell no," she says. "If it involves making that prick Torres look bad, I'm all in."

"Excellent."

SIX

Kennedy Residence; Ballard District, Seattle, WA

"You're really going hard on this," Astra says. "Like I said, dog with a bone."

"I just have a feeling about this. The bells are going off in my head," I tell her.

She nods as I pull the car to a stop at the curb and cut the engine. Astra looks at me for a long moment, a sly smile curling a corner of her mouth upward.

"Are you sure you're hearing bells? Or is this you creating work for yourself so you can avoid going home and dealing with Mark?" she asks.

I raise an eyebrow. "Are you seriously asking me that question right now?"

She shrugs. "Seems like a fair question to me."

"Come on. You should know me better than that," I tell her. "But if you'd like, I can take you back to the shop and you can help Mo and Rick track the ATM bandits I assigned them to."

"Hard pass, thanks," she says with a laugh. "I'll go with your gut on this one."

"And has my gut ever steered you wrong?"

"Not lately."

"Not ever," I correct her.

We laugh as we get out of the car. I pause and look around what looks like an upper-middle-class neighborhood. The street is lined with tall trees with wide boughs that stretch out, almost forming a tunnel over the road. All the homes are large and well-kept, the yards are well-tended, and the street is quiet. It looks like a nice place to raise a family.

We cross the street and follow the walkway lined by colorful flowers on either side up to the stairs that lead to a wide porch. There's a swing on one end of it, along with a pair of large chairs with plush cushions. The front door is white with brass fixtures and has a frosted glass window etched with flowers. It's beautiful.

I reach out and push the button. Inside, I hear the soft chime of the bell sound. A couple of moments later, the door opens, revealing a woman—or rather, the ghost of a woman. She's about five-foot-four, with disheveled shoulder-length blonde hair. Beneath her bloodshot blue eyes are dark shadows, her skin is waxy, and her face is drawn and pale. She looks like she hasn't slept in days.

"Mrs. Kennedy?" I ask.

"Paula," she replies, her speech slightly slurred.

Astra and I flash our badges. "SSA Blake Wilder, and this is my partner, Special Agent Astra Russo," I introduce us. "May we come in? There are a few questions we'd like to ask."

Without saying a word, she turns and walks deeper into the house, leaving the door open. Astra and I glance at each other and she shrugs, so we step inside. Astra closes the door behind us and we follow Paula past the formal living room on our right

THE CHOSEN GIRLS   41

and a dining room to our left. We pass the staircase and walk
down the long hallway to the back of the house.

A bonus room opens to our right. An oval oak and glass
coffee table is in front of a large couch and a loveseat sits
perpendicular to the sofa. It's a beautifully decorated house.
Everything is done in soft earth tones. A large flatscreen TV
hangs on the wall across from the sofa, currently tuned to some
trash reality show. I don't think Paula was actually watching it
though, because the sound is muted, and the coffee table is
littered with vodka bottles. The air in the room is stale, as if a
breath of fresh air hasn't passed through in ages. Underneath
that is the smell of sweat, cigarettes, and booze. But the most
pervasive odor in the air is this woman's grief.

Paula is leaning against the sink side of a floating island in
the center of the kitchen to our left. It's thoroughly modern,
with all black and white tile and stainless steel appliances. All
the bells and whistles. It's gorgeous. Makes me think of my own
kitchen, which seems tiny in comparison, I find myself feeling a
little jealous. I stuff that all down though and focus on the
sobering reason we're here. This woman clearly takes a lot of
pride in the upkeep of her home, but to see her lost and broken
like this is utterly heartbreaking.

Astra and I step over to the island and are standing on the
other side of it, across from Paula. She sways on her feet, and
even from where I'm standing, I can smell the vodka. It's
obvious that she crawled into a bottle when she got the news
about her daughter and hasn't climbed out yet. I can't say that I
blame her. I know the pain of loss well, and God knows I've
been tempted to self-medicate with booze more than once.

Paula lights up a cigarette and takes a deep drag, then
blows a plume of smoke to the ceiling. She looks at the cancer
stick in her hand like she's not sure how it got there, then shakes
her head.

"I quit, you know. Hadn't had one in twenty years. When I found out I was pregnant, I stopped cold turkey," she mentions, her voice quavering. "Not until the other night. Seems like I've had one of these damn things in my hand every single minute."

"Mrs.—Paula," I start. "We're very sorry for your loss. We can't imagine how painful it must be to—"

"I know these things will kill me, but what's there left to live for anyway?" she goes on as if I hadn't spoken. "Husband's dead—cancer, ironically enough. Now my Summer. I've got nothing left to live for, but don't have the courage to kill myself."

"Paula, I know it's hard to see through your grief right now, but you've still got a lot of life ahead of you," Astra says. "The pain will fade in time. And then—"

Paula's head snaps up and she narrows her eyes at Astra. "Have you ever lost a child, Special Agent Russo?" she spits. "Actually, have you ever had to bury a husband *and* a child?"

Astra lowers her eyes and shakes her head. "No ma'am."

"Then you don't really know what you're talking about, do you?"

Tears spill from the corners of her eyes and race down her sunken cheeks. Paula takes another drag from her cigarette and angrily blows out the smoke.

Astra cuts a glance at me, then turns back to the grieving woman. "I'm sorry, Paula. I didn't mean to presume—"

"What do you want?" Paula snaps. "I've already talked to the police. Why is the FBI involved with my daughter's case?"

"I understand. The Bureau is just assisting in the investigation," I cut in. "We just had a few follow-up questions."

"Then can we do this and get it done?" she asks as she picks up a half-empty bottle of vodka. "I've kind of got a busy day ahead of me."

"We were just looking for a little background," I go on. "We understand Summer was a student at UW. Do you know if she was having any problems with anybody on campus?"

Paula shakes her head. "No. None. Everybody loved her," she says and sniffs loudly. "She was a good girl and had a lot of friends. She wasn't having problems with anyone."

"What about a boyfriend? Astra asks.

"She didn't have a boyfriend. Summer is—was—focused on her studies," she replies. "She wanted to be a child psychologist. That was her passion. Helping kids."

Astra cuts her eyes to me before asking her next question and I can see the tension in the set of her jaw. Having to question a grieving family member is one of the hardest parts of this job.

"And you're sure there was nobody special she was spending time with?" she asks, as delicately as she can. "She never mentioned—"

"My daughter and I had no secrets from each other," Paula snaps. "She told me everything."

In my experience, no child ever tells their parents everything, regardless of how close they are. I was extremely close to my own folks and I never told them that Sean Dugan gave me my first kiss in the basement of his parents' house when I was eleven years old. There are some things that, as a kid, you just don't discuss with your folks. That doesn't mean you don't love or respect them, and it certainly doesn't mean you're not as close as you believe you are. It just means that we're all individual people with our own lives—and yes, with our own secrets too. There's nothing wrong with having things you keep just for yourself.

But I know there are a lot of parents out there who would take offense at the notion that their children were anything but one hundred percent forthright with them. They would take the secrets their children held back as proof their kids weren't who they believed them to be. They'd be upset and question everything about their relationship with their children. And I'm kind of getting the feeling Paula would definitely be that kind of parent.

Which is kind of sad in my book, simply because as a parent, I'd think you would want your child to grow up to be their own person.

"Did she live on campus or have an off-campus apartment, Paula?" I ask.

"She lived in the dorms."

"Great. And does she have a roommate?"

She nods. "Yeah, Ariel McCann. She's a lovely girl. She and Summer were very close."

I jot the name down in my notebook, and then we ask some basic background information on Summer—places she liked to spend time, groups she was involved in, the names of some of her other friends. And when we're done, Paula looks wrung out and ready to crawl back into her bottle. I hate leaving her like this, but there's nothing I can do.

"Do you have somebody who can stay with you for a bit?" I ask. "Family member or—"

"I'm fine. Thank you for your concern," she growls, not sounding very thankful at all. "Now, if there's nothing else?"

"No, I think we have everything we need. Thank you for your time," I say. "We'll show ourselves out."

Paula looks at me for a moment and I see her eyes shimmering with more tears. And as she holds my gaze, I see her lips quivering.

"Please find who did this," she whispers, her voice thick with emotion. "Please find the person responsible for my baby's death."

"We're going to do everything in our power, Paula," I say. "I promise you that we will do our very best."

SEVEN

"THAT WOMAN IS FALLING APART," Astra sighs.

"I can't say I blame her," I reply. "To lose her husband and her daughter? The grief has to be unimaginable."

After leaving Paula's home, we made a beeline for the UW campus, hoping to catch Summer's roommate before she heads to class for the day. Assuming she's going to class. In the wake of a tragedy like this and losing a good friend, going to class is probably the last thing on Ariel's mind.

"I hope I never have to go through something like that," Astra says.

I frown. "I wish nobody ever had to."

After getting Ariel McCann's dorm assignment, we make our way across the busy, bustling campus. I watch a group of guys throwing a frisbee back and forth. Another group is tossing a football around. There's a small knot of people sitting beneath a large tree talking and laughing. One of them is playing guitar. Other clusters of kids are scattered about, some of them talking. Some of them, with books and laptops open on their laps, look like they're intently studying. All around us, the students give off a powerful sense of life. They give off this powerfully vibrant energy that fills the air.

And yet, when I look at all these kids who have their lives and their futures stretched out before them, with all the hopes and dreams they're chasing, all I can see is a wide pool of victims. And predators. The fact is, there is an alarmingly large percentage of people on this campus who are going to experience some form of violence. Be it physical or sexual, there are very, very few who will make it off campus completely unscathed and untouched by violence of some kind. It's a depressing thought.

"You're thinking about all of the kids on campus who are going to be raped, beaten, or murdered, aren't you?" Astra asks.

I nod. "You must be a psychic."

"Nah. I was just thinking the same thing."

"I'm not sure if that makes us good at our jobs or just dark, twisted, paranoid freaks."

I flash her a grin. "I tend to think it's both."

"Probably so."

We make our way up the steps to Narasaki Hall, presumably named after Karen Narasaki, a Seattle-born civil and human rights activist and former Commissioner of the US Commission on Civil Rights. Seems fitting for a women's dorm. We check in with the security desk and badge our way past them after confirming that Ariel McCann is in her dorm—the students are required to use their IDs to get in and out of the building, and she hasn't checked out yet today.

Some of the students we pass give us sidelong glances as we cross the lobby and make our way to the elevators. It's as if they somehow instinctively know we're law enforcement or some-

THE CHOSEN GIRLS   47

thing because they give us a wide berth. There are a pair of girls waiting in the elevator lobby, but when the doors open, they step aside and give us the car to ourselves.

"We'll catch the next one," chirps a bubbly blonde.

I roll my eyes and we step onto the car, then take it up to the third floor. The doors open again with a soft chime and we walk out, immediately looking around for signage.

"It was room 324A, wasn't it?" Astra asks.

I nod. "It was."

"Okay, it's this way."

The building is massive. There are more rooms than you'd think looking at it from the outside. The walls are all a uniform shade of yellow with a gray linoleum made to look like marble beneath our feet. Most of the doors are decorated with photos or small, colorful decorations. The whole place is surprisingly clean. I see no graffiti on the walls—which tells me the school has a crack janitorial staff, since I know students aren't exactly paragons of cleanliness. Spaced pretty evenly on both walls are cork boards littered with fliers for tutors, things for sale, concerts, and open mic nights. It's everything a college dorm should be.

"You look like you're feeling pretty nostalgic," Astra observes.

I shrug. "I enjoyed my college years."

We find the room and Astra knocks on the door. There's a hurried shuffling inside the room and when the door opens a crack, we find ourselves looking at nothing more than a green eye pressed to that crack. We both show her our badges and the eye grows wider.

"Ariel McCann, I'm Special Agent Russo, this is SSA Wilder," she intones in her best butt-kicking, FBI chick voice. "We'd like to speak with you for a moment."

"Yeah, this isn't a good time. I'm actually not feelin' real good right now," Ariel replies, then gives us a fake cough and looks at us like we were expected to buy it. "Maybe another time."

I look at Astra. "Do you smell that, Agent Russo?"

Astra frowns dramatically. "If by smell that, you mean the overpowering aroma of marijuana, then yes, SSA Wilder, I do smell that."

Ariel rolls her eyes but looks shaken. "It's legal in Washington."

"Only for those twenty-one and older," I point out. "And I'd say you can't be more than nineteen or twenty years old—and don't bother with the fake ID. Now, you can either have a nice conversation with us or we can arrest you. It's your choice."

She hesitates and I can see the annoyance on her face, but I can also see the fear. I can tell she's calculating the odds of her parents finding out and what the fallout of that might be.

"You wouldn't want all of your friends to see you getting hauled out of here in cuffs, do you?" Astra asks, applying the pressure. "Forget your friends. What would your folks think? What would they do to you if we popped you for smoking weed in the dorms? It's been a while since I was in college, but I'm pretty sure it's against university policy, too, with pretty heavy penalties. You willing to take that risk?"

I don't like strong-arming the girl like this, but we really need to talk to her. She may or may not have important information, but I won't know until we have a conversation with her. She finally relents and throws the door open for us, grumbling under her breath. Astra follows me in, shutting the door behind us as Ariel belatedly opens a window then drops down onto her bed. The smell of pot is strong, and the cloud gathered around the ceiling is as thick as the smog in Los Angeles.

The dorm room is a tale of two women. Ariel's side is messy

and unkempt. Her bed is unmade, the blankets and sheets twisted into knots. There's a pillow on the floor that's sitting on top of a pile of clothes. The desk at the foot of Ariel's bed is cluttered with books, notebooks, pens, pencils, and cans of Monster energy drink—the drink of choice for potheads everywhere. The closet door on her side is standing open and I see shirts half-hanging off hangers and shoes tossed into a pile on the floor. Two of the four dresser drawers are half-open, with clothes hanging out of them as well.

But then, as if there is a clear line of demarcation that runs down the center of the room, the other side—Summer's half of the room—is spotless. There isn't a single hair out of place. The bed is neatly made, the corners crisp, the comforter perfectly smooth. The desk is organized and neat, and there doesn't seem to be a speck of dust anywhere. Summer's walls are adorned with pictures of beautiful landscapes and inspirational sayings, while Ariel's side is covered in a mishmash of posters of boy bands and old concert and music festival fliers—which I think are presumably shows she's been to.

Ariel herself is a bit of a mess. Her long, dark hair is askew, standing out in a hundred different directions. I would have said she looks like she just got out of bed, but she's obviously been up here smoking up already this morning. I guess much like Paula Kennedy, she's got her own method of self-medicating.

She's got pale skin with a smattering of freckles across the bridge of her nose, and green eyes that seem as dull and lifeless as Paula's had been. She won't meet our eyes and pulls a pillow into her lap, hugging it to herself almost protectively.

Astra takes the chair at Ariel's desk and I lean against Summer's desk. Both of us are trying to give her a little space and make her feel comfortable. Or at least, not crowded. I know a lot of guys—local LEOs and Feds both—who use that tactic.

But I've found that when you crowd a suspect, it can be intimidating and put somebody on the defensive right away. They're more likely to shut down and not give you anything. But when you give them a little space and try to put them at their ease, it feels more like a conversation and less like an interrogation. You're more likely to get something out of them that way.

"I understand you and Summer were close," I start.

Ariel clutches the pillow to her tighter, still not meeting our eyes. She just nods vaguely and looks as if she's fighting back her tears.

"We're very sorry for your loss," Astra says.

"Thanks," she mutters, though she still won't look up.

"We already spoke to her mother, but we thought you might know some things—"

"I don't know anything," she interrupts.

"We understand she was popular," I offer.

Ariel nods again. "Everybody loved her."

"Do you know what she was doing the night she disappeared?"

"She was with Katie and Jordyn. They were out somewhere celebrating Riley's birthday," she replies.

"But not you?"

She shakes her head. "Riley and I weren't friends. I think she's snobby, pretentious, and fake as hell," she says softly. "Riley didn't like it when I said that to her face. So no, I wasn't invited to the party."

"Did it upset you that Summer was still friends with her?" Astra asks.

She shrugs. "A little, I guess. But I wasn't going to make a scene about it. She's entitled to have her own friends, just as I am," she says. "That doesn't mean we were any less close."

It's a very mature attitude for somebody so young. Most younger girls I've run across tend to think the opposite—that if you're friends with somebody they don't like, it means you can't possibly be friends with them too. Younger girls sometimes form a black-and-white, either/or scenario in their heads. Ariel's attitude is refreshing. She has wisdom uncommon in people her age.

"Can you give us the names of some of those friends she was out with?" I ask.

She nods and then does, rattling off the names of the girls who were out celebrating this Riley's birthday the night she was taken. I jot them all down in my notebook. We're going to need to speak with these girls as well.

"So, you don't know of anybody she was having problems with?" Astra asks.

"No, there was literally nobody who had a problem with her. At least, not on campus. Like I said, she was adored around here," she replies. "But you can ask her boyfriend. She hung out at his bar a lot, so maybe there was something down there."

"Boyfriend?" Astra raises an eyebrow. "Summer's mother was certain she wasn't seeing anybody."

Ariel glances up for the first time and looks Astra like she's an idiot. "And I'm sure you told your parents everything when you were in school too, right?"

"What is her boyfriend's name?" I ask. "And where does he work?"

"His name is Dylan Betts," she answers. "He's a bartender down at the Yellow Brick Road."

A smile flickers across my lips. It's a clever name that plays on Seattle's "Emerald City" moniker. This is the point in the conversation where I feel like I've gotten all I'm going to get out of somebody and would typically ask them for an alibi. But I feel confident that Ariel is not our unsub. There's no way she could have hauled Summer from the parking lot at McGeary

Park to that pond. She's small and wouldn't have had the strength, and there's no discernable motive I can see.

But we have to do our diligence.

"I hate to ask this," Astra starts. "But where were you the night Summer went missing."

She shakes her head. "I was here studying. All night. Alone," she replies, her voice as warm as ice. "You can look at the logs at the security desk."

Astra nods. "Sorry, I had to ask though. It's just procedure."

She nods as if she understands but her expression is one of annoyance, bordering on being offended. I get to my feet and Astra follows suit. I step forward and pull a card out of my inner pocket and hand it to her.

"My cell phone number is on the back," I tell her. "If you think of anything else or just need to talk, give me a call."

She offers me a weak smile, her eyes shimmering with tears. "Thanks," she says, her voice choked with her grief.

"We're very sorry about your friend," I say, then Astra and I take our leave.

EIGHT

Baxter's Coffee House, Student Union, University of
Washington; Seattle, WA

"You were right," Astra says.

"Of course, I was," I reply. "What about this time?"

"That Summer had a life her mom didn't know about."

"I'm sure you had the same thought."

She shrugs. "I guess I like to think that somewhere out there, some kids really are one hundred percent honest with their families. I mean, I was that kid. I told my folks everything, and I kind of want to believe I'm not the only one," she tells me.

"Seriously? You told them everything?"

She nods. "I did. Still do."

"You're kidding me."

"Not in the least."

That's something I never knew about her. It's honestly a shock. But I still can't believe that she told her parents everything. Nobody does that. I look over at her and arch an eyebrow.

"You even told them about the string of men you used to bring home?" I ask.

"Of course," she replies. "Sex wasn't the forbidden topic in our home it is in some others. My parents encouraged me to be open about it. And to explore my own sexuality and—"

"Oh my God, stop," I say with a laugh. "As much as I loved my folks, I can't imagine telling them about the men I've slept with."

"That's the problem in this country. People are so uptight about sex and there's such a taboo about it that it's no wonder we deal with some of the freaks and deviants we do," she states.

"Well, I think there's a lot more that goes into it than that, but point taken."

Astra holds the door to the student union open for me and we slip inside. It took some doing, but we were finally able to track down a couple of the girls Ariel had mentioned—Katie Greer and Jordyn Kirkson. They're sitting in the campus coffee house, and when we walked up, we found them huddled over a tablet, whispering and giggling to each other like a couple of schoolgirls.

Katie has smooth, caramel-colored skin, dark, wavy hair, and eyes the color of milk chocolate. Jordyn's hair is the color of copper and her blue eyes are set in an oval-shaped face that looks perpetually young. Without invitation, Astra and I pull out the chairs and take a seat across from them. Both of the girls look up suddenly, sour expressions on their faces.

"Excuse you," Katie snaps.

Astra and I badge them, and though the girls exchange glances, they both look wholly unimpressed. They both wear the same expression of annoyance on their faces. It's so uniform and synchronized, it's hard to believe they haven't practiced it. The one thing I don't see much of on either of their faces is grief. To look at them, you'd never be able to tell one of their good friends was just brutally murdered.

"SSA Wilder and Special Agent Russo," I start. "We wanted to talk to you about Summer Kennedy. Your friend."

At that, they both shift in their seats, seeming to be uncomfortable. Katie brushes a strand of her long, dark hair behind her ear and looks at me, a small frown creasing her full lips.

"What can we do for you?" she asks, her voice soft.

"First, we heard you were partying the night she was taken," Astra says. "We need to know where that was."

"We were down at a place called the Sidecar," she replies. "We were celebrating Riley's birthday."

"We heard," Astra nods. "Was Summer's boyfriend there?"

"Dylan?" Jordyn gasps. "God, no. He wasn't invited."

"And why is that?" I ask.

"He's like—old," Jordyn replies. "If we wanted to hang out with old guys, we would have gone to one of the old guy bars."

"Old?" I ask. "How old are we talking?"

"I don't know. Thirty, I guess?"

It takes all the willpower in me to not reach across the table and slap the taste out of Jordyn's mouth. As if she's picking up on my vibe, I see Astra doing her best to stifle the smile that's flickering across her lips. I glare at her balefully for a moment before turning back to the girls. I run a hand through my hair, giving myself a moment to dispose myself of the urge to throttle the girl across from me.

The bit of information she gave us is interesting, albeit a little bit creepy. The fact that he's substantially older than her could be a reason she didn't tell her mom about him. It also could provide a motive. I admit, it seems a little thin, but like I always say, it only has to make sense to the killer.

"All right. So, he's a little bit older," I say. "It was just the four of you, then?"

Katie shakes her head. "No, there were some others there too. Riley's friends, mainly."

"And what time did Summer leave the party?" I ask.

"I don't know. I think it was around nine or nine-thirty," Jordyn tells us. "She said she needed to study for a test or something."

"Personally, I think she was going to see Dylan," Katie adds, her voice dripping with disgust.

"Why do you say that?" Astra asks.

"She was totally hung up on him," Jordyn says. "It was like her life revolved around him or something. It was kind of gross."

"What is Dylan like?" I ask.

Katie shrugs. "Like I said, he's old."

I sigh and grit my teeth, giving myself a five-count before I look up at her again. "Aside from that. What is he like?"

She shrugs. "I only met him a couple of times, but he seemed kind of creepy to me. I mean, I think you'd have to be, to date somebody that much younger than you," she replies with a giggle.

"He's a musician," Jordyn adds.

"A failed musician," Katie clarifies. "It's not like he's got a band out there touring or anything."

"What else can you tell us about him?" I ask.

"Not much. I mean, like I said, I only met him a couple of times," Katie replies.

It's a dry well, so I drop the line of questioning about this Dylan character. They obviously can't see past his status as a senior citizen to provide anything useful.

"So, you said Summer left about nine or nine-thirty?" I ask.

Jordyn nods. "That's what I said."

"And how did she leave? Did she drive? Did somebody drive her back to the dorms?"

The girls look at each other, then turn back to us, shaking their heads at the same time.

"No idea. She said goodbye to us and then she was gone," Katie says.

"So, you didn't see her leave with anybody?" I press.

"I would have said so if I did," Katie snaps.

"I'm sorry, is there some reason for the attitude?" Astra fires back. "We're here trying to solve the murder of your friend, but y'all are acting like you have somewhere better to be."

"Actually, I do," Katie says. "I have to get to class."

"You'll stay right where you are until we're done," I tell her.

"Am I under arrest?" she asks, arching an eyebrow at me.

I sit back in my chair and stare at her. "Let me guess. You're pre-law."

"And people say the Feds are idiots," she replies. "For what it's worth, I never believed that for a second."

Her arrogance and condescension are irritating. I'm sure they'll be terrific traits when she settles into her career, but right now, they're annoying.

"So, if there's nothing else," Katie says as she gets to her feet.

"Do you even care that Summer was murdered?" I growl. "I thought you were friends."

"We were. But it's not like we were besties or anything," she chirps, then turns to Jordyn. "Coming?"

Jordyn looks at us for a long moment then turns to Katie. "I'm going to stick around for a minute and talk to these agents," she tells. "I'll catch up with you."

Katie scoffs and shakes her head. "Whatever."

We watch her storm off in silence for a moment then turn back to Jordyn, who's squirming in her seat, the discomfort on her face more than clear. But there's something else I see. Now that Katie is gone, Jordyn seems more open. Her expression has changed, shifting from that Mean Girl sneer to something that looks almost bereft.

"What was that about?" I ask.

Jordyn's lips compress into a tight line. "That's just Katie being Katie," she replies. "Her personality is... forceful. And sometimes, it's hard to break out of her orbit."

"You should try harder, because hanging out with her is making you look just like her. It's hard to tell where she ends and you begin," Astra tells her.

Jordyn looks down at the surface of the table, her face etched with something like contrition. She finally raises her gaze and it's not hard to see the grief in her eyes.

"I was good friends with Summer, and this is tearing me up," she says softly.

"So why do you act like you don't care?" Astra asks.

"Because in this world, you do as Katie wants you to, or you find yourself ostracized from everybody. Cut off from all of your friends," she tells us. "Katie is the kind of girl who can make or break you socially. I've seen her destroy people and I don't want to be next. But at the same time, I don't want Summer's killer to get away. I liked her a lot, and she didn't deserve what happened to her."

I sometimes forget what it's like to be so young and so concerned with social standing. And I'm sure Jordyn is going to pay a price for talking to us since talking to the cops isn't cool. Judging by the look on Astra's face, she's thinking along the same lines.

"So, is there anything you can tell us about Dylan?" Astra asks gently.

She shakes her head. "I really did only meet him a couple of times. And yeah, he's older than Summer is—was. But I thought he seemed like a decent guy," she says. "He seemed to really care about her. And she, of course, was wild about him.

Said she was in love. I don't know about that, but she was really into him."

"Okay, that's good, Jordyn," I nod. "So, you said you didn't see her leave with anybody?"

She shook her head. "I didn't. I wasn't really paying attention," she says. "Plus... I'd had a few. I just know she said goodbye and that was it."

"Did you notice anybody watching her?" Astra asks. "Or anybody who seemed off or out of place?"

She screwed up her face as she thought about it but shook her head. "No, I didn't notice anybody. Nobody was watching her that I saw."

"Was she having trouble with anybody on campus?" Astra asks. "Anybody giving her a hard time or anything?"

"Not that I know of. As far as I know, everybody loved her. She really was a good person. She bent over backward for people and I'm just sick that this happened to her," Jordyn tells us, her eyes welling with tears.

I purse my lips and try to think of any other questions I can ask but come up empty. It's like I thought before—this is a dry well. But at least we have confirmation of a boyfriend. That gives us an angle to pursue.

"You're going to catch who did this, aren't you?" she asks.

"We're going to do our best."

As Astra and I get to our feet, I see Jordyn look down, but not before I see the tears start to spill down her cheeks.

NINE

Aggio's Italian Ristorante; Downtown Seattle

"BLAKE, it's so wonderful to see you," Aunt Annie says as I sit down at the table across from her. "It's been forever."

And there is passive-aggressive shot number one, in what I'm sure will be a night filled them.

"It's good to see you, Annie. I've missed you," I say, reciting the expected lines for my role in this little production.

"Well, I'm never too far away, you know. You don't have to miss me unless you want to," she chirps brightly.

I'm so used to hearing those exact words from her, in that exact order, I could have dropped that line on her before she uttered it. But this is the initial salvo in the coming barrage of passive-aggressive bombs she'll be dropping. This is my atonement for being a terrible niece.

"I hope you don't mind Aggio's," she continues. "I am so very fond of their eggplant parmigiana."

"No, not at all," I respond. "I enjoy the food here."

While we were interviewing Jordyn and Katie, my aunt left

a message for me, asking to see me tonight. It's been a few weeks since I've seen her, so I figure this is my penance for that sin. I'm sure it's going to be an hour of her railing on me for not making more time for the family and an hour of her telling me how much she hates my job. That seems to be the agenda for just about every family dinner. And she wonders why I don't try to carve out more time for her.

It's not that I dislike Annie. And it's definitely not that I'm not appreciative of everything she's done for me in my life. She took me in after my parents were killed and my sister, Kit, was abducted. She raised me from that point on and provided for me. I will never say that she wasn't good to me, because she was. In many ways, she became my second mother. I shudder to think where I'd be right now if Annie hadn't stepped in and taken care of me.

But she's a woman of very strong opinions and convictions. She's also got a very strong belief in what is proper work for men and women. And she doesn't think that my job with the FBI is proper in any way, shape, or form. She's tried to talk me into quitting the Bureau since—well—since before I even joined. I made the mistake of telling her back in college that I was double majoring in Criminology and Psychology because I wanted to be a profiler for the Bureau.

Shortly after that conversation, she started trying to divert my career path to something safer and more appropriate for a young lady. She tried to recruit me to be a bookkeeper like her, or a librarian like my cousin, Maisey. But then I compounded the problem by telling her I was going to join the Bureau because I was going to find out who murdered my folks and abducted my sister, and that I was going to find Kit.

That lit a fire under Annie to steer me onto another course entirely. I can't say I don't understand where she's coming from. Given the fact that my parents, who were NSA employees and were—despite the official police reports citing a robbery gone wrong—executed, for reasons I have not been able to find yet. But I will. If I can ever crack Mr. Corden's code, it will be a big step toward doing just that. As far as Annie goes though, her fears are neither unreasonable nor unfounded. I just refuse to heed them. I refuse to be a captive to my fear and anger. I have the ability to do something about it, and that's exactly what I'm going to do.

"So, what looks good to you?" Annie asks.

"I think I'm going to have the spaghetti carbonara."

"Aren't there a lot of carbs in that dish?" she asks. "And then you factor in the bread? Oh, I'd just be so bloated."

Shot number two—this one a lot closer to home though. So close, I actually feel the wind from her passive-aggressive missile whizzing by. I smile sweetly at her.

"There are a lot of carbs," I admit. "But considering I'm always in a high-speed chase or fighting off a bad guy, I could use the energy."

A frown starts to crease her lips, but she's able to catch it, replacing it with a smile that looks entirely stiff and wooden. She doesn't reply though, not willing to engage me directly. I shake my head. This whole choreographed dance is as useless as it is irritating. But this is how we do things in our family. Every family has its quirks and challenges. It's just that some—like ours—seem to have more than most.

I keep hoping one day my aunt is going to see the light. Or at least, simply accept that I'm an FBI agent and nothing she can do is going to change that. I love what I do. I'm passionate about it and I feel like I'm making a real difference in the world.

The waitress arrives and we place our dinner orders. A couple of moments later, she comes back with our wine and then departs again, leaving my aunt and me in an awkward silence for a few moments. But then the ice thaws and we're able to make small talk for a little while. We catch each other up on our lives and everything going on with us. Although I decline to tell her about my whole blowup with Mark. That's a whole other can of worms I don't want to open.

Back in the old days, they would have called her a spinster. Today, they just call her bitter. Of the two, I'd say the latter is the more accurate term. And believe me, I've tried to get her— and Maisey—out there. Annie is beautiful, intelligent, clever, and contrary to everything I've said to this point, can be kind and quite lovely; She's just used to doing things her way, as she has for so long, she has trouble remembering that her way isn't the only way. But as a strong woman on her own, raising two teenage girls, she'd had to be that. I just want her to see that she doesn't have to be that anymore.

Our conversation over dinner is blessedly normal and she's stopped hurling her passive-aggressive barbs at me. We're just two women enjoying a meal and some conversation together. It's been a surprisingly refreshing evening; I'm starting to feel a little guilty for walking in here prepared for battle with her. The waitress comes by to clear our plates and I find I'm not in as big of a hurry to leave as I normally am, so we order dessert and coffee.

"So, there is something I wanted to talk to you about tonight," she says. "I've just been sitting here trying to figure out how to broach the subject."

I immediately tense and feel my guard going up again. I knew it was too good to be true. But Annie is staring down at the table and frowning.

"What is it, Annie?" I ask. "Are you okay?"

She nods. "Oh, I'm fine. It's Maisey."

I spoke to Maisey last night, so I know she's fine. But judging by how much Annie seems to be struggling with her words, something is obviously going on between them. Maisey hasn't mentioned anything to me lately, which tells me this is something on Annie's mind rather than anything my cousin did.

"What about her?" I ask cautiously.

"I don't know. Lately, she's just been acting different," Annie says. "She's been acting strangely."

"Strange how?"

"She's been secretive. It feels like she's hiding things from me. It's not like her at all," Annie says. "Maisey always told me everything before."

A grin curls my lip and I shake my head. Maisey and Annie are close. Always have been. But my aunt has always kept Maisey under her thumb a bit. Some of her fear and bitterness was rubbing off on my cousin, and when I saw that, I made a point of talking to Maisey about it. I told her at the time that her life was her own; she needed to live it for herself and for nobody else. She deserved to be happy and experience all life had to offer. I was very clear when I told her I didn't want to see her end up like her mother—secluded, isolated, and alone.

Maisey is a beautiful girl. She's intelligent and clever. Charming and funny. She's got one of those quirky personalities that make her absolutely adorable. Yeah, she's naturally a bit shy and she's never been the outgoing type—something I blame on Annie's extreme helicopter parenting—but once you get Maisey out of her shell, she's a force of nature and you can't help but love her.

"She's never hidden anything from me before, and I'm not sure what to think about it. I don't know what's happening with my own daughter right now," Annie says.

I want to tell Annie that Maisey has hidden a lot from her over the years. More than that, I want to tell her that Maisey is a grown woman and that she doesn't need to know everything happening in her life. In this case, I know exactly what Maisey is hiding from her mother, but it's not for me to say. It's not my secret.

Annie looks up at me. "Do you know if she's seeing somebody? Is that what this is?" she asks. "Does she have a secret boyfriend? It's the only thing that makes sense to me."

I gnaw on my bottom lip for a moment, struggling with my promise to Maisey. When she first started dating Marco, she swore me to silence, and I don't want to give up her secret. But I can see how much Annie is struggling with the idea that Maisey is freezing her out of her life and keeping things from her. But I can't blame Maisey for keeping it to herself, given Annie's tendency to nitpick at everything, especially our life choices.

My aunt has been screwed over by men in her life, and while I sympathize with her and understand her feelings, I think she should have moved past it a long time ago. I think rather than continuing to dwell on it, hardening her heart and her opinions, she should have been able to let it go. If for no other reason than how her attitude has impacted her daughter's life.

"Do you know what's going on with Maisey?" she asks.

I frown, still trying to figure out how to answer her. I don't want to betray Maisey, but I don't want to lie to Annie either. I told Maisey when she started dating Marco—months ago—that she should tell her mom. But she's been hemming and hawing and dancing around the subject. It seems so silly to me that a thirty-two-year-old woman is keeping a secret like who she's dating for fear of her mother.

Things would be so much easier if people would just stop hiding and communicate with each other.

"I think you should talk to Maisey about this," I finally say. "I really don't want to be in the middle of things, Annie."

She frowns. "So, she is hiding something from me."

"I think you're both grown women and you should be able to talk to each other."

"Is she dating somebody? Just tell me that much at least."

I shake my head. "I'm not getting involved with this, Annie. I think you need to share your concerns with Maisey, and if there's something she wants to tell you, she will."

The truth is, I am kind of involved with this. After watching Maisey and Marco flirt shamelessly with each other for a really long time, I finally managed to push her to him. I was really glad to see it because Marco is a good guy and treats her like a queen. She deserves no less. But that's where my involvement ends. Everything that's come after is on Maisey. She decided to keep it from Annie. And it's not my place to violate that trust—no matter how hard Annie is trying to get me to do it.

"If she's dating somebody, why would she hide it from me, Blake?"

I shrug. "All I can say is that she knows you don't have a high opinion of men. We both know that, Annie. You've made that perfectly clear over the years," I tell her. "No man is ever good—or good enough. You find fault in every single man you come into contact with."

"That's not true," she gasps.

"It is. I hate to say it, but you can be very judgmental. And you know how gentle Maisey is," I say. "She sometimes feels intimidated by you."

She puts her hand to her chest, her face a mask of horror. "I've never intimidated my daughter. I wouldn't do that."

"Not consciously. I agree," I say. "But do you remember the boy who asked Maisey to her junior prom? I think his name was... Alex?"

"Alex Wingate. Yes, I remember him clearly," she says, the disdain dripping from her lips. "Horrible boy, that one. He was a troublemaker, and there was no way I was going to let a boy like that influence—"

"That's what I'm talking about, Annie," I cut her off. "The fact was, Alex was a good kid. He got straight A's in school. Was always polite and respectful. Nobody ever had a bad word to say about him. Except you."

Annie looks at me, positively scandalized. "I can't believe you're saying all this to me."

"I should have a long time ago—like when it was happening," I tell her. "I should have told you that you were letting your own experiences and heartache impact Maisey. Your bitterness was creeping into her soul, and it was turning her hard. Like you."

Annie's eyes welled with tears. "Blake, I can't believe this. You make me sound like a monster."

I shake my head. "I'm sorry, but it's something I should have said a long time ago. You got screwed by a man. I get it—I have too, in some ways. But at some point, you have to move past your pain, Annie," I tell her. "You're a wonderful mother in most every way, but your bitterness is poisoning your own soul—and Maisey's."

"This is outrageous," she replies, her expression dark and angry.

"I'm sorry, Annie. But somebody had to say something," I say. "I guess I drew the short straw."

Without another word, my aunt slips out of the booth and gets to her feet. She looks at me like she's about to say something, but lets the words die on her lips. Instead, she grabs her bag and bolts from the restaurant, leaving me sitting there feeling like a jerk.

The waitress walks up to the table, our desserts in hand, and looks down at me, uncertainty coloring her features.

"I guess I'll take those to go instead."

TEN

ASTRA and I got confirmation that our guy, Dylan Betts, is working the afternoon shift today, so we came down early to surveil the area and have a conversation with him. We sit in the car in a parking lot across the street that's got a clear view of the bar he works at. The sky overhead is gray, choked with fat clouds promising rain soon. A cold wind rushes down the street, carrying leaves and other litter along with it.

The outside of the Yellow Brick Road looks like any of a thousand other bars in the city. A low fence lines the front with tables set out for outdoor drinking and dining that's separated by the walkway to the front door—which is painted gold. The building itself is made of brick—and is painted parakeet yellow, with the bricks outlined in black to make it pop. The front door is an ungodly shade of green, and the walls to the other side of it are smoked glass doors that open onto the front patio. It's a kitschy little hole-in-the-wall bar I'm sure is popular with the Capitol Hill hipster crowd.

"Tell me something," I start. "Is that front door sparkling?"

Astra leans forward and stares at it, then laughs softly to herself. "They glittered the hell out of the door. So yeah, it's sparkling."

"That's tacky."

"It's eye-catching. Draws a crowd. And besides, people love tacky," she says. "Anyway, how'd dinner with Aunt Annie go last night?"

A rueful grin stretches my lips. "I'm not even sure if a total train wreck with a dash of a nuclear meltdown accurately captures the essence of just how horrible it was."

"That good, huh?"

"Oh yeah," I reply. "She knows Maisey is keeping something from her and assumes it's her secret boyfriend."

"I mean..." Astra chuckles. "Is she wrong? Your aunt is perceptive. Maybe she should have been a profiler."

I laugh softly. "Never would have happened. FBI work isn't a woman's work, according to her. She thinks it's better left to the menfolk."

"Yeah, they do a stellar job of running the show."

I crack open the file and look through the pages again. Before I went to dinner with Annie, I'd tasked our tech guru Rick with putting together a quick and dirty dossier on Dylan Betts. I just wanted to get a handle on who we were dealing with before we walked in the door. I'll have Rick do a deeper dive if I get a hinky feeling about this guy after we talk to him.

"So, what are you going to do? About Maisey and your aunt?" Astra asks.

"Stay as far away from that situation as I can. I told Annie I don't want to be caught up in it," I reply. "Really, the dinner was so pleasant until the end. But she kept asking about it and I told her to talk to Maisey about it, not me."

"Why do I get the feeling that's not the whole story?"

I sway my head from side to side, as if wondering how to phrase it. "I... may have also told her that she's a bit judgmental and bitter, and it was infecting Maisey's soul, and it wouldn't be a big surprise if Maisey was hiding a boyfriend from her. She sort of... stormed out of the restaurant."

"Yeah, that's staying out of the middle. Well done."

The flow of foot and car traffic is starting to taper off as the lunchtime crowd starts to filter back into the buildings all around us. A fairly large crowd of people exit the Yellow Brick Road—or the YBR as the kids apparently call it, according to the Internet—after a liquid lunch. We sit and wait another twenty minutes or so until the flow of the crowd thins to a trickle, then get out of the car and head across the street.

I pull the sparkling door open, allowing Astra to walk in first. I follow her in and let the door swing shut, giving my eyes a moment to adjust to the dim light inside.

"Sit anywhere you want, ladies. But you just missed out on the lunchtime specials," comes a voice from behind the bar. "Although, for you two, I might just be willing to make an exception."

As my eyes adjust, the figure behind the bar resolves itself into the form of Dylan Betts. He's tall. Six-two, maybe six-three, with dark hair that hangs to his shoulders. He's fit, has broad shoulders, a strong jawline, and sharp angular features. His black t-shirt is tight, showcasing his tattoo-lined biceps and the taut lines of his pecs. He's a good-looking guy who definitely looks younger than his years, but the flecks of gray in his goatee give away the fact that he's not a college kid.

The bar is empty, save for a few stragglers in suits sitting together and one old-timer sitting at the far end, nursing a pint of beer as he watches a game on one of the six flatscreens mounted behind the bar. The walls of the place are painted in the same obnoxious green as the door—and like the door, they've been very liberally glittered. Even in the dim lighting of the place, they sparkle.

The place isn't what I expected. It's kitschy as hell, sure, but it seems to be well kept, clean, and well ordered. There is a row of black padded booths against the wall to our left, the polished dark wood bar runs half the length of the wall to our right, and black topped tables fill the rest of the open space. There's a small stage at the back of the bar, likely for live music. It makes me remember the girls had mentioned that he's a musician.

Astra and I walk over to the bar and I'm keenly aware of Betts' eyes on us. They move up and down, taking us in, though I don't get the feeling it's in a lecherous, sexual way. He's appraising us. Taking our measure. And by the time we get to the bar, a corner of his mouth is curled upward like he's already got us sized up.

"What can I do for you, officers?" he asks.

I glance over at Astra and she chuckles. The guy is obviously street smart and knows how to pick the cop out of a crowd. His rap sheet was light. He was busted for auto theft when he was fifteen and he had a couple of minor arrests for weed. But he's obviously plugged in enough to know law enforcement on sight, which makes me wonder about what else he does for a living. And what he does that he hasn't been busted for. The grin on his face is cocky and he radiates arrogance like heat off a stove.

Astra and I flash our badges. "Actually, we're Agents. Not officers," I correct him. "SSA Wilder, Special Agent Russo."

"Well, I beg your pardon then," he replies. "What can I do for you, SSA Wilder and Special Agent Russo?"

"You can tell us about your girlfriend," Astra says.

"Which one? I mean, I've got so many it's hard to keep track—"

"Summer Kennedy," Astra cuts him off, her voice colder than ice.

A shadow crosses his face and that cocky smirk immediately melts away. He looks away and clears his throat as he picks up a rag and starts polishing a section of the bar that I didn't see a single streak on. It's obvious he's giving himself something to do while he gathers himself. It's an interesting reaction. It tells me that he's already putting together the story in his head—which makes me curious as to what he'll say. After a minute of wiping down the bar, he looks up at her, fully composed, his face a mask of cool indifference.

"What about her?" he asks.

"We heard you were seeing her," I say.

He furtively glances around the bar, as if checking to ensure he's not being overheard. And when his gaze lands on mine again, he puts that cocky smile back on with the practiced ease of a man slipping on a familiar pair of boxers. He shrugs casually.

"I see a few people," he replies. "What's this about?"

"Like 'em young, do you?" Astra asks.

He tries to cover it, but I see him swallow hard. A slight tremor passes through his body and he's suddenly crackling with an unmistakable nervous energy. He's doing his best to hide how anxious he is, but both Astra and I can sniff it out as easily as a shark smells blood in the water. His cocky swagger has evaporated, and he suddenly looks more like a caged animal than anything else.

"It's like that," he says. "I'm not like a pedophile or anything."

"You're really walking that fine line there though, aren't you, Dylan?" she presses.

"Screw you. She was nineteen when we got together."

"And you're thirty-one," I say. "That's quite an age gap. Let me guess, she was really mature for her age?"

"She..."

He lets his words trail off as he apparently realizes how stupid that sounds. It's something a lot of pedophiles say to justify their predilection. But I know he's not a pedophile. Technically speaking, he might be considered an ephebophile, which is an adult who is sexually attracted to mid-to-late adolescents. Ephebophiles are generally considered to covet those who fall between the ages of fifteen to eighteen, or so.

But we're not here to roust him about his perceived sexual peccadillos. We're just trying to rattle his cage to see if we can knock him off balance and put him back on his heels. See if we can get him to admit something he otherwise wouldn't. With us there putting the screws to him, we're hoping he'll crack and slip up. You'd be surprised at how often you can get people to absolutely fold if you apply just the barest amount of pressure.

He runs a hand through his hair and looks at us. "She was very mature for her age," he says, apparently figuring that finishing his thought would look better than not. "But her age had nothing to do with it. Summer was..."

"You're aware she was murdered just a few days ago, right?" I cut him off. "Personally, I think you seem to be fairly chipper after such a tragedy."

That nervous energy explodes back into his face again, and his eyes dart around the bar. His face is tight, and he looks like he's afraid of somebody overhearing him. He leans forward and pitches his voice low so only we can hear him.

"Listen, can we talk about this someplace more private?" he asks.

"Got someplace in mind?"

He nods then walks over to a blonde twenty-something in a short skirt and tight top and whispers something in her ear. She nods and he motions for us to follow him. Dylan pushes through the swinging door that leads through the kitchen. It's sweltering in the kitchen, but the air is redolent with a host of fragrant aromas that make my belly growl. I find myself surprised once again by the place. Who would have thought you could get a good meal in a place that glitters their walls?

We follow Dylan through a black security door that's standing propped open and out into a parking lot behind the bar. About twenty yards off is a pop-up tent that has a couple of benches, a trash can, and a standing ashtray beneath it. It's obviously the smoker's area. As soon as we reach the tent, Dylan fishes a pack of smokes out of his pocket and lights up. I can't help but notice that his hand is trembling as he takes a drag of his cigarette.

"So you want to know if I killed her," he starts.

Astra shrugs. "Did you?"

He looks at her and his face darkens. "No, I did not."

She glances over at me. "Oh, okay. Good enough for me. I guess we should go ahead and take his name off the suspect list, boss."

I laugh softly to myself, but Dylan's face darkens, and he glares hard at Astra. And when he takes a step toward her, I drop my hand to the butt of my weapon. He looks over at me, and when he sees that I'm about to draw down on him, he clenches his jaw and takes a step back, his glare harder than iron. He points at Astra with two fingers, his cigarette clenched between them.

"I didn't kill her. Why would I?"

"Oh, I can think of about a million reasons off the top of my head," she replies. "Men kill women for all kinds of stupid reasons, all the time. You ever read the news?"

"Yeah, well, I didn't kill her. I wouldn't kill her," he insists, his voice softening. "I was in love with her. I would never hurt her."

"Even men who claim to be in love with a woman have been known to kill them," I offer.

"Maybe so. But I didn't," he says. "I wanted to marry her."

"After what, six months?" Astra scoffs.

"Sometimes you just know," he says, sounding miserable as he drops down onto one of the benches.

I watch Dylan closely. His hand is still trembling as he raises his cigarette to his lips and takes a deep drag. The expression on his face is one of pure anguish and it looks to me like he's fighting back tears.

"This is a nice act," Astra presses. "But what about what you were saying inside about having a lot of other women—"

"It's an image. Nothing more than a stupid image," he mutters.

"If you were so in love with Summer, why in the hell would you want to make out like you're some big player?" Astra asks.

A wry grin curls his lips. "Because women, and some men, tend to tip better if they think you're single. Crass, I know. But when you rely on tips, you have to work with what you have."

On the one hand, it makes sense. On the other, it does still make me question his credibility. There's also the fact that he's so shaken that he's trembling. It could be a sign of nervousness, which could be an indicator of guilt. Or it could simply be that he's so rattled by the murder of a woman he loves, he's barely keeping it together. At this point, I don't have enough information to know which theory is correct. But I need to find out.

"Mr. Betts, I'd like you to come down to the field office

tomorrow," I tell him. "We have some more questions we'd like to ask you."

"Are you arresting me?" he asks, his eyes widening.

I shake my head. "No, we're not arresting you. We'd just like to ask you some questions, and I'd like to do it in a setting that's more conducive to a conversation. That's all."

He looks from me, to Astra, and back again. I can see him mulling it all over in his mind. He's scared. That much I can see, and I know I need to do something to agree to get him to come in. I want him on record so that we can either catch him in a lie or find a reason to exclude him from the suspect pool. Because let's face it, in a hell of a lot of cases, it's the significant other, be it a husband, boyfriend, or even a wife or girlfriend, who is responsible for somebody's death.

"Look, we want to find Summer's killer. I'm sure you want that, too. And the best way to do that is to gather up as much information as we can," I tell him. "And that includes information from you. You very well might have a critical piece of information that you're not even aware of right now."

He hesitates a moment longer and then nods. "Yeah. Okay. I can come in tomorrow before my shift here," he tells us. "Whatever you need. I just want her killer caught."

Dylan gets up and we watch him walk away. My mind is spinning as I process everything he said, and I frown.

"That sounded sincere," I say.

Astra nods. "It did. We may be barking up the wrong tree."

"It's the only tree we have right now."

"Well, let's shake the hell out of it tomorrow and see what falls out."

ELEVEN

ASTRA and I stand behind the two-way glass watching Dylan Betts. He's sitting at the table in the center of the room, nervously shifting in his seat. He pulls out a pack of smokes, then notices the large "No Smoking" sign on the wall and drops the pack. He starts to flick his lighter though and can't seem to stop fidgeting.

We're standing in the observation pod, giving Dylan a little time to sweat. The pod is where all the audio and visual equipment for the interrogation suites are set up. There are four two-way windows in the pod, each one overlooking one of the four interrogation suites it's connected to. A tech sits at the control board in the corner of the room, situated before two of the windows to our left.

"Nervous," Astra observes.

"I imagine being hauled in by the FBI has that effect."

"Technically, he came in on his own."

"That was the first test," I nod. "He didn't skip town, so that's something."

"True," Astra admits. "But I'm not ready to absolve this creep just yet."

The door to the observation room opens and Rosalinda Espinoza—Rosie to most of us—saunters in. She's the Special Agent in Charge, or SAC, overseeing the entire Seattle Field Office. To look at her, you wouldn't think she's quite the rough and tumble woman she is. She's got dark hair shot through with gray, rich tawny colored skin, and caramel-colored eyes. She's on the smallish side, though far from waifish, and has a quiet and unassuming manner about her. She's a straight shooter and a no-nonsense kind of woman. Rosie is tough as nails, but cares for others deeply. I have all the respect in the world for her and have never had a better boss.

"What's all this about?" she asks, then points to Dylan. "Who's Mr. Twitchy in there?"

"That's Dylan Betts. The boyfriend of Summer Kennedy," I respond.

"And Summer Kennedy is... who?"

I turn to Rosie and give her a hard look. "Do you not read the reports I every so faithfully and dutifully file?"

"I skim," Rosie shrugs. "When I get a chance."

"Sounds like you don't have to file reports anymore to me," Astra whispers.

"Yeah, that doesn't work," Rosie replies. "I may not read them cover to cover faithfully, but you know how the brass loves their paperwork."

I laugh. "Yeah, I know. We all have to give the pencil necks something to push around their desks."

"Exactly," Rosie says. "So, fill me in."

I tell her about the discovery of Summer Kennedy's body and then take her through our investigation to this point. She listens closely, nodding along until I finish. Then she points to Dylan sitting beyond the glass.

"So, why is he here?" she asks. "Couldn't you have just interviewed him at his home or place of employment?"

"I want this on record," I tell her. "That way, if he lies, we can nail him to the wall."

Rosie nods, but frowns. I can see her mind working and know she's wondering the same thing Astra has already questioned me about. She turns to me.

"Okay, so this is great and all, but why aren't you letting local LEOs handle this?" she asks. "Last I checked, SPD has a fully functioning detective's bureau. So why take this on?"

"Hey, that's a great question," Astra says. "And it sounds so familiar too."

"Stow it, Russo," Rosie barks at her, though she's grinning.

"Because I don't think this is a one-off, Rosie. The level of sadism and violence this girl went through was extensive," I explain. "Based on my experience, it feels like this isn't the first time our unsub has killed. The killer was methodical. Careful. He wasn't rash or impulsive and took care to employ forensic countermeasures. Those are all hallmarks of a serial. And if there's one thing we know about Deputy Chief Torres and the SPD, it's that they don't handle serials well. They're too busy covering their butts to work a case properly."

"So, basically what you're telling me is that you're going on a hunch. And you're running a parallel investigation to the SPD," she states.

I shrug. "Yeah, pretty much. I just have a feeling about this one," I tell her. "If we don't get ahead of it, Summer Kennedy won't be the last body to drop. As it is, I would bet my entire salary for the year that she wasn't the first, either. When we start digging, I'm sure we're going to find more."

Rosie frowns, considering my argument. I know she's only

trying to make me sweat. My gut hunches have always been good enough for her before. I get a latitude a lot of agents don't, simply because I have a solid track record. Does that mean I'm always right? Of course not. But I'm right more often than I'm wrong, which affords me a certain benefit of the doubt.

It's that latitude that's caused some friction between me and some of my fellow agents. Some of them are resentful of the opportunities I've been afforded. But I've worked my tail off to get to where I am, and I want to take advantage of that opportunity.

"And what are you doing about the ATM bandits you were so hot about a couple of weeks ago?" Rosie asks.

"I have Mo running point on that."

She looks at me with an arched eyebrow. "Mo?"

"She's fantastic at analyzing data points and finding patterns, especially with financial cases. Honestly, she might be even better than I am about that, coming from White Collar," I tell her. "I've got the utmost confidence she's going to be able to crack it."

"She's also not real great at murder scenes," Astra adds.

I look at Rosie. "We're having a period of adjustment. It's not easy to come out of White Collar straight into the blood and gore."

Rosie turns back to the window. "And you think Mr. Twitchy in there has something to do with all of this?"

I shrug. "I don't know yet. We need to get in there and talk to him."

"What does your gut tell you?"

"That he's not our guy. He genuinely seemed to care for the vic," I say. "But I can't exclude him just yet. Just because he's showing his love for her right now doesn't mean he doesn't have a monster lurking inside of him."

"That's true," Rosie nods.

"So? Do I have your blessing to run with this?" I ask.

She nods. "Yeah. You do," she says. "But if it looks like you're going to step on the SPD's toes, I want you to liaise with them. We clear?"

"Of course."

"I mean it, Russo. I don't want to talk to Torres any more than you do," she tells me with a smirk.

"You go it, boss," I say.

"All right. Then get in there and rattle his cage. See what you get."

"Thanks, Rosie."

I nod to Astra and we head through the door that leads us into the interrogation room where we've got Dylan sitting. He looks up at us, a frown creasing his face. We take a seat at the table across from him.

"Aren't you supposed to read me my rights or something?" he asks.

"Only if we were arresting you," I explain. "It's like I said yesterday, we only want to have a conversation."

"Okay, so... what?" he asks.

"We just want you to tell us a little more about your relationship with Summer," Astra starts.

"Like I told you, we were in love," he says. "We were going to get married when she finished with school."

"Yeah, that's what you told us," I nod. "Unfortunately, Summer's not here to confirm that."

"I didn't kill her," he snaps.

"You told us that too," Astra says.

"Hey, I came in here voluntarily," he fires back. "If I were guilty, would I have done that?"

"I'm not saying you did it. But you'd be surprised at what murderers think they can get away with. Granted, coming in here would take some serious stones," I say with a laugh.

But Dylan doesn't laugh. His expression darkens and he glowers at us from his side of the table. He sits back in his chair and crosses his arms over his chest.

"You weren't invited to the birthday party she was at the night she was taken," I say. "Is that right?"

He shrugs. "Even if I had been invited, I couldn't have gone. I was working."

"At the bar?"

"Until about eight," he says. "After that, I was working my second job."

"That's right," Astra says. "You're a musician, right?"

"I am," he says with a cocky smile that quickly fades. "But that night, I was working my other second job."

"And what is your other second job?"

He frowns and runs a hand over his face. "I work for a ride-hailing service."

"A ride-hailing service?" Astra asks.

"Yeah, it's like Uber," he tells us.

"Okay, and what is the company called?" I ask.

"It's called e-Ride."

I nod and jot it down in the file. "And what hours did you work there?"

"From around eight until two or two-thirty. I'd have to go back and check," he says. "But that's my usual Friday night schedule."

"So, you weren't pissed about not being invited to the party?" Astra asks.

"Nah. Hanging out with college kids isn't really my thing."

"Except for the fact that Summer was a college kid," I point out.

He frowns. "That's different."

"Okay, that's fair," I say. "But I have to say that you're handling her death pretty well."

"Just because I'm not sitting in here bawling my eyes out to you doesn't mean I'm not hurting," he growls. "Not everybody processes grief the same way."

"And how are you processing it?" Astra asks.

He stares at her in stony silence for a long moment. "I'm channeling my grief into my music. I've already written two songs about her."

"That's pretty fast," Astra says.

He shrugs. "A lot of the greats like Jim Morrison and Kurt Cobain used their grief as motivation. Their grief fueled their music and they turned out some classic hits practically overnight."

"Yeah, I think Taylor Swift does that too," Astra notes.

"Did you really just compare yourself to Kurt Cobain?" I raise an eyebrow.

"No," he snaps. "I was talking about using music and creativity to process one's grief. That's all I was saying."

"Oh, okay," I say. "How did you find out about Summer's death?"

"I don't know. I think I read it online," he replies.

"Online?"

"It was getting passed around on Facebook or some local crime blog or something. I don't remember," he says. "I'd been trying to get ahold of her since Friday night but hadn't heard back."

"Did she do that a lot? Not return your calls?" Astra asks.

"Not all the time. But there were times she dropped off the radar for a few days. It wasn't a big deal. She was a college girl," he says. "I usually figured she was studying and had her phone off so she wouldn't get distracted."

I nod and make a note to check the crime blogs from the morning after she was killed. In today's online world, hearing about the death of a loved one online isn't all that surprising.

Most of the time these days, word of somebody's death is getting passed around on Facebook and Twitter long before local news or sometimes, even the authorities know what's going on. It's just the nature of today's world of instant news for those needing instant gratification.

"You read the local crime blogs a lot?" Astra asks.

"Sometimes when I have nothing better to do, yeah. It's interesting reading."

We take him through a few more questions just to nail down his timeline and get him to commit to a few more facts that we'll check his story against. We'll see if he's lying or if we can eliminate him as a suspect. All in all, we question him for a little more than an hour before we kick him loose with the ominous-sounding, but totally unenforceable admonishment to stay around town.

"Do you believe him?" Astra asks.

I shake my head. "I just don't know right now. Part of me does. He seems pretty shaken up about her death," I say. "Maybe I'm naïve, but I actually believe he loved her."

"Yeah, I'm trying to not think about that. I mean, she was nineteen and he's thirty-one. No matter which way you slice it, that's kind of creepy," she points out.

"Agreed—and his initial reaction wasn't exactly heartening. But I don't think he would have given us all this information freely if he really had too much to hide. I'm not ready to cross him off just yet, but if our unsub is a serial, I just don't see it lining up."

We head out of the interrogation suite and make our way back to the shop. And all the while, I can't stop thinking that Dylan's not our guy and we're going to see more bodies dropping soon.

TWELVE

"Mo, how are we doing with the ATM bandits?" I ask as we come through the doors and into the shop.

"Still working on it. I'm starting to see a pattern in how they're picked, but it's far from complete just yet," she replies.

"Good, good," I tell her. "Keep working it."

The case is one I've been tracking on and off for about a year. Somebody with some serious ingenuity has figured out a way to actually break into ATMs and clean them out. It's impressive but frustrating, because I haven't been able to get out in front of these guys yet. They're good. They're organized and highly efficient. But sooner or later, we're going to catch a break. And when they do, we're going to get these clowns.

"Rick, have you been able to track the serial numbers on the cash being stolen?" I ask.

I know it's a long shot, but at this point, I'm grasping at straws with this case. It's been making me want to tear my hair out for months, and I'm hoping and praying for just one break. Just one little break. That's not too much to ask for, is it?

"Sorry, boss," Rick says. "Nothing yet. Whoever's stealing it is cleaning it really well."

"Yeah, I figured we weren't going to get that lucky."

"What are you guys working on?" Mo asks.

"Caught a body," I answer.

"And Veronica Mars here thinks it's part of a string," Astra says, tipping me a wink.

"I wouldn't be against her," Mo replies. "She's right more often than she's wrong."

"Don't encourage her, new girl," Astra cracks.

I laugh and pace the floor at the front of the room, thinking about everything that's transpired over the last few days. There are things we know, but so much more that we don't. All I have are bits and pieces. Scraps that are suggestive of bigger things, but are far from definite. All I know right now is that I don't have enough information yet to build a proper profile. I need more information.

"Rick, I need you to run a search for similar cases in the state," I say. "Look for cases that involve Caucasian college-aged women. Look for manual strangulation with acts of torture. In particular, I want you to search for cigarette burns."

"Check, check, and check," he says. "But you don't want me to run it through any of the national databases?"

"Not yet. We'll expand the search if we need to," I say. "I just have a feeling this is a local thing. The killer was way too familiar with the area he dumped Summer Kennedy in for him to not be from around here."

"That much I can agree with," Astra nods. "You don't stumble onto McGeary Park by accident."

"Oh man, they found the body in birdwatcher heaven?"

Mo asks. "There are going to be some upset blue hairs if they don't get to feed their birds."

I laugh. "Hopefully, the scene's already been processed, and they released the park."

"The way the SPD works, they'll be lucky if it's opened before next week," Mo says.

Mo used to work for the Seattle PD and came away with as bad a taste in her mouth about them as my friend Paxton, who was summarily dismissed after clashing with the brass one too many times a few years back. Mo couldn't deal with the garbage there anymore and left voluntarily, then jumped to the Bureau. And although she's still a little green when it comes to murder cases, she's got a keen mind and is starting to come out of her shell and into her own here. She's a terrific asset to the team and I couldn't be happier to have her.

"So, the guy you were in there interrogating. He good for it?" Mo asks.

"The boyfriend? Not sure yet. But I honestly have my doubts," I say. "What did you think, Astra?"

"My honest two cents are that the guy is a creep and is bordering on being a pedophile," she says. "But he didn't do this. And he's definitely not a serial."

I nod, agreeing with her sentiment. "But we still need to do our due diligence," I say. "Sociopaths are adept at imitating emotion. So, it's entirely possible he's just pullin' one over on the both of us."

She grins at me ruefully. "Don't think the thought hasn't crossed my mind."

"Are there any other parameters you want me to run?" Rick calls from his station.

I shake my head. "Not yet. We just don't have enough information," I admit. "The torture is the only thing that stands out to me right now."

"Probably going to be a few of those," Mo remarks. "There are a lot of sadistic people in the world."

"Yeah, but I'm thinking we can always narrow it down as we get more information. I'm waiting for the ME's report. That might give us a little more to work with," I say.

I think it over, going over all of the information we've gathered so far, and the thought occurs to me.

"Hey Mo, I also need to see if you can get some information from a ride-hailing company called e-Taxi," I tell him. "The boyfriend says he was driving the night Summer Kennedy went missing and I just want to verify that. I want his routes, fares, whatever you can scrounge up."

"I might need a warrant for that," she says.

"Right. I'll get one in the works," I nod. "In the meantime, can you contact them and see if they're willing to volunteer the data?"

"I'm on it," she replies.

I turn to Astra. "We've got to run down some of Summer's friends and see if there's anything they can tell us. Somebody had to have seen her leave."

"I'm not going to hold my breath, but let's do it," she says.

We head out of the CDAU and back to UW to see if we can find some of her friends, which I already know is going to be like herding cats. But that's part of running a tight, thorough investigation—doing the garbage work. I like to think that's what separates me from some of the other agents who resent me—I'm willing to roll up my sleeves and do the work they're not willing to do.

But man, sometimes it's really tedious.

THIRTEEN

Wilder Residence; The Emerald Pines Luxury Apartments,
Downtown Seattle

I CLOSE the door behind me and drop my bag next to the small table next to the door and my keys into the bowl on top of it. After that, I strip off my boots and drop them next to my bag, then untuck my shirt. I'd strip out of my shirt and bra, but the familiar trumpet of Miles Davis', "*So What*," is playing, alerting me to his presence.

And when I step into the main room of my apartment, I find Mark sitting at the dining room table with the lights all dimmed. He's got two glasses of wine poured, places set, and candles lit. His eyes glitter in the candlelight as he looks at me.

"What's all this?" I frown.

He gets to his feet and moves around to the other chair, silently pulling it out for me. I walk over and sit down, and he pushes the chair back in, then returns to his own seat. Mark picks up his wine glass and holds it up as if to make a toast. I oblige him by picking up my own glass and look at him.

"And what are we drinking to?" I ask, a little more apprehension in my voice than I intend for there to be. I still haven't fully forgiven Mark for what went down the other night, but I'm willing to at least hear him out.

"To me being an ass," he replies. "To me trying to make amends."

"I think I can drink to that," I reply, then tap my glass against his.

The cool chardonnay hits my tongue, and the flavors explode in my mouth. I nod as I set the glass back down on the table.

"That's a really nice wine," I say.

"I thought you might like it."

I take another swallow of it, just to confirm it's as good as I thought after the first sip. It is. I inhale and the heavenly aroma of food fills my nose. I turn and look at him, surprised.

"You cooked?" I ask.

"Of course not. I wanted to impress you, not poison you," he says. "I picked up the Thai food we didn't get to eat the other night."

A small smile touches my lips. "Yeah, about that," I say. "I ate it."

He looks at me for a moment, then laughs. "Well, at least it didn't go to waste."

I take a sip of my wine and stare at him over the rim of the glass. I'd expected that we'd talk at some point. I didn't think he'd show up here with wine, food, and what looks like an expression of genuine contrition on his face.

"Listen, I needed to apologize for the other night. I was just worried about you. Scared for you, actually," he starts. "The thought of you being hurt tears me up inside. I mean, I know I don't express myself well, though. And I know I crossed a line."

"And?" I gesture for him to continue. He probably

expected me to just smile and say 'apology accepted', but I want more than that.

"And I acted like an idiot, and all I can ask for is your forgiveness. I'm really sorry, Blake. I just care a lot about you, and... I should never have freaked out on you like that."

"And?"

"And?" he frowns.

"And, you're sorry for trying to center yourself in the conversation about my life and my family," I explain. "You're sorry for trying to guilt-trip me about my own feelings."

He takes a sigh and looks up at me with clear eyes. "And I'm sorry for that too. I shouldn't have prioritized how I feel about it when it's clearly your life that you have to worry about."

"That's what I was looking for. Apology accepted."

It's like the room just exhaled. I smile at him and really mean it.

"And you're sorry you acted like an idiot," I crack, winking at him to soften the blow.

He laughs and nods. "I know it. Trust me, I've been beating myself up about it more than you ever could."

I take a sip of wine and set the glass back down, considering my words. Mark is looking at me with that intense green-eyed gaze that never fails to get my heart racing. With high cheek-bones and a square, chiseled jawline, he's rugged-looking, but still somehow also has a sweet baby face at the same time. Regardless, he's a beautiful man that I've found utterly intoxicating from the day I met him, which seems like a lifetime ago now.

"I know you were just worried about me. And I appreciate that. I really do," I tell him.

"You sure could have fooled me."

I laugh softly. "It may not seem like it, but I do. I just—my parents' case is very personal to me. I lost everything that day and in large part, it's why I joined the Bureau. I know you think I'm obsessed, and maybe I am. But I know I'm never going to be able to let it go until I know who killed my folks and took my sister."

"Even if the cost of finding out is your life?"

I shrug. "Yeah. I guess so."

"It scares me to hear you say that."

"I understand, Mark. You come from an entirely different world," I reply. "But my world was shaped by violence. I'm used to it. It doesn't scare me."

He sits back in his chair and takes a drink of his wine. I don't know if his goal in coming here tonight was just to apologize or if he's trying to subtly get me to stop with my investigation. I don't like thinking he came to this with an ulterior motive and not simply put our argument to rest. I want to believe he's here because he misses me and wants to make up. Not because he's trying to manipulate me into doing what he wants me to do.

"I know you think I need to drop this investigation. But I need you to understand that I can't," I continue. "You don't know what it's like to feel like a piece of your soul has been ripped out."

"But getting yourself killed trying to find out who did it isn't going to fix that feeling, Blake," he replies. "Do you think your parents or your sister would want that? Do you think they'd want to see you get yourself killed trying to avenge them?"

"No, of course not."

"No, they'd want to see you move forward with your life," he presses. "They'd want to see you happy. And isn't that what we are? Happy?"

"Yes, of course, we are. But don't you want me to be happy? Don't you want me to feel settled and at ease?"

"I really do."

"Then you should know I won't ever truly be at ease until I figure out who killed my folks and abducted my sister. Until I solve the case, I'm always going to feel tormented."

He sighs and runs a hand through his sandy brown hair. "It's just... when you told me that not only was the guy you were meeting with murdered, but you were shot at, I flipped out, Blake. The idea of you getting shot scares me to death."

"I know you don't want to hear this, but the job I do comes with risk. Every time I'm out in the field trying to run down a bad guy, I'm at risk of being stabbed, or shot, or run over by a bus."

He arches an eyebrow at me. "Run over by a bus?"

I shrug. "There was a story once that a couple of agents out in like Kentucky or something were trying to run down some meth head, and the guy got his hands on a bus. Apparently, he ran them both over with it."

"Well, that's comforting. So, not only do I have to worry about guys with guns coming after you, now I have to worry about guys driving buses coming after you too," he says with a small smile on his face.

"The point is that my job is always going to have risks. And I don't know any other way to do my job than to be the one kicking down the door and charging in," I tell him. "That's just who I am."

"I have noticed that about you."

"That's part of the deal with me. It's who I am and who I'll always be. I need you to not just understand, that but accept it. I'm going to be shot at. I'm going to be attacked. I may even have somebody try to kill me with a bus. And I can't handle coming home to you freaking out about it. This is me, Mark.

This is my job. And you're either going to be all right with it, or maybe I'm not the girl for you."

"But your parents' case. That's not an official Bureau case," he points out. "I get that those other cases are your job. But that one's not. And that's the one I worry about the most."

"Why is that?"

"Because when it comes to your job, you're dealing with garden variety criminals, for the most part. You're steeped in the rules of that world," he says softly. "But the people who killed your folks—those aren't run-of-the-mill criminals. If I'm to go by what you told me about them, they're assassins. Your folks were executed. And I have a fear that if you dig too deeply into that, they might execute you too. That scares the hell out of me."

"I won't stop, Mark. Which is why I say, you either need to accept it—or don't," I tell him. "But it's far too important for me to give up. Ever. Not until I've gotten justice for my family."

He looks down and frowns, seeming to be considering my words. Or maybe considering whether or not this is going to work after all. At the moment, he looks like he could be going either way. And while I don't necessarily want to lose him, I'm not giving up my drive to get justice for my family.

"I can make you one promise," I offer.

"And what's that?"

"I'll do my very best to minimize the risk," I say truthfully. "And I'll do my best to avoid putting myself in dangerous situations."

He sighs heavily. "That's about the best I'm going to get out of you, huh?"

"This is me, Mark. This is who I am. I am the job, and there's only one way I know how to do it—by totally committing myself to it and accepting that every time out in the field could be my last. And being at peace with it."

"To be honest, I don't know that I'll ever be at peace with it. I care about you, Blake. I care about you a lot," he says. "And I don't know that I can ever be blasé and just accept your death. And I sure as hell can't be at peace with it."

"Then I just need you to accept it," I urge him. "Because I can't alter the way I do my job. That's just not who I am. So, if it's too much for you and you want out, I understand. Go and find somebody who makes you happy and is less likely to meet a violent death at the hands of some cracked-out wannabe bus driver."

He laughs softly. "That's what sucks about this whole thing. I don't want anybody else."

"Neither do I."

He frowns and shakes his head. "I'll try to find a way to be at peace with the job you do. I can't promise there won't be rough patches. But I'll try."

I give him a smile and get to my feet, then walk around the table and wrap my arms around him. My mouth finds Mark's and we descend into a fiery, passionate kiss that feels natural. It feels right. And it makes my heart turn somersaults inside of me.

"What was that for?" he asks.

"Because I wanted to make you shut up so we can eat."

He laughs and gets to his feet and leads me into the kitchen. It feels like we're back on track and that we can put this behind us. He may not like it, but hopefully, he can accept it.

I know this is a conversation we're probably going to be revisiting again. Probably more than once. But as long as we feel like we're moving in the right direction, I think we'll be all right.

FOURTEEN

I GRIP THE WHEEL TIGHT, turning my knuckles white. The pressure's been building up in me all day and I know there's only one way to release it. It came on quicker this time than it did last time. That gnawing hunger in me. That need. I imagine this is what druggies feel like when they're jonesing for their next fix.

"Druggies or vampires," I mutter to myself with a giggle.

The streets are crowded with both cars and foot traffic. It's both a blessing and a curse. In this part of the city, there's lots of variety. Lots of girls to choose from. It's like a buffet. But the sheer amount of people makes it hard to get away clean. But hey, like my mommy always used to say, you have to take the good with the bad. That's what I'm doing here, right? Taking the good with the bad?

"Taking the good and doin' somethin' bad with it is more like it."

I giggle again, amused by my own cleverness as I scan the

crowds on the sidewalks passing by. I'm like a Great White Shark, slowly and silently cruising through the waters, looking for my next meal. And none of the people out there on the sidewalk knows just how close Death is to them. Unlike the Great White Shark though, I'm picky about my meals. I'm not going to eat just anything. No, not me. They'll never cut open my belly and find a license plate or an old, deflated basketball. I only choose the finest morsels to sate my appetites.

I pass by the bars, restaurants, and coffee houses that line these streets. Belltown's one of the trendiest spots in the entire city, and as a result, it's never short on tasty morsels. The trick is finding that one little fish that somehow gets separated from its school. Once you spot the straggler, you have to time it just right so you can swoop in and snatch it up with nobody being any the wiser. That's something else my mommy always said— make a plan. Always make a plan. My mommy was a fount of wisdom like that.

I turn up the radio and sing along with Blondie. *"One way or another, I'm gonna find ya. I'm gonna get ya, get ya, get ya, get ya..."*

The song seems perfectly fitting. It's almost like my theme song, and I take it as a good sign that it came on while I'm on the hunt. I turn down Bell Street from Second Avenue and cruise by a line of bars. There. Up ahead. As if the angels themselves are smiling down on me, I see her. She's standing beneath a streetlight—alone. Her hair shines like spun gold and her pale skin glows like she's lit from within. She's beautiful. She's perfect. And like a moth, I'm drawn to the light she casts.

Even from where I am, I can see that she's crying. She keeps angrily wiping away the tears that are spilling down her cheeks. And the way she's swaying on her feet tells me she's had a few. Perfect. I pull to a stop beside her and roll down the passenger side window.

"Hey, are you all right?" I ask.

"Fine. I'm fine," she slurs.

She's unsteady on her feet and looks like her legs could give out at any moment. Although she's swaying like she's on the open ocean during a hellacious storm, the girl somehow manages to keep her feet.

"Hey, why don't you get in and let me get you home, huh?" I ask. "A girl in your condition shouldn't be out here alone like this."

"I'm fine," she repeats, still slurring and still swaying.

I put the car in park and pull my ballcap low before getting out of the car. I casually glance around, making sure I'm not being observed, then circle around to the other side and lean against the car, making myself look as non-threatening as possible. The girl has her face glued to her phone and is tapping away on the screen furiously. Tears are streaming down her face. Only now, she's not bothering to wipe them away and lets them fall.

"Boy problems, huh?" I ask.

She snaps her head up and looks at me like she didn't even realize I was standing there. Her eyes are unfocused, and her jaw is slack. She sways, and I'm sure she's just about to go down but manages to catch herself and stumbles a step closer to me.

"Your boyfriend givin' you grief, huh?" I ask, pointing to her phone.

"He's ch—cheating on me," she sobs, the admission triggering a fresh flood of tears.

"He's a fool," I tell her. "Don't know what he's got right in front of him."

"Right?" she gasps.

"He don't deserve you."

She shakes her head. "He doesn't."

"And you shouldn't be out here in this condition. You just

never know what kind of creeps are runnin' around lookin' to take advantage of a girl who ain't in her right mind."

She looks down at her phone again and holds it up for me to see. "I'm trying to call Uber."

"Well then, it's your lucky night. I'm a driver for e-Taxi. Same thing as Uber."

She cocks her head and looks at me, that wild-eyed, unfocused gleam in her eye. She looks at me as if she's trying to figure out some complicated calculus equation. I point to the sticker in the window of my car—the black and yellow checkered e-Taxi sticker I stole from somebody who actually drives for them.

"I should go home," she slurs.

"Yes, you should. I'll get you there," I tell her.

She shakes her head and squints at her screen. "I don't have your app on my phone."

"That's all right. I'll drop you at home and won't charge you. I just wouldn't feel right about leaving you out here on the street like this. You just never know what kind of monster might come along."

Inside the car, I hear Debbie Harry's voice, "*I'm gonna get ya, get ya, get ya, get ya,*" and smile to myself.

"That's sweet," she says, drawing out the word 'sweet' in a long, snake-like slur.

"Just doing my part to help somebody in need. What's your name, sweetheart?"

"Serena—Serena Monroe," she says, though it sounds more like a question.

I open the door of the car and let her pour herself into the back seat. As she struggles to sit up and figure out the complicated mechanics of the seat belt, I slip the syringe out of my pocket and uncap it, making sure to tuck the plastic stopper back into my pocket as to not leave it behind for somebody to find—an ounce of prevention, as mommy used to say.

I lean down, giving her a smile that she returns. The needle slips into her flesh with practiced ease, and before she even knows what's happening, I'm pumping the ketamine into her system. It starts to take effect quickly and a small gasp passes her lips. The girl leans her head back against the seat rest and closes her eyes with a blissed-out little smile on her face. I finish buckling the seat belt, then close the door.

I walk back around to the driver's side door, glancing around at the street. There are knots of people everywhere, but nobody close enough to me to see what's just happened. I climb in and drop the syringe into the plastic waste collection box on the floor of the passenger's seat. Feeling that pressure in my starting to lighten already, I look in the rearview mirror and see the smiling face of Serena Monroe. Her eyelids are fluttering closed, and she's wearing a nearly euphoric expression as she murmurs to herself.

"You're trash," I tell her. "You're dirty."

Serena mutters something I can't make out. Not that it matters. She has nothing to say that I'd be interested in anyway. She's one of those filthy girls mommy used to warn me about. Sluts. Spreaders of disease. Those kinds of girls who go out partying all night, hoping to find somebody to go home with because they can't wait to spread their legs. Girls like that are all trash. Garbage. Girls like that serve no purpose.

Serena's voice is soft and breathy. It's the voice of somebody who is descending into a deep, peaceful sleep. Her smile flickers across her lips and her eyes close as the warm grasp of sleep reaches up and pulls her down into the comfort of its dark embrace.

I'm really looking forward to wiping that smile off her face. Forever.

FIFTEEN

I STEP off the elevator and am walking through the underground parking garage, my eyes darting everywhere as I search for threats. It's so ingrained into me by this point, it's as much an unconscious reflex as breathing is. Being a woman, you always need to be alert and on your toes. Being an FBI agent, you're trained to be paranoid and expect an attack to come at you. So being a female FBI agent has made me obsessively vigilant.

I make it to my car without incident and toss my bag onto the passenger's seat as I climb in. I'm just about to put the key in the ignition when my phone rings. I quickly turn the key to start the accessories, then push the button to route the call through the speakers.

"Blake Wilder," I answer.

"Blake, it's Rebekah."

"Hey," I reply. "Kind of early for you, isn't it?"

"A little bit, yeah. I guess," she says. "Actually, it's late. I worked overnight last night. I'm just getting off now."

Her voice is hushed but hurried, and there's an edge of fear in her tone.

"You all right, Beks?" I ask.

"Yes. No," she says. "I mean, maybe."

"You sure about that?"

"I'm flipping out there, Blake. Like, I'm having a full-on mental meltdown right now."

"Okay, what's wrong?"

There's a pause on the line and I watch an older couple walking through the garage, hand in hand. I've seen them in the building before and have exchanged greetings, but I'd never say I know them. They've always just struck me as a couple who is in love. And knowing they're still deeply in love at their age gives me hope that maybe one day, I can have that. Maybe one day, when my life has settled down some, I can find the sort of relationship that, like the couple I'm watching, has not just survived, but flourished over the many years they've been together.

But those thoughts are always followed by the inevitable voice in my head that says that sort of love isn't in the cards for me. That I don't deserve it. I've tried arguing with that voice on several occasions, telling it that Mark's presence in my life disproves its opinion. But the voice always ends the argument by saying it's only a matter of time before I do something that will make my relationship with Mark implode spectacularly.

"Rebekah, what's wrong?"

"Not on the phone. Can you meet me for coffee?"

"Yeah, absolutely," I reply. "Just tell me where."

"Do you know where the Urban Bean is?"

"I can find it," I tell her.

"Good. I'll be there in twenty."

"I'm on my way."

I disconnect the call and start the car then pull up the GPS on the dash-mounted display. I type in the name for the coffee house and let it pull up the route for me. It's a little bit off the beaten track and is well away from the ME's office, making it less likely that Rebekah would run into anybody she works with. The precautions pique my curiosity, as did the near panic I heard in her voice. Wanting to find out what in the hell is going on, I put my car in gear and pull out of the garage and merge into the flow of traffic.

A little more than fifteen minutes later, I pull into the Urban Bean's parking lot. I pull alongside Rebekah's VW Beetle and shut off the engine, then climb out. The coffee house is round, like a donut. Large plate-glass windows wrap around the front half of the donut, with tables at each of them. The back half of the donut is brick and windowless and is presumably where the offices are.

I see Rebekah through the windows, already sitting at one of the tables. She gives me a nervous wave when she spots me walking in. I move straight to the counter and order a coffee drink and a blueberry scone. When my order comes, I take it over to the table and sit across from her, and take a bite of my scone, washing it down with my coffee drink.

"So, what's up?" I ask. "You seemed pretty freaked out on the phone."

She nods and takes a drink of her coffee—taking a few beats to put her thoughts in order, I suppose. She finally raises her gaze to me, and I can see how freaked out she is. Whatever happened, it left her shaken.

"Beks?"

"I had a visit from Deputy Chief Torres last night," she starts. "And he's none too happy."

I feel my blood run cold. It wasn't all that long ago that

Torres pulled me over on the street and had all but threatened to kill me outright. Suffice it say, we won't be exchanging Christmas cards anytime soon. Torres is a snake who would rather let killers run rampant through the streets of Seattle than do what's necessary to catch them. His only concern is in playing department politics and climbing the ladder.

So, he does what he can to minimize the bad news and talk up his achievements, regardless of how minor they are. The man is a natural-born snake oil salesman. And yet, he plays politics so well and knows exactly which butts he has to kiss, so he continues to advance. Torres is a disgrace and yet, it won't be too long before he's running the entire SPD. It's a shame.

"What did he want from you?" I ask.

"He said that he knew about our connection. Our relationship," she says. "He said he knows I've been feeding you information about our cases."

I swallow hard, knowing just how intimidating and vindictive Torres can be. Rebekah isn't used to that sort of thing—she's just not that kind of person—which is why she's freaking out right now.

"What did you say?"

She shakes her head. "I didn't say anything. What could I say? He's not wrong."

"But he doesn't know that."

"It sounds like he does to me," she replies. "He said he'll arrest me if he catches me doing it again. I don't want to go to jail."

"He's blowing smoke, Beks," I tell her. "He has absolutely nothing. What's more, I don't think he can arrest you for providing information to the Bureau. He's just trying to intimidate you. Scare you."

"Yeah well, he did a pretty good job of it."

I nod. "He can be very forceful and intimidating."

I tell her the story of him pulling me over and everything that happened. She listens, completely aghast. And when I'm done, she shakes her head.

"God, I hate bullies," she mutters.

"You and me both," I nod. "He's got nothing, and he knows it. If he were going to arrest you, he would have. He wouldn't have given you warning about it first."

She frowns but nods, the logic getting through to her. Rebekah takes a bite of her pastry and chews on it for a long moment as I watch a myriad of emotions scrolling across her face. I really don't want to cut off the information pipeline, but I know that I don't want Rebekah getting tossed out of the ME's office even more. Torres might not be able to arrest her like he's threatening to do, but he can certainly move against her to make her job hell—or even get her fired.

"Listen, I don't want you getting caught up in all of this garbage," I tell her. "So, I understand if you want to get out of the information-sharing business. No sweat all."

It's a lie. It would be a hardship without eyes and ears in the ME's office. But I'll get by. I always do. More than anything, I just don't want Rebekah to be collateral damage in this little behind-the-scenes war I'm having with Torres.

She thinks on it for a moment and shakes her head. "Maybe we just need to be a little more circumspect," she offers. "Maybe you shouldn't come into the ME's office like you're storming the Bastille."

My mouth falls open, shocked. "I do not come into the ME's office like that."

"Oh, you so totally do sometimes."

We share a laugh, but I let out a silent breath of relief knowing that she'll continue to slip me the information I need.

"I propose that when we need to pass information back and forth, we meet here," I say. "It's out of the way, quiet, and I'm sure Torres' guys would stick out like a sore thumb here."

She nods. "That's true. It's kind of an insular little community around here. It's one reason I like it."

"Listen, Rebekah. I don't want you doing something you're not comfortable doing," I tell her. "If you want to stop, I have no problem with that."

"Are you eventually going to take Torres down?"

"I hope so. I'm hoping I can build a case," I reply.

"Then I'll keep passing you information. Mostly because I want to be around when you drop the hammer on him."

I laugh. "And here I thought I had the market cornered on vindictiveness."

She rolls her eyes. "Please, I've got you beat in that department, hands down."

"Yeah, if you say so."

Rebekah reaches down into her bag and pulls out a thick file then slides it across the table to me. I look at it for a moment, unsure if I should take it. I don't want to get Rebekah into any more trouble than I've already caused her.

"That's the tox screen and the official report," she says. "Everything you need for Summer Kennedy."

"I thought the tox screen wasn't coming back for a while yet?"

She shrugs. "Somebody called down and made it happen. I'm guessing Torres. He's one of the few who have the juice to make it happen."

"But why, is my question? Why jump the line for this case?" I ask.

"That is an answer I do not have, my friend."

"And you haven't seen any other bodies that came in like Summer's?"

"Babe, I see bodies come through that are all torn up in a lot of different ways," she replies.

"But the torture—the shallow cuts and cigarette burns," I clarify. "Seen any with those markers lately?"

She frowns. "I haven't."

"Well, we'll start with this," I say and tap the file. "I can't thank you enough."

"Sure you can," she says with a grin. "Buy me a scone to go."

"Comin' right up," I reply.

SIXTEEN

Criminal Data Analysis Unit; Seattle Field Office

"So, Torres is coming after Rebekah now," Astra says after I've filled her in on my meet with Rebekah this morning.

"He's trying to get at us any way he can," I say with a shrug.

"He's persistent. I'll give him that."

"He's a piece of garbage," Mo adds.

"He is that for sure," I nod. "Anyway, we got the case file, and based on the stomach contents, it looks like our unsub kept her for a least a night."

"Makes sense. He'd want maximum time to dole out the punishment," Astra notes.

I nod. "And we also got the tox screen back." I toss the file Rebekah gave me onto Astra's desk, where it lands with a hard thump. "Ketamine."

"What about it?" Astra asks.

"It was found in Summer Kennedy's system," I answer.

Everybody whistles low in unison, like they rehearsed it, drawing a laugh from me. I pace before the monitors at the front of the bullpen and process everything we know so far. Which sadly, isn't all that much. But it's enough to give us a start. And knowing that the killer used ketamine to subdue her gives us a pretty good data point to add to the list.

"Okay, so what do we know about ketamine?" I ask.

"It's a pretty powerful sedative," Mo says. "They use it to help keep patients anesthetized. It's also supposed to help with OCD, so it's often prescribed."

"And because it can produce a near trance-like state, it's sold on the streets. I heard it's a popular party favor for students these days," Astra says.

"Nice. Not sure a party with a house full of people in a stupor is exactly my idea of a good time, but that's just me," I comment. "So, who can purchase ketamine?"

"Doctors, obviously," Astra says. "And of course, anybody with a prescription."

"Veterinarians can buy it as well," Mo adds.

"Actually, you don't need a prescription anymore. You can buy it online pretty cheaply and easily," Rick chimes in. "Or so I've heard... from friends."

"That's lovely," she replies. "A generation of kids who can easily buy drugs that turn them into zombies. What could possibly go wrong with that?"

"All right, how many of these online stores sell it?" I ask.

"There are only three major websites that ship into Seattle," Rick replies.

"Wow. Your friends sure do know a lot," Astra says.

Rick coughs and looks away, unable to meet my eyes, making me laugh. "Okay Rick, get in touch with these online retailers to see if they can give us a list of customers. Exclude doctors and veterinarians for now," I tell him. "Right now, I want to look for end-users."

"I'll give it a shot, but these people are touchy about the

privacy of their customers. We may have a hard time getting the names," he says.

"Just tell them if they don't cooperate, you'll take your considerable business elsewhere," Astra offers with a grin.

"Right. Okay, Mo, start working on getting a warrant," I say. "Rick, are any of these online stores headquartered here in Seattle?"

Rick turns back to his screen and his fingers flurry on the keyboard.

"Just one," he answers.

"Okay, we're going to focus on that one for now," I say. "Give Mo the pertinent details so she can draft the paper."

"You got it, boss," he nods.

"Also, we need to add ketamine to the parameters of what we're searching for," I say. "Rick, expand that search. Caucasian women. College-aged. Torture and ketamine."

"No sweat."

"Any word from that ride-hailing company?"

He shakes his head. "Not yet. They're slow-walking it, even with a warrant."

I nod, having expected that. Online companies are loath to give up their client lists. They hold onto their names like they're gold for as long as they can—even in the face of a murder. On one hand, I get it. They want to protect their clients. It makes sense. On the other, we're not some random person looking. We're the FBI and we're trying to stop people from being murdered. You think they'd get that and would help us out.

"What are you going to do?" Astra asks.

"I'm going to talk to Fish."

"And who is Fish?"

"If you ever need to know who's dealing what out in the

streets, you talk to Fish," I say. "And you never deal out in the streets without the blessing of Fish."

Astra grins. "Let me guess, Fish gets a cut of every deal out there?"

"It's true. And when you're a legend like him, you get away with it."

"I've never heard of this guy," Mo says. "How is it that this guy is a legend?"

"Because he did some things back in the day that cemented that status," I say.

"Allegedly," adds Astra.

I laugh because it's true. "He was tried six different times," I say. "He was acquitted six different times."

"Weak cases?" Mo asks.

"More like bought and paid for judges and jurors," Astra says.

"The guy didn't take chances and covered all his bases. He's smart, crafty, and does not take no for an answer. He's ruthless. Or rather, he was. Now, he's living the high life of a retired man. Semi-retired, anyway. And yet the street thugs continue to pay tribute to him. Because if they don't, they know the consequences. Fish may be kind of retired, but he's still the leader of a ruthless army."

"Comforting," Astra remarks. "And how is it exactly that you know this notorious outlaw?

"Let's just say our paths have crossed a few times over my career," I offer with a laugh.

A chime sounds from my phone so I slipped it out of my pocket and felt my heart sink. I sighed and looked up.

"Body dropped," I announce.

"Great," Astra mutters.

"Okay, Fish is going to have to wait. Astra, you're with me,"

I say. "Rick and Mo, can you start tackling your to-do list? We've got a little bit of steam up and I want to keep it rolling."

"Aye Aye, Cap'n," Rick responds with a salute for good measure.

Mo rolls her eyes. "I'm on it, boss."

"Thanks, guys. Keep up the great work."

I turn and head for the door, Astra by my side. It's strange in that for knowing so little right now, I feel like we're at the point of the case where the momentum is starting to build. It feels to me like events are picking up steam and are starting to move faster. Or at least, we're not at a complete standstill anymore.

There's still so much we don't know and so many different moving parts right now, but it feels to me like some of the boxes are starting to fill in. And that feeling always puts a charge in my belly.

SEVENTEEN

Perry V. Wilson Memorial Park; Seattle WA

"So, you get alerts when a body drops now?" Astra asks. "Kind of morbid, don't you think? I mean, the only way you could take your work home with you any more would be to bring the actual body back to your place."

I laugh. "It's a prototype of an app Brody developed," I tell her. "It uses the software that monitors police bands, interprets the codes, and voila, I get a message telling me where it's at and some of the basic details, like whether it's natural causes or a homicide."

"Wow. That's actually pretty ingenious. And where did he come up with an idea like that?" she asks.

"It was my idea. I asked him a while back to see if it was even possible," I tell her. "I got tired of the SPD freezing us out and wanted to know when they got calls for homicides. It sure beats having to rely on tips or gathering information after the fact, doesn't it?"

She nods, looking quite impressed. I give myself a mental

pat on the back for having had the idea in the first place. When I pitched it, Brody wasn't sure he could pull it off, but he sent it to me last night and this first test drive worked like a charm. But we won't know for certain until we get to the crime scene. If there is one. As morbid as it sounds, I'm hoping this isn't a call out for a fender bender or a death of natural causes. I'm tired of Torres having the jump on us and want to get ahead of him.

We badge the cops working the barricade and pull the sawhorses aside, allowing us to drive into the parking lot. As with the last scene, there is a double barricade, but minimal emergency response vehicles. It's odd that the scene is set up in this way again.

"I guess Torres thinks if they don't call attention to it, maybe people just won't notice the brutal murder in a public park?" Astra gives voice to my thoughts without me even having to say anything.

"That must be it. But at least we know Brody's app works," I shrug. "This is, in fact, a crime scene."

"Hooray for silver linings."

We park next to one of the squad cars, then make our way to the second set of yellow tape that's been strung across the entrance to the park. We badge the cops at the tape, and he holds it up, allowing us to slip under it and head further inside. Trees and bushes are scattered all around through the park. A little way to our left is a large open field where people gather to play soccer or football, or what have you. There's also a play-ground set about fifty yards off to our right with swings, monkey bars, a merry-go-round, and other equipment. Beyond that another twenty-five yards or so is a workout station. It sits just off one of the running trails. I know from having used this park to work out before, there are half a dozen more workout stations along the path.

We follow the concrete trail we're on through the trees and

THE CHOSEN GIRLS   121

bushes and find ourselves standing at the edge of a small pond. It's fed on one end by a swift-moving stream and flows out through a small channel that had been cut a while back to keep the pond from overflowing its banks. It keeps the water in the lake circulating so it doesn't get stagnant and become a breeding ground for mosquitos.

Unlike the pond at McGeary, this is in a wide-open space. Trees ring the water, but they stand back about twenty yards from the edge of it. Out in the middle of the pond is a large concrete fountain that shoots water ten feet into the air, along with smaller jets encircling it shooting water half that high.

It's a popular place. People come every day to wade and play in the water, or play with radio-controlled boats and drones. I seem to recall them even holding tournaments here. Boys and their toys.

I follow Astra over to where they're fishing the girl out of the water. We're standing about fifteen feet away as they haul her up to the laid-out body bag and gently set her down. Once the divers step away, Astra and I walk over to the body to do a quick external examination.

The girl's blue eyes are wide open, glazed over in death. Her blonde hair shimmers like gold over her delicate bone structure. I'm immediately struck by how much she looks just like Summer Kennedy. She had been a beautiful girl in life.

And also, like Summer Kennedy, she was tortured. Cuts and puncture marks litter her body. It seems like there are even more than what had covered Summer's body. Same for the cigarette burns. They're everywhere. She's bruised and beaten to hell, and judging by the awkward angle her right arm is protruding, the monster who took her broke it. And like Summer Kennedy, there are distinct finger-shaped bruises around her throat.

"This is just pure rage," Astra mutters. "This is a man who does not like women."

"Or one particular woman," I reply softly. "Notice how alike this one looked to Summer Kennedy?"

"This one would be Serena Monroe."

We turn at the sound of his voice to find Detective TJ Lee standing behind us with a nervous look on his face.

"Are you all right, Detective?" I ask.

"What are you two doing here?" he asks, his jaw clenched and flexing.

"Investigating a crime scene," I reply. "You know, our jobs?"

"How did you guys even know we had a body drop out here this morning?"

"There's apparently an app for that," Astra says and chuckles at her own wit.

I have to fight to keep myself from laughing along. It's not appropriate to the time or current setting and I need to maintain a professional demeanor.

He ignores her, his eyes laser-focused on me. "Seriously, you can't be here right now."

"I hate to break it to you, but I can," I reply. "This is an active crime scene, we are both law enforcement—"

"No, it's not that. It's Torres. He's here, and if he sees you, he's going to lose it. You're like his newest obsession and the man is on a warpath, determined to make your life a living hell. Seriously, for your own sake, you guys should get out of here," Lee implores us.

"Too late," Astra mutters.

I lean around Lee's body to see Torres coming our way with all the delicacy and grace of a charging bull. I glance over at Astra and grin.

"Got a red cape by chance?" I ask.

"Sadly no, it's in my other coat. As is my *espada*," she says, referring to the ceremonial bullfighter's sword. "I really, really wish I had that right now."

"Wilder, what in the hell are you doing on my crime scene?" Torres huffs when he finally reaches us.

"That would be Supervisory Special Agent Wilder, Deputy Chief Torres," I snap.

"I don't give a damn what your title is. This is my crime scene and you're on it, without my permission. Now kindly pack up and get your ass out of here, Supervisory Special Agent Wilder," he spits.

I step closer to him, a malicious grin on my face. "You do realize the FBI is a federal organization, don't you? Federal authority, in most cases, supersedes local authority. So, if I wanted to, I could step in, claim jurisdiction, and kick you off *my* crime scene."

Torres looks at me, his mouth hanging open for a moment as he seems unable to process what I just said. But the moment passes, and his bluster comes back with a vengeance. He glares hard at me, his already beady eyes growing smaller and more malevolent.

"May I have a word with you in private, SSA Wilder?" he asks.

I look around at the wide-open space of the park pointedly. "Not sure there's much privacy to be had here, Deputy Chief."

He sighs and walks away, fully expecting me to follow. So, I don't. I wait until he's standing about twenty feet away and turns around, thinking I was right behind him. He looks up, his face twisted and contorted with rage.

"SSA Wilder," he calls. "A word, please."

"You should really be careful with him, Blake," Lee says, low enough so only I can hear. "Pissing him off is only going to make things harder on you in the long run. Like it or not, the man plays the game and is really well connected."

I wave him off. "Let him do his worst. Trust me, Detective Lee, nobody, and I mean nobody, can be more petty and vindictive than me. I made it an art."

He looks skeptical and shakes his head. "Your funeral. But don't say I didn't warn you."

I leave him chatting with Astra and walk over to where Torres is waiting for me, glowering, his expression dark. I have to keep myself from laughing. I stop a couple of feet away from Torres and watch as he physically transforms. His face loses the heat, as do his eyes. He unclenches his jaw and releases his fists, and a sense of calm descends over his face. I'm sure it's a Herculean effort. Going from rage to calm—or in this case, the appearance of calm—is no easy feat. I'll give him kudos for trying to keep himself under control for a change.

"What can I do for you, Deputy Chief?" I ask.

"I suppose asking you to get off my crime scene nicely won't have any effect, will it?"

"I think we've already established whose crime scene this actually is," I reply. "But I'll let you stay on it. I'm not that petty."

"Hey, you remember that little chat we had outside your car a while back?"

"Oh, you mean when you stopped me, threatened me, then really gave serious thought to shooting me by the side of the road?" I fire back. "Is that the little chat you're talking about?"

"Characterize it how you want, but my point remains. I'm not going to let you grandstand out here and besmirch the hardworking men and women of the SPD because you want the headlines," he spits. "I will not let you run roughshod over my department or try to make us—or me—look bad."

"See, that's the problem with you, Deputy Chief Torres—

this isn't about you," I hiss. "It's not about you and it's not about me."

I turn and point to the body of the girl lying on the opened body bag, then glare at him.

"This is about her. This is about finding the monster who did this to her and bringing them to justice," I all but shout. "This isn't about your political fortunes or who gets the headlines. Because unlike you, I actually give a damn about these victims. I actually want to solve this case and put a monster in a cage."

"How dare you?" Torres growls. "Who in the hell do you think you are?"

"I'm somebody who doesn't think hiding the information about murders in the city is good policy!" I yell at him. "I'm somebody who doesn't think of myself first and foremost in all things. I'm not an arrogant, pompous ass like that. Like you."

And then Astra is there beside me, pushing me backward until she can take my arm and start to pull me away. But I fight her, trying to get back to Torres to finish my litany of insults. I don't have to go far though, because he's following close behind, his face twisted with rage.

"You'd best watch yourself, Wilder. Keep pushing me and see what happens."

"You threatening me, Torres? Again?"

"It's not a threat. I'm just saying I might finish what I started that day I pulled you over."

I lurch at him, but Astra is there, holding me back. I don't think I ever realized quite how strong she was until that moment. Detective Lee is also there, putting himself between me and Torres, helping to keep the Deputy Chief at bay. He turns to Astra, disbelief on his features. All around us, I can see people stopping what they're doing to watch the spectacle unfolding. I can feel the weight of their stares; I know I should get myself back under control but can't seem to stop. He's managed to trigger that "on" switch in me and now I'm ready for a fight.

"You should get her out of here," he says.

Astra nods, then drags and pulls me out of the park, not stopping until we're next to our car. When she finally lets me go, I immediately start back for the park. But then my head is rocked to the side and there's a sharp sting in my face. I put my hand to my cheek and look at her, eyes wide, mouth hanging open.

"You slapped me," I say.

"Yeah well, I didn't have a bucket of cold water handy," she says. "Get in the car."

Numb with shock and disbelief, I do what she says. She drops in behind the wheel and turns to me. I can see she's fighting like hell to keep herself from smiling and laughing. Though for the life of me, I can't figure out what's so funny.

"Well," she says. "That was interesting."

EIGHTEEN

"WHAT IN THE hell were you thinking?" Rosie growls.

"I wasn't. Simple as that," I reply. "I let him get under my skin and I just reacted. I was wrong and I apologize."

"Damn straight you were wrong, Blake."

I nod. "I know."

Rosie taps the screen on her tablet and the wall-mounted monitor springs to life, showing me and Torres getting into it. I look down at my hands in my lap, listening to both of us shouting at each other. On the screen, Astra and Lee are separating us, but Torres and I are still struggling to get back at each other, rage upon our faces. It looks like a freaking free-for-all. We're both lucky somebody didn't get hurt.

I'd been aware of the crowd at the crime scene watching us trying to kill each other, but I hadn't seen anybody filming. But apparently, they had, and then threw it up on YouTube well before I even got back to the field office. By the time I hit the

CDAU, there was a message from Rosie telling me to get to her office immediately.

"Four hundred thousand views," Rosie says, shaking her head. "And it's been what, two hours since this happened? How does it feel to go viral, kid?"

"Not very good, to be honest."

"No, I wouldn't imagine it would," she says. "Not for something like this. Something like this makes me look bad. You know that, don't you?"

"I do. And I apologize for my part in this mess. It wasn't my finest moment."

She scoffs. "You don't say?"

Rosie plays the video again from the start. I guess having to relive that moment over and over again is one form of punishment. I'm sure there will be others, though. I can't believe I lost my cool the way I did. That's not me. I'm calm. Logical. Stoic, even. I don't let people like Torres push my buttons, and I certainly don't blow up like Krakatoa in public like I did. I don't know that I've ever felt more embarrassed or ashamed of myself than I do right now.

As I sit in the chair across from her, watching Rosie watching the video again, I can't help but feel like a kid in the principal's office, waiting for the punishment to be doled out. Or even better—one time when I was a kid, I accidentally threw a ball through the window after my folks had told me not to play in the house. But it was raining, and I was bored, and one throw got away from me. After that, I'd had to sit in my dad's office, just waiting for him to drop the hammer on me— just like I'm doing right now. The two scenarios couldn't be more alike.

"You're a supervisory agent, Blake. You know better than this," Rosie says.

"I do. I screwed up."

"I'll say. I had Torres on the phone screaming that he would take this all the way up to the Director if I didn't fire you."

I look up, feeling the knots in my stomach tighten painfully. This job is my life. This job is who I am and if I lose it, I don't know what I would do. Just the thought of losing this job is soul-crushing to me. Rosie looks at me and smirks, then waves me off.

"I've already spoken to the Director. You're not going anywhere. This time," she says and points to the screen. "But do anything like this again and I can't guarantee your head won't be on the chopping block."

The wave of relief that washes through me is profound. I slump back in my seat feeling utterly wrung out. It's all I can to do keep myself from sobbing my eyes out with joy that I'm not going to get canned. I take a moment to gather myself, then sit back up again when I feel able.

"I swear nothing like this is ever going to happen again, Rosie. You have my word," I stammer.

"It better not, kid, or I'll throw you out the front doors myself."

I nod. "You won't have to. I'll leave on my own," I say. "If you need me to issue a formal apology—"

She scoffs. "To Torres? Screw that. He didn't get half of what he should have," she said. "No, I'm not going to have you apologize to that pig. He doesn't deserve it."

She watches the video again. My face is burning with embarrassment so hot I'm surprised my head hasn't burst into flame. I want to tell her to turn it off. Especially as I watch the view count scrolling as the numbers continue to rise. But Rosie seems to be enjoying herself by torturing me. I continue to sit there though, waiting for the other shoe to drop.

"Am I suspended without pay? Administrative leave?" I

ask. "Am I being assigned to anger management courses or anything?"

She waves me off again. "You're punishing yourself far harder than I ever could. So as far as I'm concerned, I've given you the firm talking to I had to give you as your boss, and you've paid your penance."

"Thank you, Rosie. I appreciate this."

She nods and then chuckles as she points to the screen. "Right there. His chin is perfectly lined up. I totally thought you were going to take the shot."

"If I had, I'm sure I'd be cleaning out my office right now."

She nods. "Probably so. That this didn't go further than a verbal altercation was your saving grace, kid," she says, then turns to me. "What did he say that set you off like that? I've never seen you so angry."

I shrug. "I honestly don't know. I guess it's just a combination of a lot of things," I reply. "And when he threatened me again, I just snapped. Lost it."

"He threatened you again?"

I nod. I told Rosie about what happened when Torres pulled me over. I honestly thought he was going to shoot me, and given that I was banged up after the case we'd just put to bed, I was in no condition to fight back. At least, not very well or effectively. And in that moment, I'd never felt weaker or more powerless in my life. It's something I've carried with me since that day. It's a feeling I despise in myself. And I hate Torres with every fiber of my being for making me feel that way. So yeah, there's probably a bit of baggage I'm hauling around after that.

"Said he's going to finish what he started," I tell her.

"That bastard."

"Yeah, but I have no proof. You can't hear it on that tape," I sigh. "It's my word against his. There's nothing I can do about it except hope he breaks into my house one night to make good on his threat, giving me the excuse I need to shoot him."

"We need to do something about that," Rosie says. "I won't stand by while he threatens the lives of my agents and gets away with it scot-free. One of these days we're going after Torres. We're going to make him pay."

"Maybe we should just let it all go," I offer. "The last thing I want is to go viral again. Or worse, end up in court for doing something I can't take back."

Rosie looks at me, arching an eyebrow. "Don't worry, Blake. He's going to get his. I'll see to it. Personally."

That sets a grin back on my face. Mild-mannered though she may be, Rosalinda Espinoza is somebody I would not want to get on the wrong side of.

I'm just grateful to be on the right side of her. For now.

NINETEEN

When I walk into the CDAU the next morning, Astra immediately begins to check out my backside, inspecting it closely until I burst into laughter and push her away.

"What in the world are you doing?" I ask.

"Just seeing how big of a chunk Rosie bit out of it when we got back yesterday."

"Big enough," I reply. "Probably won't be sitting right for a week."

"That's my girl," Astra chuckles. "Way to go, slugger."

I laugh and throw a pen at her. "Can we get to work, please?"

"Only if you promise not to beat me," she flashes me a mischievous grin.

"Am I ever going to live this down?"

"Definitely not," Mo says with a quiet chuckle.

"*Et tu, Brute?*"

"We're going to be dining out on this for years, babe," Astra adds.

The four screens on the wall at the front of the bullpen flash to life and are filled with the video. Except these ones are remixed, set to music from techno, to screaming death metal, to a power ballad. And as Rick plays them, one after the other, Mo and Astra break out into hysterical laughter. My face flares with heat once again.

"Did you do those?" I ask.

Rick shakes his head. "Not me. I personally think I would have gone with a nice Yanni remix if I had," he says, laughing. "But no, not me. The internet is sometimes a beautiful place."

"The internet is full of sick, deranged psychopaths," I mutter.

"That too," Rick nods.

"Okay, are we going to do some actual work today or just sit here and mock me all day?"

"Do we have the option?" Astra asks.

"No," I say. "Rick, cut the videos."

He's still laughing to himself as he pulls the videos down. I take a moment to compose myself—and to give Mo and Astra time to stop laughing. And when everything seems to have settled down, I look up at my team.

"All right, where are we on previous cases involving torture and ketamine?" I ask.

"We've found three over the last five years who were dosed with ketamine and were then sadistically tortured," Rick says, and the screens light up with the crime scene photos of three women—two brunettes and a blonde.

I step closer to look at the case files. One of the two brunettes was found inside a house almost five years ago. The other brunette was found in a campground three years ago.

Both bear signs of torture, and the bruising on their bodies is extensive, but to me, they don't seem to fit.

"Cause of death on the first brunette?" I ask.

Mo's fingers fly over the keys of her computer as she pulls up the autopsy report for the victim. She squints as she reads the small print.

"Monica Saldano, age thirty-seven. Looks like COD was an overdose," she reads out.

"And the second?" I ask.

"Megan Stills, age forty-two. Blunt force trauma," Mo reports.

An image of the back of her head pops up on the screen. It looks like somebody took a baseball bat to it. The skull is partially caved in and there's a gash opened down to the bone. I take it in and think about it.

"Could be our guy," Astra says. "Maybe these were his early kills, and he was just figuring out his kink. Wanted to experiment before he settled on one method."

"It's possible, but I don't think so," I reply slowly.

"Why's that?" Mo asks.

"Bring up the third girl. The blonde."

Rick calls up the photo and I'm struck right away by how similar she looks to Summer Kennedy and now Serena Monroe. She's young and blonde, and can't be older than twenty-one. She would have fit right in with some of those UW girls Astra and I were interviewing. I look at the stamp and see this kill was just over a month ago.

"COD?" I ask.

"This is Emily Tompkins. Age nineteen," Mo says. "Cause of death was manual strangulation."

I glance over at Astra who suddenly perks up, then turn to Rick. "Can you call up the photos of her body?"

The screens are suddenly filled with images of the girl's

body, moving from the crime scene to her autopsy. I notice that Emily was found in a river, hung up on a pile of rocks. Her body, like the others, had been pierced, sliced, beaten, and burned with cigarettes. She endured so much untold pain and suffering just like Summer and Serena. It breaks my heart

"This is our first victim," I say. "Emily Tompkins was the first victim. She looks just like the other two. Was beaten and tortured in the exact same way. And then she was unceremoniously dumped. And all had ketamine in their systems. The coincidences are piling up and we can't ignore them."

"Our guy hasn't evolved much over his three kills," Astra notes.

"He hasn't had to," I reply. "I'd guess that based on his proficiency, he's studied forensics at the very least."

"Maybe he works in an ME's office or a morgue," Mo wonders.

"I don't think so. This guy is filled with rage and hatred," I say. "I think the hate for women he carries around with him would be noticed by other people."

"Or he could be the kind of sociopath who knows how to turn it off when he needs to. The kind of sociopath who is adept at blending in," Astra offers.

"That's definitely possible. We can't discard that out of hand," I say. "But something tells me this guy works alone. I don't have anything to back that up. It's just a hunch right now."

"So, what about the brunettes?" Mo asks. "Why don't you think those are his kills?"

"Because they're not his type," I reply. "If you look at the three I'm positive are his—Emily, Summer, and Serena—they all look virtually the same. Or close enough, anyway. All of them blonde, young college-aged girls. All of them thin and gorgeous. Line up the blondes and they could all be sisters. I'm pretty comfortable saying he's a preferential offender, and thin, pretty, blonde girls are his type."

"So, is he fantasizing about killing a sister or his mother?" Astra asks. "Or an ex?"

"That's something we're going to have to find out on our own," I say. "We just need a little more data."

"I think we need to question Emily Tompkins' family, as well as Serena Monroe's. We need to find out where they were abducted from. If we can figure that out, maybe we can find his comfort zone. That could lead us close to where he lives."

"What's up with the water?" Mo asks. "Is that just a forensic countermeasure?"

Rick pulls up the crime scene photos from the blonde girls. I step closer and study the bodies of water they were dumped in and frown. Yeah, it could definitely be partly about forensic countermeasures. But as I study the photos closer, something inside of me tells me it's more than that. A lot more. This is his pathology on display for the world to see.

I shake my head. "This is his signature. The water," I say. "For some reason, the water is important to him. It's not only a forensic countermeasure—if it is at all—but water is important to him completing his ritual."

"Water?" Astra asks. "Why would water be important to him."

I shake my head. "I don't know for sure yet. But something about it is. I'm guessing it has to do with something in his childhood. Something left this impression on him and water became important. Critical to his life. even. What that is, I don't know yet."

I frown and continue studying the photos, looking for something to stand out to me. But nothing else does right now. I know I'm on the right track, though. I can feel it. The pieces of the puzzle are starting to come together and fall into place. I walk over to the whiteboard and pick up the green marker, then start to write down what I know of this guy so far.

"Caucasian. Late twenties to early thirties," I say the words as I write them.

"How can you predict the age?" Mo asks.

"You can't really, but don't get hung up on that. Age is the hardest thing to predict," I say. "But that's my guesstimate, because you don't typically see this level of rage combined with organization in somebody younger. It wouldn't shock me if he were older than I'm calling out."

Mo nods. "That makes sense."

"He's also going to be physically fit. He probably works out. Maybe even obsessively," I say. "He's charming. Socially adept. He can talk people into things."

"Why do you think that?" Mo asks.

"Because he got three young women to go off with him without raising an alarm," I point out. "These young women didn't cause a fuss, draw attention to themselves, or do anything that gave anybody the impression they were being abducted. That takes some social skill."

"It also means he's probably going to be attractive," Astra chimes in.

"Our boy's got game," Rick remarks.

"Maybe he can give you a few tips when we catch him," Astra says.

Rick gives her the finger but laughs. I give it a little more thought, trying to pull all these scraps together into one coherent picture.

"He's also going to have a place in a remote area. Somewhere off the beaten path. I'd guess it's going to be a cabin in the woods," I say.

"Why do you think that?" Mo asks.

"He's keeping the girls for a day and torturing the hell out of them," Astra explains as she nods along. "He's going to need privacy to do that because the girls will likely be screaming. A lot. I'd reckon that's what this guy gets off on—their screams."

"I'd wager you're right," I nod. "And I wouldn't be surprised if we found audio and videotapes of the torture sessions. He's going to want to relive it as often as he can."

"Damn. That is just brutal," Rick mutters.

"All right, Astra, I want you to go interview Serena Monroe's family and friends. See if you can dig anything up. Also, find out if you can figure out the last place she was seen," I say. "And Mo, I want you to go to the family of the first victim —Emily Tompkins. Same thing. See if you can pin down where she was taken from."

"Me?" she asks.

I nod. "You got this. You're intuitive and have great interviewing skills. You'll be great."

"And where are you going?" Astra asks.

"Going to see Fish."

TWENTY

Jade Pearl Billiards House, Chinatown-International District; Seattle, WA

I WALK through the front doors of the Jade Pearl and am immediately overwhelmed by the combined stench of cigarette and incense smoke. I give myself a moment to adjust, then walk through the billiards hall, aware of all the eyes on me. This is more of a locals-only establishment; not many Caucasian women just casually stroll through this place. Frankly, I can't see why any woman, regardless of ethnicity, would come in here.

The ground floor has a bar, a dozen pool tables, and a side room loaded with video games. Although the place is busy, with all the pool tables in use and a decent crowd at the bar, this is all a front. A façade hiding the real action, which is upstairs. I make my way through the billiards room, doing my best to avoid choking and/or contracting cancer from all the secondhand smoke. It's been a long while since I've been here but, if I remember right, there's a staircase at the back near the kitchen, hidden behind a steel door.

As I come around the corner, I'm assaulted by the odor of frying foods, which adds another layer of horrible to the smoke and incense hanging in the air. My eyes are watering so badly, I almost run into the man sitting on the stool beside the steel door. I rub my eyes and wait for my vision to clear before I'm able to get a look at him.

He's as tall as he is wide, with fawn-colored skin, dark almond-shaped eyes, and not a lick of hair on his head. He's got a round, smooth babyface, and possibly the biggest hands I've ever seen. He might be able to palm two basketballs with one hand.

"Well. You're new," I mutter.

The man looks me up and down, a roguish smirk on his face. "You lost?"

"I wish," I reply. "I'm here to see Fish."

"What you want with Fish?"

"A conversation about proper air filtration, to start," I tell him. "Other than that, my business is with him."

"He's not seein' nobody," he says.

"He'll see me."

"Doubt it."

"Call him."

"Don't have to. Fish ain't seein' anybody," he snaps.

I run a hand through my hair and count to five. Letting my temper get out of control probably isn't a good idea, knowing there are probably Triad men—Chinese mobsters —all over the place. Then again, coming here probably wasn't a good idea in general. But if there's anybody who knows, or can get me, the correct answer to my question, it's going to be Fish. Which is why I need to get man-mountain here to let me through the door so I can get to the upstairs gaming room, which is where I know I'll find him.

"Fish will see me. Now go upstairs, find him, and ask him. My name is Blake Wilder," I say through gritted teeth.

"Fish ain't seein' anybody right now."

I clap my hands over my face and rub my eyes again, my frustration growing hot.

"An," a sharp voice sounds.

Man-mountain and I both look up at the staircase to see Huan Zhao, aka Fish, standing there in a pair of silver pants and a black silk shirt. He's scowling at the big man, and lets loose to him in rapid-fire Chinese. I don't know what he's saying, but it sounds angry. The next thing I know, the large man is opening the door and stepping aside for me.

I cast him an "I told you so look," as I pass him and ascend the stairs. Fish is waiting for me on the next landing with a wide smile on his face.

"Agent Wilder. Lovely to see you again," he says, his English crisp and precise.

"Silver pants. That's a bold choice," I say.

"I'm a bold man."

"It's good to see you too, Fish," I reply with a smile.

He laughs and shakes his head. "Nobody has called me that in years," he says, then gestures to the stairs. "Please, go ahead."

I take a step up and he grabs my arm, turning me to face him. I look him in the eye and feel my stomach churn. His face is smooth and passive, his features giving none of his thoughts away. Huan is tall and lean, with dark hair cut stylishly short, tawny skin, and dark eyes. He's fit and takes care of himself, mainly through the practice of martial arts. Last I knew, he held black belts in four different martial art styles and has a body of taut, corded muscle as a result. He says it's as much for physical and mental discipline as it is for exercise.

"You're not here to bust me again, are you?" he asks.

"Me? Seriously?"

"You're a Fed. That's what you do," he replies.

"Not tonight I'm not," I tell him. "Tonight, I'm just Blake and I'm looking to have a conversation with an old friend."

He laughs. "Is that what we are? Friends?"

I shrug. "I like to think so. At least, we're not enemies."

"That's very true," he says, his laughter rich and elegant sounding. "Please, let's go upstairs and get a drink.'

When I was new to the Field Office, I briefly worked with an organized crime unit. I met Huan Zhao—Fish—on that one and only case I worked with OC. He was an informant for us—though I later found out, he was only informing on his business rivals, clearing the board for his eventual takeover. I want to be mad at him, but the guy played us by using our own ignorance, arrogance, and vanity against us. He gamed the system and he won. And in the process made the FBI look like we're a bunch of bungling idiots. Some of us learned a hard lesson from that. Others, not so much and have wasted their careers chasing—and never catching—him.

He got the name Fish when he was young and fled his native China, emigrating to Seattle. The story goes that he scraped together a living as a fishmonger, but eventually grew tired of the nickels and dimes he was making, so he turned to selling drugs. He eventually scraped enough money together to open his own fish cart and started to use the fish to transport the drugs he was selling. Business boomed, and he made his first fortune by the time he was eighteen, which was the seed he used to grow his empire. The rest, as they say, is history. That is, if you believe the legend—and I do.

Fish is a clever, intelligent guy. He's good-looking for his age—I'd say he's in his mid-fifties—and even though he never went to school here, you'd think he has a world-class education.

He's a colorful character. Big on personality and with charm to spare. He taught himself to read and speak English. In every sense, a self-made man. It would be even more impressive if he used his powers for good, rather than the illegal things he's gotten up to in his life—like this gambling hall.

I know I'm supposed to dislike him. He's a criminal. He does bad things. But I've found it's hard to dislike the guy. I've used him as an informant from time to time—he has his finger on the pulse of Seattle every bit as much as Marcy does. Though his finger usually strays more toward the underbelly than hers does. But every time I've needed information, Fish has always provided. And over the years, I like to think that we've developed a decent working relationship. There's a mutual respect between us. On my end it's not for what he does, but for what he overcame to get to where he is. I know very few people with his level of intelligence and gumption.

He leads me through the tables of card games, roulette, craps, and other games I can't even name. I have to weave around the waitresses carrying drinks to their thirsty customers, and past wildly gesticulating gamblers. This place is like Vegas with less neon and fewer hookers.

"Here we are," he says.

Fish holds the door open for me, then follows me into his office. It's large and windowless, done in polished wood and soothing earth tones. He drops down behind his desk, a massive oak monstrosity that somehow seems to suit him. I fear I'd look like a little kid playing grown-up if I sat behind it. He gestures to the chairs across from him so I take a seat.

On the wall to his left is a bank of monitors giving Fish a view of the floor outside his door as well as the billiards hall downstairs. To his right is a bookcase filled with books on topics ranging from history to current events, to biographies, to structural engineering. The spines on all of them are cracked, making it easy to see they've been read. Perhaps numerous times. And on the wall right behind his desk is a large framed black and white picture of the fishmongers in Pike's Place. I point to it and smile.

"Reminder of where you came from?" I ask.

He turns and looks at it, a faint smile upon his face as he turns back to me. "And a reminder of how easily I could be back there."

"If you're worried about losing it all, maybe you should consider giving up all the illegal stuff then," I say. "Just a thought."

He laughs softly. "Would you believe me if I told you that gambling hall outside this door is the last of my illegal activities?"

"No. Not really," I say. "Not at all, actually."

"You wound me, Blake."

I laugh. "I know you've still got a finger or two in the drug trade."

"Ahh, but I'm neither buying nor selling," he counters. "I'm merely facilitating meetings between consenting adults."

"You sound like a pimp."

"Is that what they sound like? I never got into running women," he shrugs. "It's barbaric and as far as I'm concerned, those who peddle flesh should be shot."

"That might be one of the first things we've ever agreed on."

"That's not true. We've agreed on a great many things," he replies. "Oh, by the way, I saw your clip on YouTube. Can I just say how amusing it was watching you trying to take Torres' head off? If there ever was somebody who deserved to be put in his place, it's that man."

I shake my head. "I'm never going to live it down."

"Don't try. Wear it as a badge of honor," he tells me. "You

stood up to evil and corruption. Quite literally. There is no shame in that. In fact, it's something that should be praised."

"You only say that because you hate Torres as much as I do."

"That I hate him as much as you do is irrelevant," he offers. "Torres represents everything wrong with the SPD. And you stood up to him. People will see that, and they will praise you for it. And rightly so."

"Well, I'd like to see that come about because as of now, I'm only being roundly mocked for it," I admit with a rueful laugh. "You have seen the remixes, I assume?"

He nods, suppressing a laugh. "Yes, and I particularly liked the techno mix. It was clever and catchy."

I sigh and roll my eyes as Fish laughs. Eventually, it tapers off and we're left staring at one another in silence. I shift in my seat and sit up.

"So, I need some information," I say.

"If I have it, I can help."

"I know you're a facilitator only now, but I'm looking for a guy who's buying up ketamine," I say. "I know it's uncommon, which is why I thought you might have a line on it."

"Ketamine. That went out of fashion a few years back," he shrugs. "Honestly, I can't think of the last time I even heard of somebody buying that foul stuff."

"Well, that might make my job a little easier then," I replied. "If you had a name for me anyway."

"May I ask what sort of case you're working on?"

Fish is as into true crime as my cousin Maisey. Both of them just can't seem to get enough of it. If he weren't, you know, a criminal, I totally would have been willing to introduce them and let them bond over serial killers and murder in general. But I'm not going to have my cousin wrapped up in an illegal gambling hall with a guy who's got a shady as hell past and is still technically involved with the drug trade in some fashion. I think deep down, Fish is a decent guy, but he's like a shark—and just behind those charming eyes is a mind more ruthless than I can even imagine.

"It's a murder," I tell him. "Actually, three murders now."

"Oh, a serial killer. Fascinating," he replies. "So, this man—he injects his victims with ketamine and then..."

"Tortures, rapes, and them strangles them to death," I finish for him. "He beats these women. Stabs and slices them. He puts cigarettes out on their skin. And then when he's done bearing them senseless and breaking their bones, he strangles them."

Fish looks at me with wide eyes and the sheepish look of a man who is endlessly fascinated by something he knows he shouldn't be fascinated by.

"There's a chance he's buying it online, but I tend to think he's buying it on the street," I continue. "This guy is careful. Meticulous. He doesn't leave evidence behind, which suggests to me that he wouldn't leave an online paper trail. He'd prefer paying cash."

"What else can you tell me about him?"

"He's probably white. Late twenties to early thirties. He's going to be physically fit. Strong," I tell him. "He's also likely going to be handsome and be very sociable. He's smart, but there is definitely going to be something off. If you're paying attention, you'll see that something's not right about him. You'll see that he's faking any emotion. That he's acting a part."

"That describes half the white men in Seattle," he points out with a laugh.

I frown at him and he holds his hands up in mock surrender.

"I haven't personally run across anybody like that," he says.

"But I'll ask around. Like I said, ketamine isn't fashionable these days, so perhaps that description will stand out."

"Thank you, Fish. I appreciate it," I say. "And I owe you one."

"Of course," he replies, then his smile brightens. "I meant it when I said I was going legit, Blake. And my first business is going to be a museum."

I arch an eyebrow. "A museum?"

He nods eagerly like a child who's dying to show off his new toy. "For the last couple of years, I've been collecting serial killer memorabilia. You wouldn't believe how much is out there."

"Actually, I would," I tell him. "Freaks come in all shapes and sizes."

He chuckles. "Well, I'm going to be displaying it in my own museum. I would love it if you'd come to the grand opening."

I laugh softly. "I'm surrounded by this stuff every day."

"Not like this," he replies. "I think you'll be surprised. Come as my special guest."

I think about it for a moment and realize how much Maisey would love to see something like that. It would give Annie heart palpitations, but Maisey would die of excitement. I look up at Fish and nod.

"All right," I say. "We'll set it up."

TWENTY-ONE

Golden Sun Restaurant; Downtown Seattle

ON MY WAY back to the shop, Detective Lee called me and asked that I meet him at his family's restaurant, the Golden Sun. I've eaten there before, and the food is actually pretty outstanding. The restaurant is done in light woods and bamboo with rows of red and gold Chinese lanterns hanging from the ceiling. Everything is well kept and tidy, and the aromas wafting out of the kitchen are making my mouth water.

A short, stout Chinese woman in a gray chef's coat and black pants approaches me. Her dark hair is shot through with gray and she's got dark eyes in a smooth, tawny face. She's wearing a white apron over the coat and has her hair tied back beneath a black skull cap with the restaurant's logo emblazoned on the cuff. I remember her from the last time I was here.

"Ms. Wilder?"

"Yes, it's nice to see you again."

She gives me a small smile, then turns and walks away, apparently expecting me to follow. Which I do. She leads me to one of the rooms in the back, pulls aside the rice paper door, and ushers me inside, closing it quickly after me. Detective Lee is sitting at the table sipping a glass of hot tea. I give him a smile as I take a seat across from him and he pours me a glass of tea. I pick it up and blow on the surface, scattering the tendrils of steam rising from the cup.

"Still ashamed to be seen with me in public, huh?" I ask with a grin.

"More like afraid to be seen with you," he replies—sans the grin. "You're toxic, Wilder."

"Yeah, listen. I'm sorry about what happened in the park—"

"Frankly, I wish you would have knocked him out. Might have been better if you had," he says. "Maybe it would have humbled him."

"Things bad around the precinct?"

He nods. "Real bad. And you're the main topic of conversation," he replies. "He's not real happy with the fact that your YouTube clip is nearing a million views. And do you know how I know it's nearing a million views?"

"How?"

"Because Torres keeps reminding us of the count," he says. "He's obsessed with it. Checks it constantly. He can't get over the fact that you made him look like a chump. And he's furious about it."

"I didn't make him look like a chump," I protest. "We argued. Loudly. But there was nothing that made him look like a chump. He's either delusional or he's way too sensitive."

Lee looks at me, one corner of his mouth quirked upward. "Have you actually seen the clip?"

"Just what's on the news. Why?"

"I'm sure it's selective editing, but it seriously looks like he's flinching away from you," he goes on. "The video makes him look like he's cowering in front of you while you're going all caveman on him."

"Shut up," I chuckle. "That's not even true."

"Wish it weren't," he replies. "But it is and ever since that video dropped, everybody at the precinct is walking on eggshells, trying to avoid the next explosion. Torres was on a warpath before, but now he's a total nuclear meltdown. And that's all thanks to you."

I shrug slightly. "You're welcome?"

"I just wanted to meet to give you a heads up. Torres is coming for you."

"He has been for a while. And I'm no more afraid of him now than I was then."

"You'd be foolish to not take precautions."

"I never said I wasn't taking precautions," I say. "I just said I wasn't afraid of him. He's been threatening me for a while now."

I relay the conversation I had with Torres after he'd pulled me over as well as a few things he said to me at the park before everything went sideways. Lee listens to it all, sipping his tea and nodding along with me. And when I'm finished, he sets his teacup down. He sits back in his seat, his gaze fixed on mine.

"About ten or fifteen years ago, Torres was transporting a prisoner from prison to his precinct to await trial in the morning," he starts. "Everything's goin' fine, but somewhere along the way, somethin' happens, and the prisoner ends up shot. Thirteen times. Four times in the back. All while still cuffed. That's a pretty neat trick, huh?"

"I'll say," I nod.

"Anyway, Torres' story is really vague and unconvincing. But he's got friends in high places. Namely, the Internal Affairs unit, as well as the Office of Police Accountability. They run a dog and pony show investigation and voila, no charges are filed.

They ruled the suspect somehow managed to get hold of a gun —while his hands were cuffed behind his back, mind you—and Torres acted out of fear for his life. They ruled it a good shoot."

That's a story I haven't heard before. It chills me to the bone. To think that Torres murdered somebody in cold blood and got away with it is monstrous. And to think he's got enablers in both IA and the OPA who signed off on this extra-judicial execution is even more so. No wonder Torres thinks he's bulletproof. He apparently is.

"That's not even the best part of the story," Lee continues.

"There's more?"

He nods, his expression sober. "Torres' partner at the time, Peter Light, is the one who blew the whistle. He disappears. He just vanished without a trace," Lee goes on. "There was no investigation into it. Nobody even batted an eye. Everybody just went on like he never existed."

I shake my head. "How does this happen?"

"Connections. Power. Influence. Torres has them and you don't," he says. "That's why I'm telling you that you really need to watch your ass, Blake. Torres can kill without fear of conse-quences."

Lee's words rattle around in my head, and although I'm not naïve enough to not think that things like these happen, I still don't want to believe it. That this man murdered one, possibly two people, and not only got away with it but was still able to keep his job—and move up the food chain to the point that he's one heartbeat away from being the most powerful man in the city of Seattle? It's unbelievable to me.

"I know what you're thinking," Lee says. "And just because you're in the Bureau, it doesn't mean you're protected. You don't get to where Torres is without making friends in even higher places. You may think you're safe, but you're not."

"This can't be happening," I say.

"It not only can, it is," he replies. "Torres is going to be gunning for you. He's obsessed with you now that the world thinks you showed him up and made him cower to you. And when I say obsessed, I mean Fatal Attraction-type obsessed. I think—no, I know—he hates you more than he hates Paxton now."

I drain the last of my tea, letting both my fear and my anger swirl around inside of me. I set the cup down and lean back in my seat, still not sure if I'm more scared or pissed off right now.

"I'm telling you this because even though we have our differences, I like you, Blake. I respect you," he says. "And I don't want to see you get hurt."

"The way you're talking, it doesn't sound like I'm going to be able to stop it. Between Torres and the cops who do his dirty work for him, to hear you tell it, I don't have much of a chance," I reply with a wry grin on my face.

"Just keep your head on a swivel. Make sure you are aware of your surroundings at all times," he tells me. "And if you have the ability, don't go anywhere alone. Don't let him catch you out by yourself, Blake."

"Is this the way I'm supposed to live the rest of my life? Looking over my shoulder?"

Lee shrugs. "At least until he finds something new to obsess over. And he will," he says. "It's just going to take some time to blow over."

"Great."

The door to the room slides open and Lee's mother comes in with a cardboard box filled with plastic bags and containers. She sets it down in front of me and offers me a smile. I look at the mountain of food and feel my mouth watering. It's amazing that Lee just told me his boss put a greenlight on me and I'm thinking about food.

"Thank you, Mrs. Lee," I say as I reach for my bag.

She waves me off. "No. You enjoy."

"Thank you very much. That's very kind," I say. "And I will definitely enjoy."

She walks out of the room, leaving me alone with Lee again. I look from the box to him and grin.

"I guess if this is my last meal, this is a really good one to end things on."

TWENTY-TWO

Wilder Residence; The Emerald Pines Luxury Apartments, Downtown Seattle

THERE's something about waiting for the Grim Reaper to show up and snatch the life out of you that makes you feel a little nostalgic, I suppose. Mark is at work tonight, so I'm all alone. And with nothing better to do, I started to pull the boxes containing the last of my family's things that I kept, out of the closet.

I held on to a lot of their things for a long time. I kept an entire storage locker filled top to bottom with things. It's really only been over the last couple of years that I've started to purge a lot of stuff that I probably shouldn't have kept to begin with. Bed sheets. Plates and dishes. My mother's old perfume bottles. My dad's cologne. My sister's hair ties. I finally made the decision to part with things that made no sense for me to keep and things I haven't looked at in years.

So I spent a weekend down at the storage facility and

started to sort through everything. I had a keep pile and a toss pile and had to make some really difficult decisions. But I did it. I got through it all and pared everything down to the boxes I store in the closet of my spare bedroom. Eight total boxes, and most of them are filled with photo albums and envelopes of pictures. There are, of course, some personal things I wasn't able to part with, but what I kept didn't even fill half of one of the boxes.

I open one of the boxes I know contains photos and indulge myself with a trip down memory lane. There are pictures of the whole family from the time we went to Disneyland. All of us at the top of the Space Needle. A smile crosses my face as I look through all the pictures and remember happier days. It fills me with a sense of joy, but also a sense of longing. I can't help but wonder what my life would be like if my parents hadn't been killed. If my kid sister hadn't been taken.

Would I be working for the FBI? Or would I have chosen to pursue another career path? Would I have become an artist or a chef? What would I have done had they not been killed?

I push those thoughts away, but that void is immediately filled by thoughts of Torres. The stories Lee told me today. He said they happened ten or fifteen years ago, which means Lee wasn't on the force at the time. So those are stories he heard second hand. Which means it's possible they're not entirely true. I don't doubt that some elements are true. But all of them? Would Torres really have been allowed to get away with two murders? Or one murder and one disappearance?

I run out to the living room and grab my laptop, then dash back to the bedroom. My service weapon sits in the holster nearby—just in case. I won't lie. Lee's stories, as well as his insistence that Torres is coming for me, got me spooked. Who wouldn't be? To know that the Deputy Chief and all his minions are gunning for me is a terrifying thought. I'm only one person. And if Lee is right, I'm facing at least half of the SPD. Maybe more.

I crack open my laptop and do a search for Torres's former partner. There are a couple of articles detailing the disappearance, but the slant of the pieces make it seem like he'd simply had enough and had gone off the grid. None of the articles I skim even raise the idea of foul play. That doesn't mean there wasn't any. It simply means either the SPD covered it up that well, or there really was no foul play. And after reading several pieces, I have no idea which one is right.

I clear out of that and run another search. This one for the prisoner killed by Torres. And there is a lot. Most of the articles from back in the day just tow the company line—the prisoner had gotten hold of a weapon and Torres fired in self-defense. A few of them raise the questions Lee mentioned. Specifically, the fact that the prisoner had his hands cuffed behind his back and the official story stank to high heaven. But those were written off as cranks and conspiracy theories pretty quickly.

I search and search, but can't find anything conclusive. I can't find anything to support or refute the accusation that Torres murdered the man. All I have is the official findings, but to me, they still leave open-ended questions I can't answer. I don't know if Torres killed the prisoner and his partner. What I do know is that he's an out-of-control loose cannon who thinks he can do what he wants and get away with it. What I do know is that he is coming for me. Of that, I have no doubt.

I set all of that aside and go back to all the photos, trying to recapture those feelings of happiness that enveloped me before. I pick up one of the photo albums and look at it for a moment. It's not one I remember seeing before. Back when I was culling the stacks and getting rid of everything, it's not like I went through everything in detail then and there. I probably threw this one in there without thinking about it.

I open it and see photos of my mom and dad. My vision blurs and my eyes well with tears. I flip through photos of them when they were dating, smiling, and even laughing. Gosh, they were so young. Not to mention their goofy clothing. The book moves from their dating life to the wedding. I have to believe my mom was telling their story as she put this book together. It's adorable and so sweet, and I can't help but wonder if I'm ever going to be able to put a book like this together. I can't help but wonder if I'm ever going to find a love as pure as the one my parents had for each other.

I flip the page and a couple of pictures fall out, so I set the book down and pick them up. The first is another picture from their wedding. This one is a candid shot of them staring into the camera, laughing hysterically. I trace the tip of my finger along the edges of their faces.

"I miss you guys. I think of all three of you every single day," I whisper.

The second picture is stuck to the back of the wedding picture, so I carefully pry it loose and hold it up, frowning as I try to place the faces I'm seeing. Other than my parents and Mr. Corden, I don't recognize anybody else in the photo. But they're all obviously good friends; they're having the time of their lives at somebody's backyard barbecue. And that's when it hits me: these people must be my parents' work family. This must be their NSA work group.

I flip the picture over and feel a lump rise in my throat when I see my mother's neat handwriting on the back of the photo. She lists out all their names. It's almost like she knew I would be at this point someday, and she wanted me to have a signpost to guide me.

"Thank you, Mom," I whisper.

Pulling my computer back into my lap, I type in the first name on the left. Gary Rodgers. A quick search shows me that he passed away. I don't see a cause of death in the obituary I'm reading, but I note that he died about a week after my parents. The next name on the photo is Lindsey Haskins. I search her online and find an obituary for her as well, dated about a month after my parents died. As I look up the third name on the photo, Michael Pratt, I get a sinking feeling in my stomach. That feeling is confirmed when I pull up the obituary for him—two weeks after the death of my folks.

"What in the hell is going on?" I whisper.

I look at the list before me in stunned silence for a long moment, trying to comprehend what I was seeing. Trying to understand what was going on. Of the eight people I don't recognize in the photograph, seven of them are dead. Seven out of eight of my parents' NSA work group are dead. And all of them within a year of my parents' murders. Eight out of nine, if you count Mr. Corden's death a few weeks ago. I don't know what the others died of; I haven't done a deep dive yet. For now, it's enough for me to know that practically every person in this photo died within a year of my folks. It's a coincidence of staggering proportions. As far as I'm concerned, it strains the bonds of belief.

The one survivor of the group is a woman named Gina Aoki. A quick Google search tells me she's here in Seattle and has been for quite some time. She's a freelance software and app designer who has apparently made a lot of money in the private sector. According to her website, she founded her company less than a year after my folks were murdered. It can't be a coincidence that while my parents' work group was apparently being purged, Gina fled and got as far away from the NSA as she could. There has to be something there.

I check the time and see that it's too late to call her tonight, so I make a mental note to call her the minute I have some time. She has to know something about what happened. And I intend to find out what it is.

TWENTY-THREE

Criminal Data Analysis Unit; Seattle Field Office

"Mo, what did you find out?" I ask.

"I found out that I don't like teenage girls very much," she tells me. "Does that count for anything?"

"Not so much," I reply.

"Fine. Okay well, Emily Tompkins was nineteen, in hairdressing school. She worked as a waitress at the Mermaid's Gentleman's Club," she reports. "The night she was taken, she was out with some friends. According to those teenage menaces, they were at Sin, a trendy nightclub in Belltown. They said she stepped out for a smoke and never came back. She was found two days later and—well—we saw how that all played out."

"Sounds like you were having some horrible high school flashbacks, huh?" Astra asks.

"You have no idea," she replies.

"Did anybody see anything?" I ask. "Did anybody see her talking to anybody? Leave with anybody?"

Mo shakes her head. "Nope. She just vanished."

I chuckle to myself as I pace at the front of the bullpen, absorbing the information Mo is reciting. So, just like Summer Kennedy and Serena Monroe, Emily Tompkins vanished without a trace. At some point, they encountered their killer, were apparently comfortable enough with him—or at least, not threatened by him—that they ended up being injected with ketamine and were taken without so much as a scream.

"Rick, can you pull up any street-level cameras around Club Sin the night Emily went missing?" I ask. "Or can you access the club's surveillance cameras?"

"On it. I'll let you know," he calls out.

I nod then turn to Astra. "Your turn. What did you get from Serena Monroe's friends and family?"

Astra smiles wide. "You're going to love this."

"Hit me."

"I talked to her parents—lovely people, by the way—and they directed me to some of the friends that she was out with the night she went missing."

"Uh-huh... and?"

"The only piece of information you need to know is that the night Serena went missing, the last place she was seen was —are you ready for this?"

I let out an exasperated growl. "Oh my God, you're killing me. Tell me already."

"The last place she was seen before she went missing was The Yellow Brick Road Tavern."

My eyes widen and my mouth falls open. I gape at her, every neuron in my head firing as I make the connections. It almost seems too good to be true. And my cautious mind thinks it seems too easy to be true. Though it's not conclusive of anything, it's certainly suggestive. And it's definitely worth another conversation.

"So... two of our three victims tie directly to the boyfriend," Mo says. "What was his name again? Dylan..."

"Betts," I say. "His name is Dylan Betts."

"Oh, oh, oh," Rick calls out. "But wait, there's more."

We all turn to him as one and Rick straightens up in his seat, a wide smile on his face and a mischievous glint in his eye.

"Are you ready for—"

"Spit it out already," Mo, Astra, and I all shout in unison.

He laughs out loud and claps his hands. "I finally heard back from e-Taxi," he announces. "And according to their driver information, Mr. Dylan Betts, driver number 430293, on the night Summer Kennedy went missing, logged off the app—meaning he wasn't taking new fares—from nine-thirty until eleven-thirty that night. Which, if I'm not mistaken, blows a big ass two-hour hole in the man's alibi."

Silence descends over the bullpen for a long moment and I exchange a look with Astra. Both of us smile at the same time.

"Is today my birthday?" I ask.

"Funny, I was thinking it was mine," she says. "Either way, I'd say that Dylan Betts has just taken the lead in our prime suspect race."

"Oh yeah. I'd say he's up there," I reply. "Let's go pick him up. I think we need to have another chat with Dylan. Excellent work, everybody. Really. Great job."

———

Interrogation Suite Alpha-2; Seattle Field Office

"Aren't you guys like, supposed to give me an attorney?" he asks.

"Do you need an attorney, Dylan?" Astra asks. "Did you do something you might need an attorney for?"

"Well, the way you two are coming at me, you certainly seem to think I did something I need an attorney for."

"We're just having another chat, Dylan," I say. "I told you last time that we might be following up with you. This is us following up."

He eyeballs us closely, looking for all the world like a cornered animal trying to decide whether to fight or try to flee. We're sitting across the table from him, the same positions we were all in the last time we had him in here to chat. But he's right. There is a tension in the air this time that didn't exist the last time we had him in. He's a pretty perceptive guy.

I open the file folder sitting in front of me and pull out the first DMV photo on the stack. It's Emily Tompkins, the first victim. I turn it around so he can see her and lay it down on the table. I do the same for Summer and then Serena's photos. Dylan stares at the three pictures; I notice his eyes lingering on Summer's face. His expression darkens and I can see the emotion welling up within him. It strikes me then that perhaps the emotion isn't love and the pain of loss, but guilt. Perhaps he's coming to grips with the fact that he did something horrible to the woman he professed to love and he's having a hard time with it now.

He manages to keep himself in check though and looks up at us with his cocky swagger. "So, what's with this? Who are the other two?" he asks. "They related to Summer or somethin'?"

Without saying a word, Astra opens the file folder in front of her and withdraws the autopsy photos. First, she lays the picture of Emily's lifeless body on top of her DMV photo and then does the same with Summer and Serena's pictures. With each one she lays down, Dylan's face grows slightly paler, and his eyes widen that much more. He stares at the pictures and licks his lips nervously, then looks up at us.

"What in the hell is this?" he croaks.

"We were hoping you could tell us," Astra says.

He looks at her, his expression stricken. "What the hell is wrong with you? Why would you show me these? Are you sick? Do you get off on this or somethin'?"

"What's the matter, Dylan?" Astra asks. "Don't like admiring your handiwork?"

"My handiwork? What in the hell are you talking about?" he gasps.

I tap the DMV picture of Serena and hold his gaze. "Do you recognize this girl?"

He glances at her briefly, then looks up at me. "I've never seen her before in my life."

"That the story you're going with?" Astra asks.

"It's not a story. It's the truth," he practically shouts.

"Never seen her before? Ever?" I ask. "Are you sure about that?"

"Are you deaf or something? I've never seen her before in my life."

"Would it surprise you to know that the night she went missing, the last place she was seen was The Yellow Brick Road Tavern?" Astra chirps.

"Correct me if I'm wrong, but isn't that where you work?" I ask.

"Oh no. No, no, no, no," he says. "I see what you're trying to do, and that's bullcrap. That's not going to work. You are not going to hang this on me. I'm not going to let you do that to me. Oh, hell no."

"We're not doing anything, Dylan," Astra says. "You have direct connections to two of our victims. Can you see how that looks?"

"It looks like that because you two are trying to frame me," he snaps. "I didn't do this. And you can't prove anything."

"Spoken like somebody who's terrified that we can prove everything," Astra says.

"There is nothing for you to prove because I didn't do anything," he growls. "Why can't you get that through your thick skulls?"

"I need you to walk me through something, Dylan," I say. "The night Summer went missing, you said you worked at the tavern until..."

"Until eight. And then I jumped onto my e-Taxi account and worked until around two," he says. "Same as I do most every Friday night."

"Yeah, that's what I thought you said. In fact, I remember you saying that," I nod. "But do you know what I don't remember you saying?"

"Enlighten me."

"That you signed off of e-Taxi for two hours."

His face pales immediately and his mouth falls open. But he quickly recovers and runs a hand through his hair. Dylan clears his throat and tries to regain some of that cocky swagger.

"I didn't say it because I didn't do it," he says. "I worked straight through, only stopping to grab some food and a coffee once."

"See, that's funny," I say as I pull a page out of the folder and set it down in front of him. "Because e-Taxi's records show that you did indeed log out for two hours. Specifically, between the hours of nine-thirty and eleven-thirty."

"And coincidentally, Summer was last seen around nine-thirty," Astra adds. "We believe she was taken right around that time."

He shakes his head, trying to deny it. "I didn't do this," he says. "I didn't do this."

"Then help us understand," Astra says. "You were Summer's boyfriend and she goes missing. Serena is in your bar the night she goes missing. You're the common denominator."

He looks up at us and taps Emily's photo—which is the weak point in our case. I was actually hoping he'd save us all the trouble and confess.

"What about her?" he asks. "What's my connection to her? And spoiler alert, I've never seen her before in my life either."

"Our people are digging into that. We know this girl had an e-Taxi account, so we're waiting to get her rider information from them," I reply. "If she ever took a ride with you, we're going to find it."

"I didn't do this."

"So, you keep saying," Astra says. "But don't you see how lying to us kind of makes you look bad? You never told us you logged off for two hours—the very same window Summer went missing. Don't you see how we might think you lied to us about other things—like you telling us you didn't kill these women?"

Dylan crosses his arms on the table and buries his face in them, moaning and muttering to himself. Astra and I shared a glance with each other. She looks more confident than I feel right now. Everything we have is circumstantial. There are still big holes in our theory. On the surface, it looks good. It looks like Dylan is our guy. But there are still lingering doubts in my mind that I can't quite put to rest. The biggest of which is that we can't find a connection between Dylan and Emily. Yet.

Dylan raises his head and looks at us, his expression one of pure misery. He let out a long, loud breath.

"Fine. I logged off that night because I spent those two hours with my sidepiece."

"Your what?"

"His sidepiece," Astra interprets. "The woman he's banging behind the back of the woman he professed his undying love for."

I glare at him and shake my head. "You're such a pig."

"We're going to need her name," Astra says.

"H—her name?"

"You didn't think we were just going to take your word for it, did you?"

"W—well, yeah."

"You really are stupider than you look," I say.

"Name," Astra demands.

"I can't. She's married," he says. "Please don't make me tell you that. If her husband found out—"

"This story just keeps getting classier by the minute," I growl.

"You either give us a name so we can verify your alibi," Astra says. "Or, we can charge you and you take the full weight of all three murders."

He bangs his head on the table, groaning to himself. He finally raises his head and looks at us again.

"Fine," he says. "But if you can keep this between us and not tell the husband—"

"Name," Astra demands again.

Dylan blows out a frustrated, scared breath. "Haley. Haley Edmunds."

"There. That wasn't so hard now, was it?" Astra chirps brightly.

"We're going to detain you until we can verify your story," I tell him.

"Please don't tell her husband," he repeats.

Astra smiles wide at him. "We'll do our best."

TWENTY-FOUR

SSA Wilder's Office, Criminal Data Analysis Unit; Seattle Field Office

"Great," Astra mutters. "Now what?"

I shake my head. "Now we go back to square one."

"I thought for sure he was our guy."

We looked into Dylan's alibi and it checked out. After a couple of tense moments with Haley Edmunds—wife of Tyler Edmunds, of MMA fighting fame—we managed to corroborate Dylan's story. He was with her for those two hours on the night Summer went missing, and she had the compromising photographs taken in her hotel suite to prove it. He also had an airtight alibi for the night Serena Monroe was grabbed. So in other words, we were totally boned and had no choice but to kick him loose.

"Part of me hopes Tyler finds out Dylan's been schtupping his wife," I say.

"Only part of you? Every last bit of me wants Tyler to find out about him," Astra says. "I'd like to see Dylan go a few rounds with ol' Animal Edmunds. Pretty sure he'd be eating through a straw for the rest of his life."

"Animal?" I raise an eyebrow.

She laughs. "Benjamin's a big MMA fan. I've seen Edmunds fight before. Let's just say the nickname is fitting."

I lean back in my chair, laughing to myself. It is frustrating though, to have built up all this momentum in the case, only to come crashing into a dead end. Now we're back at square one with nothing. No leads, no suspects, no nothing. I toss my pen down on my desk and blow out a disgusted and frustrated breath.

"You started to tell me about something you found last night," Astra says.

I wave her off. "It can wait. We need to find a new lead. We need to get ahead of this guy before he kills again."

"Sometimes getting your mind off it and thinking in a different direction helps," she offers.

I nod, knowing she's right. Sometimes you can think so hard on a problem, you only get frustrated, which oftentimes only makes it worse. In cases like this, I've found the best way to solve a situation is to avoid thinking about it. I've had a lot of answers just come to me out of the blue when I've been letting my brain work in the background while I'm focused on something else.

"Yeah. I was looking through some of the boxes of my family's things that I kept. Pictures mainly," I say. "Anyway, I found some photos I'd never seen before. Specifically, I found one of their NSA work group—and Mr. Corden. It was shot at a backyard barbecue at a house I'd never seen before."

"Okay, so what's so troubling about that?" she asks. "You knew they kept their NSA family separate from the real family."

"So in that photo are my parents, Mr. Corden, and eight people I don't recognize."

"Okay?"

"Seven of those eight people are dead, Astra," I tell her. "And they all died within a year of my parents' murder."

She sits back in her seat, a look of stunned surprise on her face. "All of them?"

"Except for one. Gina Aoki," I tell her. "She apparently left the NSA during this—purge—and settled here. She's been a software engineer and app developer for almost twenty years now."

Astra whistles low. "Do you know what the others died of?"

I shake my head. "No, I wasn't able to come up with CODs, but I only gave it a cursory search. The coincidence is enough for me," I tell her. "It just seems too strange to be a coincidence. Don't you think?"

She opens her mouth to reply but pauses, seeming to think better of her words. Astra looked off into the distance for a moment, seeming to be thinking of a better way to phrase things. She finally looks at me and I can't help but see the skepticism in her eyes.

"So, you think this conspiracy that killed your mom and dad," she says. "Also, in fact, killed their entire work group."

"I do," I tell her. "There are just too many coincidences piling up all around me. At some point, the simplest answer has to be the right one."

"Or it could just be a series of unfortunate events that add up to a lot of coincidences."

"I admit, that's a possibility. But the fact that seven people in my parents' work group died so soon after their murder—it defies belief."

Astra nods, perhaps conceding the point. "We won't know for sure, though, until we have somebody look into the CODs on those seven," she says. "Otherwise we're putting carts before horses again."

Honestly, I want to know. I want to know if these were natural deaths—which, given the timing, I'm kind of doubting—or if there was something sinister about them. I want to know if there's something that will put me onto the trail of this conspiracy—a conspiracy I'm coming to believe in the more I learn.

"I know you're not a big fan of conspiracy theories, but hear me out," I start.

"Should I go and grab my tin foil hat?"

"Shut up. Listen to this and then try to apply it to any other case we work. Use the same processes of logic. Can you do that?"

"Of course."

"All right. So, if you were presented a case in which there are eleven employees of a company, and nine of those employees were killed—"

"But we don't know if they were killed. Sorry."

"It's all right. Just bear with me. Two killed, then seven more within a year," I go on. "And then let's say you were going out to meet one of the two survivors of the entire group, who said he had critical information for you—and you find that he has been murdered. More than that, you take fire from some unknown assailant. Would you still scoff at the idea of a conspiracy?"

Astra looks away and seems to be thinking about it. She finally turns back to me. "No. With that set of circumstances, put that way, probably not."

"All right, then. We've got some common ground to work from."

"And what's the next step?" she asks.

"First, I'll task Rick with looking into the deaths of the

seven," I tell her. "I want to know if it was natural causes or something else. Second, I'm going to keep trying to reach Gina Aoki. I left a message earlier, but haven't heard back yet. She's the key. She's going to know what happened. Or will at least, have some idea or perhaps a clue for me to follow."

"Blake, I don't want to sound like I'm paranoid or trying to get you to walk away from learning your truth. But have you stopped to consider that maybe if there is a conspiracy, that the people behind said conspiracy—maybe the very same people who murdered your parents—don't want you looking into their business?"

I nod. "I've considered it. And I reject it."

"They killed your folks, Blake. What's to stop them from killing you too?"

"I don't know. Nothing, I guess."

"Is this really worth risking your life over?"

"You're sounding like Mark now."

She shrugs. "That's not necessarily a bad thing right now. If this conspiracy exists, I don't know how smart it is to kick the hornet's nest."

"It's wise if you want to see who comes crawling out of it."

"Or it's exceptionally stupid."

"It's a fine line."

"There's no way I'm talking you out of this madness, am I?" she sighs.

I shake my head. "I need to know. I need to put this festering hole that's been torn inside me to rest once and for all."

"I understand you wanting answers, Blake. I'm just worried that you're going to get yourself killed."

"Well, right now, that's all cart before the horse. I need to hear what this Gina Aoki has to say before I'll know anything one way or the other," I say.

We sit in silence for a moment, marinating in all that has just been said. I won't lie, the idea of stirring up the folks who killed my parents does scare the hell out of me. But this is a life-long quest. I'm not going to stop just because I'm scared. I'll handle whatever comes my way. I owe my mom and dad this. I owe this to Kit. And I'm going to make good on it.

"Hey, you were right about distracting my mind by thinking of something else," I announce. "I just had an idea about our unsub."

"See? I'm always right. I told you that you would," she replies.

"You do have your moments," I say. "Let's get out of here and see if we can't solve the case."

"Somebody's feeling ambitious all of a sudden."

"Yeah. I guess I am. So, let's ride this wave before it dissipates."

We get to our feet and laugh together as we head out of the office. There are things to do, people to see, and murderers to catch.

TWENTY-FIVE

The Yellow Brick Road Tavern, Capitol Hill District;
Seattle, WA

WE WALK into the bar and are immediately met with a wall of
ice from the staff. The bartender glares at us, as do the waitresses on duty. Other than the same older man sitting at the far
end of the bar we saw the last time we were here, the place is
empty. We timed our arrival to coincide with the end of the
lunch rush so we'd have everybody's undivided attention.

"I'm going to go out on a limb and say they heard we hauled
Dylan in," Astra comments.

"I'd say you're probably right."

We walk over to the bar and the bartender on duty, a lanky
man with dark eyes and long dark hair that's tied up into a man-
bun looks us up and down, a sneer on his lips.

"Going to accuse me of killing her now too?" he asks.

"Not at the moment, but never say never," Astra chirps.

He scoffs and folds his long arms over his narrow chest.
"What do you want?"

"We need to know if you have internal and/or external surveillance cameras."

"None that work," he says. "They're there for show."

"Well, that sort of defeats the purpose of security cameras, doesn't it?" Astra asks.

"That's above my pay grade," he says. "You'd have to talk to the owner."

"All right, can we talk to the owner?" I ask.

"No. She's not here."

"When will she be in?" I press.

He shrugs. "No idea. She doesn't keep a schedule."

I sigh. "All right. Can we leave a message?"

"If you want."

"Better question," Astra says. "If we leave a message, will you make sure she gets it?"

"We'll do our best."

That's encouraging. I'm fairly certain if we leave a message, it'll be torn up and in the trash can before we ever walk out the door, so there seems to be no point. It doesn't matter, though. If the cameras are there for show and aren't recording anything, it'd be a waste of time anyway.

"Why are you guys hammerin' on Dylan so hard?" he asks. "He just lost his girlfriend. Do you even know what it's like for him to have you idiots accuse him of being the one who killed her?"

"Would that be the girlfriend he was cheating on?" I ask.

"I never said he was perfect," he says. "He's a good guy, though. He doesn't deserve you guys hassling him like you are. His other girlfriend even broke up with him because of what you did."

Astra looks at him. "Are you even hearing yourself right now?"

"Look, the bottom line is that we're trying to solve a

murder, and he lied to us. Multiple times," I say. "The odds are good that if you lie to the authorities, you're going to be a suspect. Or at the very least, somebody we're going to want to talk to. So, take what happened to Dylan as a cautionary tale."

"Yeah, whatever."

He turns and walks off, huddling with the pair of waitresses who are standing in the sidewell, casting dirty looks our way. I turn to Astra and we both head for the door. I glance up at the corner and see a camera mounted there. But there's no indication it's on. The guy was telling the truth. Some wonders never cease.

We push through the doors and step into the bright afternoon. The sidewalk is busy with people taking advantage of a nice day by getting out and about. Fat, fluffy clouds lazily drift by overhead, and there's a slight warmth in the air. It is a beautiful day, that's for sure.

"So, what now, boss?" she asks.

I look around, frowning and trying to figure out what our next step is going to be. And that's when I see it.

"That's it. That might help," I say.

"What?"

I point to the four ATMs set into the wall of the bank across the street. ATMs all have front-mounted, forward-facing cameras. Astra spots what I'm looking at then turns to me and smiles.

"You're a genius," she says.

"Yes, I am," I reply. "Or at least, I will be if those cameras picked anything up."

We have to wait for a break in the traffic before we scamper across the street. Nobody is anywhere close to us, but that doesn't stop a couple of people honking and shouting obscenities at us as they rolled by.

"I feel like we just played a real-life version of that old school video game, Frogger," Astra says.

"Except out here, you don't get to hit the reset button if you get squished."

"Yeah, that's the downside."

We reach the door of the bank and go inside. The air inside the bank is quiet, calm, and as hushed as a library. A lean man in a gray suit with a vibrant pink tie makes his way over to us. He's got a wide smile on his face that looks as fake as the Rolex on his wrist.

"May I help you, ladies?"

We flash our badges, which immediately brings a frown to his lips. He looks around and acts like he's guilty of something.

"We'd like to speak with the manager, please," I say.

"Right away."

The man walks away and goes to an office at the far end of the building. I can see him pointing in our direction. The man behind the desk gets up and heads our way. He's a small, bookish man, dressed in a dark suit and tie. He looks more like a funeral director than a bank manager to me. But what do I know?

"Good afternoon, Agents," he says. "How may I help you?"

"The ATMs out front," I say. "Do you store the footage from the cameras?"

"Yes, of course. It's stored digitally for a year."

I feel a surge of excitement in my belly and look over at Astra, who looks like she's feeling the same way. This could be our next lead. And it could be the break we need to crack this case wide open. I'm keeping my fingers crossed that it is, anyway.

"That's great," I say. "We're going to need to see some of that footage."

"Of course," he replies.

We follow him into a medium-sized, windowless back room. It contains nothing but a desk and a video monitor separated into different grids that show different sections of the bank. A second computer sits on the desk as well, and I can see by looking at the pictures on a screen that's divided into four squares that it's the footage from the ATMs up front.

"Excellent," I say, feeling a surge of hope.

The manager gives us a quick lesson on how to use the computer before he leaves us to it. We scroll back in time to the day Serena was abducted. We know from her friends that she arrived at the YBR with her boyfriend at about eight that evening. Once inside, she and her friend partied for a while. At some point, she and her boyfriend had a blowout, because she learned he was cheating on her. She threw a drink in his face, slapped him, then stormed out. The trouble was, she was pretty inebriated herself and was calling a ride-share to take her home. That's when I imagine our unsub struck. Unfortunately, her impaired state made her the perfect target for the predators out there looking to take advantage of women.

"Okay, I have them going in," Astra announces.

I lean down and look at the monitor. The footage from the ATM cameras is grainy and choppy. It's not a clean image in the least. We can barely make out the scene across the street unless we squint and look really close at it. But I remind myself it's better than nothing.

"There," she points. "She's coming out alone and it's eleven pm."

We watch her standing at the edge of the sidewalk. She's swaying and unsteady on her feet. She walks away from the front door of the bar and down the sidewalk with an awkward ad uneasy gait. It's then I see she's holding something in her hand—one of her heels. She's near the edge of the camera's field of vision. I'm afraid we're about to lose her, but she stops and leans against a streetlight. It looks to me like she's on her phone. Maybe she's sending a text to her boyfriend telling him what a pig he is.

A couple of minutes later, a dark sedan comes into view. It pulls to a stop next to her and though I can't see what's happening, I'm sure the driver is leaning over and speaking to her through the passenger's side window. A moment later, he gets out of the car. He pulls the brim of his ballcap low to cover his face. Smart. Very smart.

He is as I thought he would be, though. From what I can see of him, he's got broad shoulders, though it's hard to see them under his thick hoodie. We watch as he talks to Serena. I would kill to know what he's saying to her. Whatever it is, though, it works. He opens the back door of the sedan and she gets in. I can't see what's going on but a moment later, he closes the door and dashes around to the driver's side, climbs in, and is gone. All without ever having revealed his face.

"Damn," Astra mutters. "The guy is good."

I nod. "Scarily so. It's like he's had some practice at that."

"I'd say so."

"Roll it back a bit for me," I tell her.

Astra does and I watch it again. This time, I'm looking at the car, looking for any identifying marks. Unfortunately, the picture is too grainy for me to see the license plate, which seems unusually dark anyway. He might have mudded out the plate—literally smeared mud over it—to keep it from being identified.

"Wait, stop. Pause the tape," I say.

Astra does and I lean closer to the screen. In the lower left-hand corner of the rear window.

"What is that?" I ask.

Astra blows up that section of the screen, but it's too grainy and pixelated to make out what it is.

"I don't know," she frowns. "Some sort of ID sticker? School sticker, maybe?"

"Possibly, yeah. If it's one we can track, that would be fantastic."

Astra snickers. "Look at you being all optimistic, thinking we'd catch a lucky break. It's adorable."

I sigh. She's right. If it weren't for bad luck, I'd have no luck at all. Even still, knowing that, I'm still crossing my fingers anyway.

"Do we have what we need?" Astra asks.

"I think so. Can you make a copy of that tape?"

"Sure thing."

After getting what we came for, we thank the manager and leave. I want to get this back to the shop and let Rick start working his magic on it as soon as possible. I don't know why I feel like I do, since our luck is usually horrible. But I have a good feeling about this.

TWENTY-SIX

SSA Wilder's Office, Criminal Data Analysis Unit; Seattle Field Office

AFTER SETTING Rick to the task of cleaning up the picture to see if we can ID that sticker in the sedan's window, I walk back into my office and drop into my chair, feeling wrung out and exhausted. I just want to go home, crawl into bed, pull the covers over my head, and sleep for the next twelve hours. At least. But there's still work to be done.

"You can sleep when you're dead," I mutter to myself.

I sort through all my emails, returning those that need it and deleting those that don't. After that, I look through the small pile of phone messages that have accumulated over the last few days and discard most of them. With that done, I turn my attention to the ever so tedious paperwork that comes with the job. This is the only real drawback to being promoted and running my own team—there seems to be a never-ending pile of paperwork to be done and reports that need to be filed. There's always so much, I feel like I'm never going to be caught up on it. Ever. Like Rosie said, the brass loves their paperwork.

As I'm shuffling the piles of paper about on my desk, I see the card for Detective Moore. He's the one handling Mr. Corden's murder investigation. It's been a while since I've heard from him and I've had no update in a long time. Moore had promised to keep me apprised of the case but has apparently fallen down on that count. I know that things get busy. There are always cases that needed to be worked, and you don't always have time to follow up with people. But I was adamant about how important this case was to me and he swore he'd keep on top of it.

I pick up my office phone and punch in the number, then press the receiver to my ear. It's picked up on the third ring.

"Moore," he answers, sounding grumpy and on edge.

"Detective Moore, this is SSA Blake Wilder," I greet him. "I spoke to you the night Mr. Corden was murdered out at the Cascades RV Park. Do you remember me?"

"Of course. How could I forget?" he replies. "Not many people are as persistent as you."

"Well, that's why I'm calling. I haven't heard from you in a while, and I wanted to get an update on Mr. Corden's case."

"The update is that we don't really have an update," he responds. "There unfortunately hasn't been any movement. We don't have a suspect as of right now, and given the lack of evidence, witnesses, or anything, I have a feeling we're not going to. I'm sorry."

"So, you're just going to drop the case in the circular file?"

"No, it'll remain open. But barring any new evidence or witnesses, we don't have anything to go on. You know how these things go, I'm sure," he says.

I gripped the phone receiver so hard I thought it might break. The thing is, I do know how these things go. Without an eyewitness or any sort of physical evidence, the case is dead in the water. Whoever murdered Mr. Corden and shot at us knew what he was doing. He left no trace of himself at the crime scene, despite having torn through all of Mr. Corden's stuff to find whatever information that was supposed to come to me. All of that tells me that we're dealing with a professional hitter. What it doesn't tell me is whether the hitter was there for Mr. Corden or us.

Knowing what I know about him now, the fact that Mr. Corden was a CIA spook, makes me wonder if the killer was indeed there for him. Over his long career, he very likely made some very powerful enemies. No doubt, so have I, but I run down killers, bank robbers, and child abductors. The sorts of enemies I make are on a completely different level than those Mr. Corden would have made playing his spy games.

"Agent Wilder, are you there?"

The Detective's voice brings me back to the present; I ease the death grip with which I'm holding the phone.

"Yeah. Yes. I'm here, sorry," I say.

"Like I was sayin', I'm sorry I don't have more for you."

It would have been nice if you had anything for me. The words are on the tip of my tongue, but I manage to bite them back—but just barely.

"No, I understand. Like you said, I know how these things go," I tell him.

"Yeah. I'm awful sorry again."

"Just keep me informed if anything changes?"

"Absolutely."

"Thank you, Detective."

I hang up the phone and sit back in my chair, scrubbing my face with my hands. It just seems so wrong that somebody who gave everything he had to this country would be forced to die an anonymous death like that. Without justice and therefore, to my mind, without genuine peace. It makes me feel awful for him. It makes me wish I could do something about it. But Moore is right—without evidence or a witness, there really is nothing that can be done.

My cellphone rings and I look at the caller ID. A spark of hope surging within me, I snatch up the phone and connect the call.

"Fish," I say. "Tell me something good."

"Something good?" he asks. "Well, I won the auction for Jeffrey Dahmer's refrigerator. I should be getting it delivered next week and I know exactly where I'm going to put it."

I laugh softly. "I certainly hope you're not going to be eating out of it."

"Of course not. I'm talking about my museum. You remember, right? You're going to be my special guest when I open."

"How could I forget?" I ask. "Also, I'm going to be bringing my cousin with me. She's as into this as you are. Fair warning, she's off-limits. Not just to you, but to anybody. You got me?"

"I will be a perfect gentleman. And I will make sure everybody else is as well."

A smile creeps across my face. The thing is, I believe him. He's involved with some shady business, but the one thing I can say about Fish is that he's never lied to me.

"Great. I'm looking forward to it then," I say. "So, what's up?"

"I told you that ketamine was out of fashion, right?"

"Yep. I recall."

"Well it's because of that a friend of mine remembers a man trying to buy it from him recently," he says.

I sit up in my seat, suddenly alert. "Yeah? And did he get a name by chance?"

He chuckles. "You know there are no names in this business."

"Of course," I reply. "A girl can dream though."

"The man you are looking for is large. He's maybe five-ten, with dark hair that's graying, and blue eyes. But he is a man who works out. A lot. He's very strong. Very broad," Fish says. "He is also very angry. When my friend said he did not have ketamine, this man threatened to beat him to death. He spoke with a slight accent. My friend says it is Czech. He's very good with accents."

"Fish, this is amazing. That's great information, thank you," I say. "That's a terrific help."

"Of course," he says. "You've helped me many times in the past. I am still indebted to you many times over."

"Thanks, Fish. You're a good man for a crook."

He laughs. "An alleged crook."

"Well, I'll look forward to the day you're one hundred percent legit."

"I may be able to get to ninety-nine percent. One hundred may be a bridge too far."

"Fair enough," I say with a laugh. "Thank you, Fish. Seriously."

"You're most welcome. Goodnight, Agent Wilder."

I disconnect the call and set my phone down, absorbing the information. Now we know what our guy looks and sounds like. I'm sure it's him. I glance at the clock on the wall and decide to make another call. Rather than use my cell this time, I pick up my office phone again and punch in the number I've already committed to memory. The phone rings once. Twice. Three and then four times... and then she answers.

"Hello?"

The blood in my veins turns to ice and I feel my stomach fold over on itself. I suddenly realize that I hadn't actually expected her to pick up the phone. She hasn't all day; I figured this call would go unanswered like all the others. And now that

I have her on the line, my mouth is dry and my throat locked up.

"Hello?" she says again, her voice colored by irritation.

I know if I don't say something, she's going to hang up. And if she does, who knows how long it will be before she answers her phone again. I silently will myself to calm down and to speak. This is what I've been waiting for, after all.

"M—Ms. Aoki. Hello. Hi," I start, instantly cringing at how ridiculous I sound.

"Yes? Who is this?"

"My name is Blake Wilder," I say. "And you knew my parents."

She goes absolutely silent, and I can feel the nervous energy inside of her ratcheting up through the telephone line. I close my eyes and picture her face. She's probably white as a sheet, with wide eyes and her mouth hanging open. If she's standing, she probably sat down, and she probably stared at the phone like it was a grenade in her hand, just waiting to go off.

"Y—you worked with them a long time ago," I go on.

"What do you want?" she asks, and although she's trying to make her voice sound authoritative and commanding, I can hear the tremor in it, betraying her fear. "How in the world did you find me?

"Answers. I want answers. And I think you might have some," I tell her. "And as far as how I found you, I live in Seattle as well and I work for the FBI—and I'm very good at what I do."

"I'm sorry, I don't—have answers. I don't have anything I can give you," she stammers.

Interesting that she knows what kind of answers I'm looking for before I even give voice to the questions.

"Ms. Aoki, please," I say. "I need to understand some things. I need to be able to move forward with my life. But I can't do that with all these questions hanging over my head. I need your help."

"I'm sorry," she says. "I don't know what it is you're looking for, but I can assure you I don't have the answers you're seeking."

"I disagree. Please," I implore her. "Meet me for lunch and let me ask you some of the questions I've had for the last twenty years."

"No, I'm sorry. That's out of the question. I don't even know you," she replies.

"Do you know what I looked at last night? A picture of you and my folks, and the entire NSA work group. You were all at a barbecue at somebody's house," I tell her. "You all looked so happy. My parents used to refer to you guys as her work family. You were family to them."

There is a long silence on the other end of the line. I wonder what sort of memories are being conjured in her mind. Are they of the barbecues? Maybe of laughing at somebody's joke in the office? Perhaps a memory of a singular conversation she'd had with my mother? Or my father? I wonder what the first memory she conjures up when she thinks of my folks is.

"I truly am sorry for your loss, Blake. But that was an awfully long time ago," she says. "I've moved on with my life. I suggest you do the same."

"I'm so glad you've been able to put it all behind you. But how can I move on when I don't understand why my parents were executed in cold blood," I hiss. "How can I move on when I know that seven of the eight members of my parents' work group are now dead. That you're the only survivor. How am I supposed to move on, when I feel like you have the answers I'm looking for but won't say?"

"I'm sorry, Blake. But like me, you have to find a way to let the past remain in the past," she says. "Now please, I have to go. And I beg you... don't call me again."

The line goes dead in my hand and I stare at the receiver for a long moment, my emotions swirling around inside of me and coalescing into something dark. Something angry.

Before I'm even aware of what I'm doing, I grab my office phone and hurl it across the room. It hits a picture frame hanging on the wall and rebounds with a horrendously loud crashing sound. The frame hits the ground and the glass shatters with a sharp tinkling noise.

I lean forward with my elbows on my desk and bury my face in my hands. I try to stifle the tears but can't, so I give up the fight and let them flow. Gina Aoki was the last chance I had to get the answers I have so desperately wanted for so long. And she drop-kicked me. Refused to answer a single question and told me to never call her again.

What kind of person does that? What kind of a person can hear the anguish in another person's voice and tell them it's time for them to move on?

"Everything all right in here, boss?"

I look up to find Rick standing in the doorway of my office, his face etched with concern. I offer him a weak, faltering smile.

"No, I'm not all right," I say. "This will never be all right."

TWENTY-SEVEN

Criminal Data Analysis Unit; Seattle Field Office

"Hey Rick, how long is your snazzy photo enhancing program going to take?" Astra calls from her desk.

"Excuse me, but would you walk into Gordan Ramsay's kitchen and ask him when his amazingly delicious meal would be ready?" he returns.

"Yeah, I would if I was hungry," Astra replies.

"You cannot rush genius, is my point," he says. "Do you know what my program is doing? It is breaking the photo down, pixel by pixel—"

"Forget it. Forget I asked," she cuts him off.

"Did he really just compare himself to Gordon Ramsay?" Mo asks.

"I believe he did," Astra says.

I hear their voices but don't really comprehend what they're saying. My mind is otherwise occupied at the moment. After my meltdown in my office last night, I went home and actually got a decent night's sleep. It's amazing what being physically drained and emotionally spent will do to you. Rick promised to keep my meltdown just between us and building facilities already found a new phone to replace the one I smashed last night. The only thing left out of place is the picture frame I also smashed, but I'll replace it soon enough.

My hands clasped behind my back, I pace at the front of the bullpen. We're still waiting for the digital cleanup of the picture from the ATM to complete its cycle, and until it does, we're stuck twiddling our thumbs. We've reviewed the evidence, have read the murder books Rick was able to purloin for us, and have gone over everything there is to go over every which way to Sunday. There isn't any aspect of this case that I don't know by memory.

Fat lot of good all that knowledge is doing me, though. I'm no closer to naming a viable suspect, let alone catching the killer than I was before we got word that Summer's body had been discovered. Frustrated doesn't even begin to cover it. As I pace, I'm saying a silent prayer that when that photo is resolved, we can actually identify the sticker, and it leads us somewhere relevant—like to a suspect.

At this point, we're grasping at straws, just waiting for some actionable information. And in this case, actionable means we're waiting for another body to drop. I'd rather avoid that happening and grab this guy before he snuffs out another young life. But at the moment, he's a ghost. Right now, all I have is the profile I'm putting together in my head, but it remains nameless and faceless.

And of course, mixed in with all of that are all of the feelings I have about Gina Aoki. There's some small part of me that wants to go storming over to her office and demand she speak with me. At the point of a gun, if I have to. But the practical side of my brain quashes that one right away; I'm not too keen on spending the rest of my life in prison.

I just don't understand how she can hear the desperate pleading in my voice and be okay with that. She could clearly hear that I was suffering. That I'm in tremendous emotional pain. But rather than try to help me salve my wounds, she kicks me in the teeth.

Is it because of a cruel, unsympathetic nature? Is it because she doesn't want to meet the same fate as everyone else in her work group?

Or—is it because she might be the only survivor for a reason? Maybe she knows exactly what happened to my parents all those years ago—and thinks I'm out for revenge.

"I'm thinking it's a scorned lover," Astra says.

Mo is nodding along. "Yeah, I can see that. That makes sense."

"What do you think, Blake?"

I turn at the sound of Astra's voice but look at her blankly. I'm so lost in my own head, I have no idea what she just said.

"Sorry, what?" I ask.

"Somebody's off in la-la-land today," Astra comments with a grin.

"Yeah, I suppose I am. Sorry." I shake my head to clear my thoughts. "What was the question again?"

"We were talking about our unsub," Mo explains. "Astra and I are both in agreement that the killer is symbolically destroying a lover every time he murders somebody. An old girlfriend who did him wrong."

"What does the superstar profiler think?" Astra asks.

I shake my head. "I don't think it's a lover he's destroying. I think it's somebody much closer to him. A sister or a mother, perhaps."

They all look at me like I've lost my mind. And maybe I have. But as I've been going through all the facts of the case, I've come around to a different conclusion.

"You think he's symbolically killing his mother?" Mo asks, sounding horrified.

I nod. "I do. The rage we're seeing him inflict upon these girls is personal. And it's way over the top," I say. "The extremeness of the violence is the key for me. I personally don't think you can be that enraged by a lover. I think the depth of that violence can only come from one place—somebody who was supposed to love you unconditionally and didn't."

"So, you think he's killing his mother because she didn't love him?"

"Not the way she should have, no. Think about it. With a lover, no matter how deeply in love you are, there is always the understanding that things between you can end at any time. There truly is no expectation of forever," I explain. "But with a sibling or a parent, the expectation of their love is forever. You expect that your mother will be there when nobody else is. So, from our unsub's perspective, his rage stems from the fact that his mother, or his sister, were not there. The expectation of their forever love was broken."

"I'm not sure that makes sense," chimes in Astra. "All these women are very young. College girls. They fit a very specific profile. If it was his mother, wouldn't he be targeting older women?"

"There is that," I acknowledge. "Which leads me to believe it could be a sister as well. In either case, the specific techniques of torture used just don't fit with the profile of a lover. Rick, call up the crime scene photos."

Rick taps a few keys and displays the bodies of Summer, Serena, and Emily on our screens.

"The cigarette burns," I point to each of them. "That's my clue. I think our unsub got cigarettes put out on him as a kid and is now symbolically taking revenge by doing the same to his victims. If the trigger was an ex-lover, the torture pattern would be more explicitly sexual in nature—like the Suban case a few weeks back. Cigarette burns are more indicative of a persistent pattern of abuse, over the long term. That doesn't fit with the theory of a spurned lover. It has to do with child abuse."

The room falls silent as everybody processes what I just said. It's a theory that only occurred to me in the shower this morning. But as I formulated it in my head, and even more so as I was just saying the words, it feels right to me. This one has the ring of truth in it for me. But there's one last layer to this I'm about to hit them with— one that I think will blow their minds.

"I also believe that when we catch our guy, we're going to find that not only was there physical abuse, but sexual abuse. I believe that our unsub had a longstanding sexual affair with his mother. Or his sister. One of the two," I continue.

"Wow. This just got a whole lot darker than I expected it would," Rick says into the silence that followed my statement.

"And we're also going to find that water played some role in all of this. The fact that all three bodies have been found in water is significant to our unsub," I continue. "I just don't know what that significance is to him yet."

"Huh," Astra says. "That's an interesting theory."

I give her a smile. "You don't sound convinced."

"I'm still stuck on it being a girlfriend or maybe a fiancée who set him off," she says.

I shrug. "We're all allowed to be wrong."

Mo and Rick let out a long, drawn-out, "Ooooooohhh," like we're back on the playground. It makes me laugh. I'm so grateful for these people in my life. They can usually always pull me out of whatever dark place I'm in and get me laughing again. It's something I very much need with all the emotional clutter in my head right now. I need the distraction.

"I smell a bet coming," Rick announces.

"A bet?" I ask.

"I'm in," Astra says. "And I'm willing to back it up with a hundred bucks."

"Betting on a profile?" I ask, arching an eyebrow. "Don't you think that's a little tacky?"

She screws up her face for a moment then looks at me. "Yeah, probably. But I'm still willing to—"

"Lose money? Sure, I'm in," I shrug. "A hundred bucks on it being his mother who touched this off in our unsub."

Astra laughs. "Any other takers on this action?"

"I'm going to throw a hundred on it being a girlfriend," Mo says.

"Pot's getting rich," I say. "What about you Rick?"

He shakes his head. "I'll leave all the profiling stuff to you guys. I'll stick with something that makes sense to me," he says and taps his computer.

My cellphone rings, and when I look at the caller ID, I see a call coming from a blocked number. I move to the side of the bullpen and connect the call.

"Wilder," I answer.

"Do you know who this is?"

Although I've only heard her voice once, I immediately know who it is on the other end of the line.

Gina Aoki.

"Yes, I do," I say.

"Ozuma Tea Garden. One hour. Not one minute later," she says. "And if you're not there at the appointed time, I'm gone, and you'll never hear from me again."

The line goes dead in my hand and I look at my phone like it's a bomb set to go off. I look at the clock on the wall. One hour. Not one minute later. Ozuma is about twenty minutes from here. Plenty of time. But wanting to account for every possibility so I'm not late, I rush into my office, grab my things and head out, leaving my team staring after me.

TWENTY-EIGHT

Ozuma Tea Garden, Queen Anne District; Seattle, WA

WITH FIVE MINUTES until our meeting, I get out of the car. I've been parked here for more than half an hour, waiting for our designated time. I wasn't about to risk missing my window to meet with her, so waiting half an hour was no hardship. I still don't know what changed Gina's mind and why she's suddenly agreeing to speak with me after being so curt on the phone. Whatever it is was that changed her mind though, I'm grateful for it.

I walk to the admissions gate and find a pleasant-looking Japanese woman behind the plexiglass smiling at me.

"Blake Wilder?" she asks.

I nod. "Please, go through the gate."

"Thank you."

I push through the gate and am met by a young man in khakis, a blue button-down shirt, and a blue blazer emblazoned with the garden's logo on the breast pocket. He's got a two-way radio in his hand.

"Follow me please, Ms. Wilder."

I follow him through the gardens, soaking up the atmosphere as we pass cherry trees, copses of bamboo stalks, and a giant pond filled with reeds, lily pads, and koi fish, larger than any I've ever seen. The place is beautiful, there is no doubt. And it's tranquil. Everything is so quiet and still. You can't help but soak up the natural beauty of the place.

I follow my guide up a set of stairs that had been cut into the side of a small rise that leads up to a traditional Japanese tea house. The tea house is surrounded by thickets of bamboo and flowering bushes that lend a sweet, delicate aroma to the air around us. The man steps to the rice paper door and pulls it aside, ushering me in. And when I cross the threshold, I find Gina Aoki sitting cross-legged at the low table in the center of the room.

"Shoes, please," she starts.

I take off my shoes and set them and my bag down at the door, then cross over to where she's sitting. I take a seat on the giant cushion, folding my legs beneath me. Gina reaches out and pours me a cup of tea. She's an older woman, probably a few years younger than my mother would be if she were still alive. If that. She's got straight black hair flecked with gray, fawn-colored skin, and dark, almond-shaped eyes set into a smooth, wrinkle-free face.

"I apologize for all of the cloak and dagger, but I can't afford to be seen with you. My security team didn't want me to meet with you in the first place, but it is my duty. It's nothing personal, but I'd like to live," she says bluntly.

A grin pulls the corner of my mouth upward. "I've been getting that a lot lately."

We both take a moment to sip our tea and reflect internally on why we're there. I've tried to put my questions in some sort of orderly fashion but now that I'm faced with this moment, I'm completely at a loss. But I sit up a little straighter and look at Gina, whose face is pinched and drawn. She looks sick to be sitting here with me at all. But she also looks grimly determined.

"Thank you for meeting me," I say.

"Don't thank me. I'm not here because of you," she replies. "I'm here because I made a promise a long time ago."

"A promise to whom?" I ask.

"To your mother," Gina says. "And like her, you're annoyingly stubborn."

Her words are harsh, but there's a sense of affection in them as well, so I say nothing. Her words also send a charge of electricity shooting straight down my spine. I feel myself trembling. I open my mouth to ask another question but Gina cuts me off.

"She made me promise that if anything happened to her and your father, that I would tell you what I knew," she says. "But I will tell you right now I don't know much, Blake."

It's like my mother knew, even all the way back then, who and what I would eventually become. It's like she knew I would dedicate my life to figuring out who murdered them and how to bring them to justice. It sets my pulse racing and my heart spinning to know that even all those years ago, that my mother was thinking ahead enough that she wanted me to know what happened to her.

"I joined their working group a few months before they were killed. The working group was very tightly=knit," she continues.

"Like a family," I echo the words my parents always told me.

She nodded. "Very much so. They welcomed me in from the start and I never felt uncomfortable around any of them. In many ways, I did love them like my family. But when they were killed, I knew something was very wrong, and that things would get much worse. So, I ran. I ran all the way here and haven't looked back. I have security that keeps me safe, and I live a quiet, comfortable life."

"Do you think they'll still come for you? Even after all these years?"

"I don't think they'll ever stop. Ever. I think, like you, they believe I know more than I do," she says. "That's why I exercise as much care and caution as I can. It's selfish I know, but I don't want to end up like the others."

"Who is this, 'they' you keep referring to?"

"The organization that killed your parents and the rest of our working group," she says as if it's the most obvious thing in the world.

"I get that. But who are they?"

She shook her head. "I don't know. But if you ever find out, tell me," she says, then pauses. "Wait. On second thought, don't tell me. I actually don't want to know."

"What happened out there, Gina?"

She shook her head. "I don't know for sure. But after your parents were killed, the other members of the work group started to die. And that's when I knew they were purging our work group. And that I had to get out of there."

"What were my parents looking into? And was the entire work group looking into the same thing?"

"They all tended to examine the same things, yes," she replies. "As for what they were looking into, I don't know the specifics. I was still a junior researcher at the time. I only came into the group a short time before they were killed."

"Tell me what you can. What you remember," I urge her. "Please."

"The working group had become suspicious of elements within the government. They were looking into certain people who they believed had ties to an organization known as The Thirteen," she says.

For the second time in the last few minutes, her words send a charge of electricity coursing through me. I think about Mr. Corden's notes and the mentions of the Thirteen in them. I feel the connections forming in my mind as some of the gaps are starting to be filled in.

"And what is the Thirteen, Gina?"

"They suspected there was an organization within the government, made up of high-ranking officials, who were orchestrating world events—political assassinations both here and abroad, regime change in other countries, and of course, getting the right people to pass certain pieces of legislation favored by the Thirteen. The end goal was power and wealth."

"Power and wealth," I say. "Those are powerful motivating factors for people to do all sorts of evil things."

She nods. "It is. This group, so far as they could tell, had no real political ideology. They did what they did purely to enrich themselves," she says. "I've discreetly kept tabs over the years, and I think that's changed. Oh, the core ideal is still power and money. The Thirteen is all about accruing wealth and consolidating their own power. But I also see more political bents to the events I believe they are engaged in than before."

"Who are they? The Thirteen? Who makes up its membership?"

"That's a very good question. And before you decide you really want an answer to it, you should make your peace with whatever god you may or may not believe in," she replies. "You open that door you are inviting untold evil into your life. You're inviting your own death into your life. Look at what happened to your parents and our working group. That should be example enough to you of what happens when you start poking around the Thirteen."

I sip my tea and consider her words, letting them all rattle around inside my head for a moment. Before I can ask another question though, she speaks first.

"That is truly all I know, Blake. I wish I knew more I could tell you. I wish I could make you understand why your parents are dead. But I can't," she says, her voice suddenly thick with emotion. "My advice to you is to drop this. You can't bring your parents back, and believe me when I say that if you open this can of worms, you will be putting a target on your back. They will come for you and they will kill you. They're probably watching you already."

I shake my head. "Why would they be watching me?

"Because of who you are. Because of who your parents were," she says. "I can already tell the apple did not fall far from the tree. And if I can see that, I know they can. And they will see you as a threat to them. To their power and wealth. And they will stop at nothing to eliminate those they view as threats to those two things."

"I've never seen anybody watching me," I say. "I'm good at spotting tails—"

"They're better at evasion. You'll never see them coming, Blake. They won't be ham-handed about putting surveillance equipment in your home. They'll insert people into your life to keep tabs on you. And these people will stay with you for years," she says. "That is how committed they are to their cause."

Insert people into my life? To me, that sounds far-fetched; more like something from a book than real life. I can't believe that somebody would give up years of their life pretending to be somebody they weren't, all for the sole purpose of keeping an eye on me. That just sounds flat-out paranoid.

"That's all I have to tell you, Blake. That's all I know. All I will say is: be careful," she says. "Watch your back. Because they are out there. You may not see them, but they see you. They're watching you, and if you prove to be too much trouble, they will kill you."

This all sounds so crazy. And I feel crazy for even considering it. But there is a ring of truth in her words. I believe she's being honest with me. I believe she's being sincere. And that scares the hell out of me.

"Wait five minutes before you leave, please. Finish your tea," Gina says. "And for the love of God, do not contact me ever again. I no longer exist to you."

I hand her my card. She hesitates but takes it. I look her in the eye, holding her gaze.

"If you ever need help with anything, call me, Gina. If you're in trouble, call me," I tell her. "My cell is on my card. I mean it. I'm here to help you."

"Thank you, but I very likely won't be calling," she says, but I notice she slips my card into her pocket anyway.

At the doorway, Gina hesitates and looks back at me, the ghost of a smile upon her lips.

"You really are like her. Your mother," she says. "Seeing you is like seeing her again."

And with that, she's gone, leaving me with even more questions than I had walking in here. But at least I got a few answers. It's not much, but it's something to build on. I know Gina thinks I need to give this up, but I can't. Not that I now know the truth. Or at least some of the truth. It's up to me to reveal the rest of it.

I owe it to my mother and my father. To Mr. Corden. And to the rest of their working group, who were slaughtered for daring to seek the truth.

TWENTY-NINE

*Wilder Residence; The Emerald Pines Luxury Apartments,
Downtown Seattle*

STILL CHARGED up after meeting with Gina, I went home and
immediately got to work. I moved my whole operation into the
second bedroom in my apartment, rearranging the furniture to
give me more working space and to make it easier to hide what
I'm doing from anybody who happens by. All I have to do is
close the door. This is my war room.

I make a mental note to buy a new doorknob. One that has
a lock on it, so I can be sure the room and all the files in it are
secure. As I look around, I realize I'm also going to want to
install surveillance equipment. If even half of what Gina said is
true, if the Thirteen tumble onto the fact that I'm looking into
this, they'll do whatever they can to stop me from getting to the
truth. I wouldn't put it past them to break in and take everything. Cameras may not stop them, but at least I'll have some
faces.

That also means that I'll need copies of everything I'm

working on stored in a secure location outside of my home. I run through a mental list of everything I'm going to need to get and install. Once I get this ball rolling, I'm going to need to be as smart about it all as I can be. And I'll need to protect myself as well. That means leaving instructions with somebody I trust in case something happens to me.

I sit down on the edge of the bed and try to clear my mind. But Gina's words continue rattling around in my head on a non-stop loop. I'm exhilarated and terrified at the same time. This proves my parents were killed as part of some conspiracy cover-up. They'd gotten too close to the truth and were eliminated because of it.

And as I have that thought, I have another. My parents were smart. They planned for every contingency—such as my mother telling Gina to pass onto me what she had. If they were deep into this conspiracy, they would have kept notes. They would have done something to light the path that led to what they were doing. Which means I'm going to have to take a look at everything I kept from the storage unit and look at it with fresh eyes. Surely there has to be a clue somewhere in with the photos and papers I kept.

It worries me, though. When I purged the storage unit, I threw out a lot of things. The vast majority were household goods. But there were other things, too. Lots of things they could have hidden a clue in. All I can do is hope I didn't throw out the wrong boxes. I'll have to dig through the boxes in the closet again at some point soon. There has to be something in there. There just has to be.

With my war room set up, I sit down at the desk and force myself to concentrate. I pore over the files I took from Mr. Corden's RV and I take another run at deciphering his notes. I still can't crack his code entirely, and it's frustrating me because

I'm sure there's important information contained within what looks like total gibberish. But I can't interpret it.

I open the file and look at the dossiers of the Supreme Court Justices again. I know they're significant, otherwise Mr. Corden wouldn't have put them in the file he intended to give to me. I know one old trick spies used to use is to load a file up with a lot of useless information and red herrings. That way, if the file falls into the wrong hands, the person who got it won't know what they're looking at. But Mr. Corden intended for me to have the file the night he died. And because it's so thin and he'd had it hidden, I'm confident there isn't anything superfluous in it.

I walk over to the whiteboard I set up in the corner and write the three Supreme Court Justices names across the top—Ellen Sharp, Reginald Boone, and Jonathan Kettering. Below their names, I write their cause of death and the day they died. Heart attack, stroke, and car accident respectively. Kettering was the first to die, a couple years ago. Boone died of a stroke eighteen months ago, and Sharp had a heart attack just in the last couple months.

Boone, Kettering, and Sharp were replaced by Justices Wilfred Orman, Kenneth Brighton, and Angela Lorane. Outwardly, I don't find anything that suggests they all have some wild political agenda. They actually seem to have very bland, very non-controversial judicial records. Nothing about them screams extremist or activist. From what I can tell, they're well respected and judge fairly.

But not everything is as it seems. Something I'm very familiar with. Just because they're not wild-eyed, frothing at the mouth conservatives or liberals, it doesn't mean they don't come in with not just an agenda, but marching orders as well. Yeah, it's kind of Manchurian Candidate-ish, but it's not something I'm willing to rule out just yet either. Right now, every option is on the table.

The fact that three Justices all died so close to each other is a pattern that troubles me. It's almost like they were on a schedule. The other thing that bothers me is that each of them died of something easy to set up and mimic. You can stage a car wreck. And you can give somebody drugs to induce a heart attack and a stroke. But the question is, why would somebody want to remove these three Justices specifically?

"The answer has to be in the cases they decided," I mutter to myself.

I sit down in front of my laptop and call up a search engine, then call up all the SCOTUS decisions over the last few years. Most of them are mundane and won a clear majority one way or the other. There weren't a lot of one-or-two vote decisions. But I do find a couple of cases that the newly-minted Justices were the deciding factors in. One had to do with property rights, with the SCOTUS ruling that a land claim by a large corporation was valid even though it decimated what had been to that point, a private land holding. The other ruling was also very favorable to a corporation—a defense contractor this time.

Those two cases netted the big companies millions. Tens of millions, probably. And if what Gina said is true—if wealth and power is at the core of the Thirteen—they would have to be very happy with the outcome of those cases. It makes one wonder if the Thirteen somehow engineered all of this to happen exactly as it's unfolding now.

I know it seems preposterous. Like something out of a Jason Bourne movie. And maybe it is. All I'm saying is that the confluence of these different events, all coming together at the same time, benefitting people allegedly trying to influence if not outright orchestrate major events, is interesting to look at. To say the least.

It's a good starting point. An intriguing one. But ultimately, it's rumor, innuendo, and conspiracy theory until I have something to back it up. Which I obviously don't have right now. Like I said when we were grilling Dylan Betts... it's all certainly suggestive, but nowhere near conclusive. Not yet anyway.

As I look at the whiteboard and all the papers I've hung on the wall beside it, I feel that tingling thrill start to course through my veins. The ball is finally in motion and things are starting to come together.

I might finally start to get some answers to questions that have haunted me my entire life. It's exciting. At the same time, it's terrifying. Because if Gina is right, opening these doors will put a target on my back.

And what's worse, is I have no idea what will be stepping through them.

THIRTY

SSA Wilder's Office, Criminal Data Analysis Unit; Seattle Field Office

"Okay, breathe, girl," Astra says. "Seriously, take a deep breath and let it out again slowly. Focus on your breathing."

I arch an eyebrow at her. "I'm not trying to give birth here."

"No, women giving birth are generally a lot calmer than you are right now."

A rueful smile crosses my lips and I shake my head. "How can you not be freaked out—even a little bit—by the idea that there's a cabal inside our government doing heinous things and killing lots of people just to get rich and maintain power?"

She shrugs. "I suppose because I already figured that was the case," she says with a small laugh. "I mean, I assume that's basically what political parties are. So why is this different about this Thirteen Club or whatever it's called?"

"It's just called the Thirteen. As for what's different, the last I checked, political parties weren't out there assassinating sitting Supreme Court Justices."

"Maybe not directly no, but..."

I laugh. "And you have the nerve to tell me I'm a tinfoil hat conspiracy theorist?"

Astra flashes me a mischievous grin. "Of course, I do. And that's because we can smell our own, you know."

"You're such a jerk."

"Yeah, I know. It's part of my charm."

I spent hours last night digitizing copies of everything I have. I printed out copies that will be put into a safe deposit box under a false identity. A copy has been sent to my cloud storage. And I'm giving a thumb drive to Astra. I'm also giving her a key to the safe deposit box and the password for the cloud storage.

Common sense would dictate that I spread those three copies among three different people. But I trust Astra and know she can take care of herself if they come for them. Besides, I am likely going to make more copies and spread them around a little bit wider. I just didn't have the time to do it last night. I've still got a murderer to catch, after all.

"So, let me get this straight. You're afraid that trained assassins will be coming for you and this treasure trove of documents to kill you to protect their secrets. That about right?" Astra asks.

I purse my lips and nod. "Yeah, pretty much."

She holds up the thumb drive. "And you're giving me a copy of all this trouble because... you want them to suicide me too? What a great friend you are."

I laugh. "What, you didn't think I was going to let them take me out without you coming with me, did you?"

"Uh-huh," she mutters.

"Don't worry, Paxton will be getting a set as well."

"Oh, wonderful. So, when the assassins come, everybody closest to you is going down with you. Awesome."

"I just didn't want to be lonely in the afterlife."

"You're such a giver."

I sigh and lean back in my chair, trying to get my churning mind and belly under control.

"What is it? What's wrong?" she asks.

"For so many years, I've been floundering around, trying to solve their murder. And I'm still not close, don't get me wrong, but it suddenly feels like everything is happening so fast. This thing seems so much bigger than I imagined it was going to be. I'm just overwhelmed and feel so far out of my depth right now," I tell her honestly.

"Well, to be fair, you kind of are," she says. "I mean, government conspiracies and this murderous cabal. Anybody would be out of their depth."

I nod and run my fingers through my hair. She's right. Anybody would be. But for some reason, I suddenly feel more ill-equipped to handle it than anybody. I feel like the last person in the world who should be investigating this. And that annoying voice in my head has been on me non-stop, telling me I should listen to Mark, and Astra, and Gina, and let this go. That this isn't going to have a happy ending for anybody.

"But you know what else I know?" Astra adds.

"That you were right, and I need to get out of the deep end of the pool?"

"I've already conceded that you're not going to do that," she chuckles. "No, what I know is that you are the smartest, strongest, bravest, and most determined person I know. If there is anybody who can solve this case and bring this cabal down, it's going to be you. And I know that because I've known you for a long while now. I'm comfortable saying that you don't know how to quit. And you don't know how to lose."

Astra's words touch something deep inside of me and stir my soul. They are the exact words I need to hear right now and somehow, she seems to know that. Though, that shouldn't surprise me. She's always had the best words for me whenever I needed to hear them. It's one of the things I love her for.

"Thanks, Astra," I say, fighting back the tears. "That really means a lot to me."

"And you know I've always got your back, don't you? I'm not letting you go into this fight alone. Whatever happens, I'll be right by your side."

I get to my feet and come around my desk then pull her to her feet. I throw my arms around her and pull her into a tight embrace. She laughs and hugs me back, and suddenly—even though I'm still feeling overwhelmed and terrified about what's to come—I no longer feel so alone.

The sound of Rick clearing his throat draws my attention and I step back, discreetly wiping at my eyes.

"I didn't realize it was hug it out therapy hour," he cracks with a lopsided grin on his face. "Can I get in there and get one of those?"

"Not even if you paid me," Astra quips.

"What is it?" I ask.

He shrugs. "Oh, nothin'. I mean, if you want to go back to your hug therapy, that's cool," he says. "I just thought you might want to catch a murderer."

I feel that tingle of excitement in my belly I get when a case starts coming together. Astra and I exchange a quick smile and I know she's feeling the same thing.

"You got the picture cleaned up?" I ask.

He nods. "Sure did. Come see."

We follow Rick out to the bullpen and as he returns to his workstation, we walk to the screens on the wall at the front of the room. A moment later, a picture pops up. It's not perfectly clear, but it's a lot better than before. I can actually make out the logo on the sticker.

"Rick, this is amazing," I tell him. "You did it. You actually did it."

"Hey, don't say that like you're surprised. I mean, you did hire me to be your resident genius, didn't you? Well, voila. Here's your return on investment," he chirps.

Astra turns to me. "I thought you hired me to be the resident genius."

"I did. Just don't tell Rick," I fake-whisper to her. "It makes him happy to think he's the one."

"I heard that," he calls over.

Smiling, I step to the monitor and take a closer look. There are two hands clasped in a handshake with what looks like it could be a sun behind it, and in the middle of the sun is a cross. Just below the hands are the words, "Helping Hands." I frown and turn back to Rick to ask, but it's Mo who steps up.

"Helping Hands is a faith-based women's shelter and support group—"

"Women's support group?" I frown.

She nods. "That's what the website says."

"So, what's it doing on this dude's car?" Astra asks.

I shake my head. "Maybe it was already on it when he bought it."

"That car's a 2019 model," Astra points out. "That's a pretty quick sale."

"Maybe it's his girlfriend's car or something," Mo offers.

"It's possible. But the best way to find out is to go check out this support group ourselves," I say. "Mo, do me a favor if you would and dig deep into this group. I want to know everything there is to know about them."

"On it," she says.

Astra looks at me. "Field trip?"

I nod. "Field trip."

THIRTY-ONE

Helping Hands Women's Shelter, Riverview District;
Seattle, WA

THE RIVERVIEW DISTRICT in Seattle is a very middle-class neighborhood. The houses are nice and somewhat well-kept, but they're not sprawling estates or anything. It's just south of South Seattle College, so a number of students live in the area, but they're not the wild partiers UW students are. It's also near the old Industrial District, which had its heyday decades ago.

It's not necessarily a rough neighborhood, but it's not exactly a gated community either. The overall vibe is of a community that was once fresh and vibrant maybe back in the '70s and '80s, but these days doesn't amount to much. There are the occasional hipster tattoo parlors or craft brew places here, but nowhere near the amount you'll find in trendy, affluent places like Capitol Hill or Belltown, which have been gentrified to hell and back.

What I can say about Riverview is that even if it's not pristine by Seattle's standards, it's still light years better than a lot of other places in the country. Seattle's idea of a "bad neighborhood" is sometimes skewed by places like Laureltown and Fremont.

"You get the feeling we're being watched?" Astra asks.

I turn around in the street and see the curtains fall back into place in a house to our right—and on our left. Some people just love to be nosy.

"Pretty sure we are," I mutter.

We cross the street and head for a large white house. Four pillars line the front, giving way a wide porch under a red door. Green shutters frame the windows on the New England-style clapboard house. It's a cute place and looks well-tended to. A tall, sprawling oak tree sits in the front yard —or rather, takes up most of it—and there are planters of flowers that run along the entire front of the house, adding a riot of color to the yard. A small red brick staircase leads up to the porch, where a pair of oversized rockers sit with a small, round table between them, and a porch swing sits at the far end.

"This place is cute," Astra notes. "Are you sure we're in the right spot?"

Two tall, narrow windows sit on either side of the front door, and I point to the lower panel on the right window. It's the same sticker we saw on the back of our unsub's car. Astra nods. It's placed in a low, discreet spot to help identify the shelter to women on the run, but in a place that most men wouldn't tend to notice it.

"Well, I guess that clarifies that, then," she says.

I raise my hand to knock, but the door opens before I get the chance and I find myself staring at a girl who can't be more than sixteen. She's tall and pencil-thin, with dark red hair, pale skin, and blue eyes—and is sporting a black eye and busted lip. Despite her injuries, she gives us a wide smile anyway.

"Hi," she greets us, though her fat lip is giving her a bit of a lisp. "Can I help you?"

We show her our badges and she looks at them with wide eyes and an expression of awe on her face.

"You two are really FBI agents?" she gasps.

We nod. "We really are," I say. "What's your name?"

"Sydney," she replies.

"Nice to meet you, Sydney. I'm Blake and this is Astra," I introduce us. "Is this the Helping Hands shelter?"

Sydney looks around furtively, then turns back to us, gnawing on her lower lip. "I'm not supposed to say."

"Of course, I'm sorry," I reply.

I'm mortified that I'd just asked this girl to violate the most important rule of the shelter—you don't tell anybody about the shelter. It's a common-sense rule, one I should have thought about before asking. The problem is that we need to speak to the shelter administrator, but I have no idea who's in charge. I look over at Astra and see that she seems just as lost as me at the moment, so I try a different tack.

"It's all right, Sydney," I say. "We know what this place is, and we'd never tell anybody about it. But can you do me a favor and get whoever is in charge here? We really need to speak with her."

"Sure," she says slowly. "I'll go get her."

"Thanks," I say.

She closes the door, so Astra and I take a step back. She follows me over to the railing that lines the porch and we lean against it. Shelters like these survive on secrecy. Women come to these shelters, cleverly camouflaged in residential neighborhoods because they feel safe. Because nobody is supposed to talk about it or mention where it is.

I recall seeing a magazine article once that focused on one of these shelters and the demand for secrecy was so great, the photographer wasn't allowed to take pictures of any distinguishing features. It was such a strict rule, they couldn't even photograph the fence or the trees in the yard.

And for good reason. These places exist so women and children have someplace to run. Someplace to feel safe and get away from the men who are beating on them. The men who threaten to hurt them worse, or even kill them. These shelters are a safe haven for so many. I love that abuse victims have a safe place to go. But I hate they have to exist at all.

The front door opens and a woman steps out, pulling it closed behind her. She's a small woman, five-three, maybe five-four, but is stout and has a grandmotherly look about her. She's got iron-gray hair that's pulled back into a tight bun that sits atop her head. Her cheeks are ruddy, and she's got a warm smile on her face.

"You must be the FBI agents Sydney was so excited about," she says. "I'm Marjorie Bell."

"SSA Blake Wilder," I introduce myself. "This is Special Agent Russo."

We all shake hands, expressing the usual pleasantries. Marjorie has a firm handshake and a steely glint in her eye. She seems warm and friendly, but I can tell she's fierce when it comes to protecting her shelter and the women within its walls. This is a woman who does not take crap from anybody. Although she's small, I have no doubt she's willing to throw her body into the middle of a fight to save her girls. I have to respect that about her.

"So, what can I do for you, Agents?" she finally asks.

I pull my phone out of my pocket and call up the picture of the sticker. "This is one of yours, right?" I ask.

She nods. "Looks like it."

"Do you have any men on staff? Janitorial? Security? Anything?" Astra asks.

Marjorie shakes her head. "We don't have security. It'd be a dead giveaway, and we rely on keeping a very low profile," she says. "As for men on staff, none. Not permitted."

I nod. "Fair enough."

I call up the next picture—the one of the car in full—and let her have a look at it. She studies the photo for a minute, squinting at it.

"Sorry for the quality. This is an ATM photo. Unfortunately, we weren't able to get a better one," I say. "But do you happen to recognize the car?"

She nods. "Yeah, that looks like Helen Svboda's car. She worked here for more than ten years," she said.

"Worked?" Astra asks. "Past tense?"

Marjorie nods and an expression of grief touches her features. "Yeah, unfortunately, she passed away about a month ago. Maybe a little more now," she says. "She was the sweetest woman ever. She's sorely missed."

Astra and I exchange a glance. That somebody else is in possession of the car means it's still in play as far as our suspect goes. That excited burbling inside of me is starting to build to a furious boil as I feel the momentum of the case picking up even more speed.

"Do you know who has the car now, Marjorie?" I ask.

"Of course. She left it to her son, Tony. She left everything to him," she says. "Tony is a prince among men, I tell you. He's such a good boy."

Yeah sure, if you consider a triple rapist-slash-triple murderer a good boy. I guess the bar for a prince has been lowered. But I'm practically bouncing out of my shoes as we stand there. I feel like we're closing in. But I know better than to put the cart before the horse. I've burned myself far too many times in the past to let myself say case closed, mission accomplished, or anything else. There is still a lot of work to do.

"So, what is this about, Agents?" Marjorie asks.

"Mrs. Svboda's car was seen near the scene of a crime," I say smoothly. "We're just rounding up witnesses right now."

"Oh my," she gasps. "I hope it wasn't serious."

"We're not sure just yet," Astra chimes in. "We're still gathering the facts."

"Can you tell us where Mr. Svboda lives? We'll need to speak with him," I say.

"Of course," Marjorie says. "Let me just go back inside. I have her old address in my office."

"Thank you," I say. "We appreciate it."

Marjorie disappears inside again, leaving Astra and me on the porch doing our best to keep ourselves from getting too excited. The door opens and Sydney comes back out. She stands before us, a shy smile on her face.

"Do you think I can be an FBI agent too?" she asks.

"Of course you can, babe," Astra winks. "You can be anything you want to be."

I nod. "Work hard. Don't let anybody put you down, and never forget how amazing you are," I tell her. "And don't ever, ever, ever, let anybody tell you what you can and cannot do. If you put your mind to it and work hard, you can do anything you want to do."

"She speaks the truth," Astra nods.

"Sydney, go back inside, dear," Marjorie says when she steps back out onto the porch.

Astra and I both give her a card and tell her to call us anytime if she needs advice—or help. Sydney gives us a smile, then disappears into the house. Marjorie smiles after the girl and I can see just how much she cares about her.

"She's quite taken with you two," Marjorie says.

"She seems like a wonderful girl," I say.

"She is. She and her mother have just had a rough go of it in life," Marjorie replies.

"Well, I'm sure being here with you, in a safe place where she's genuinely cared for, is going to do wonders for her," Astra says.

Marjorie looks down at the porch, her cheeks flushing. She is a woman who does great work but obviously isn't one who accepts praise very well. She hands me the paper with the address she had for Helen Svboda.

"Thank you for this," I tell her. "This is going to help a lot."

"I certainly hope so," she says. "I didn't have a current telephone number for him."

"That's all right, we can take it from here," Astra says.

I'm so excited I feel ready to burst. But I stuff it all down. There's work to be done yet. I won't put the cart before the horse. But I feel like we're close.

THIRTY-TWO

Criminal Data Analysis Unit; Seattle Field Office

"TONY SVBODA, thirty-two years old, works as a personal trainer at Rock Solid Fitness," Rick announces. "It's a gym he opened six years ago."

I pace at the front of the bullpen, hands clasped behind me, listening to Svboda's bio being read out for me.

"Degree in Psychology from Oregon, has a reported IQ of 139," Mo adds.

"You're kidding me," Astra says.

"Not according to his school files," Mo says. "Papa Svboda was a big shot union boss. Died when Tony was two years old. It's just been him and his mama until she died a month and a half ago."

"There's the stressor," I say.

Astra nods. "Has he been married? Engaged? Anything?"

"Not according to anything I can find," Rick chimes in.

We've been doing loose surveillance on Tony for the last couple of days. Mo put a tracker on his car so we can keep tabs on him, even when we can't be there in person. I had Rick do a deep dive on him and put together a dossier. I want to know everything there is to know about him, because the more I know, the better I'll be able to predict his next movements. I need to get inside his head, and to do that, I need information. And since I obviously can't have a conversation with him, a digital dossier will have to do.

But every instinct I have is telling me he's our guy. His description matches the one Fish gave me, right down to the fact that he's Czech. If he's not our guy, I will throw myself off the Space Needle. But as sure as I am, I know we need evidence. We need proof. Everything we have—which truthfully isn't much at this moment—is pointing to Svboda as our rapist/killer. But it's all circumstantial. It would be laughed out of court in the blink of an eye. Hell, I don't think we even have enough yet to get an arrest warrant. I can't think of a single judge who'd sign off on one with what we have.

"Okay, what else? Does he have a criminal record?" I ask.

"Has a juvie record, but it's sealed," Mo says.

"He has been arrested for grand theft, assault and battery after a bar fight, and vandalism. He threw a chair through a plate-glass window at the mall," Rick answers.

"None of that adds up to being a serial rapist and murderer," Astra admits.

I shake my head. "No, it does not. Not at all," I reply. "No history of escalating violence. That's unusual."

"I think we need to see what's in that juvie file," Astra says.

"Agreed," I say. "Rick, can you make that happen?"

"Do we have a warrant?"

"Can you pretend we do?" Astra asks.

I get it. Rick isn't exactly a boy scout, but he's not one to break the rules all willy-nilly either. He likes things to be ordered, and most of all, legal. He's not like Brody, who will break any law just because it's a challenge and he can. Rick is more cautious about covering his own backside. He worries about going to prison for doing some of the things I ask him to do. Which is why I ask him to do very little that crosses a line. Sure, I'll send him into that gray area. But I've stopped asking him to do anything blatantly illegal. I just go to Brody for that.

But this is time-sensitive. I don't have the time to wait for a judge to sign off on a warrant. We have a killer who, for all we know, is out on the hunt right now, and I don't believe we have the time to waste trying to get a warrant.

Not that getting a warrant in this case is a slam dunk. With what we have, it's iffy that a judge would sign off on us breaking the seal on his juvie record. And then we would have wasted all that time and arrived back at the same place we began.

No, we don't have time for that.

"Can you break the seal on it?" I ask.

"Of course, but—"

"I'll get a warrant and have a judge sign off on it retroactively. We're pressed for time right now and I need to know what's in there," I say. "Can you do it, Rick?"

He sighs and runs a hand through his shaggy brown hair. He frowns, but nods.

"Yeah, I can do that," he says. "But if this blows back on me, don't you think for a moment I won't sell you guys out to save my hide."

"I would expect nothing less."

We watch him working, his fingers flying over the keyboard. Like Brody, the man is a technological wizard. I wish I had a fraction of the skill they have.

"All right, here," Rick says.

I turn and look at the monitors as he pulls up his juvie arrest record and whistle low.

"Two arrests for assault and one for arson," I read. "Wow. Got off on all of them with probation?"

"How is that even possible?" Astra asks.

"Good question," I reply.

"Friends in high places," Mo answers. "Says here the Svboda family is connected to local politicians, judges, lawyers, cops. It's quite the legal cornucopia."

"Enough to keep a troublesome kid like Tony out of trouble," Astra says.

"Also, enough to make a kid think he's bulletproof," I add.

"Not entirely. He was mandated to attend court-ordered anger management counseling," Rick says. "He did that until his probation was up and apparently never went back."

"Yeah, seems like those worked well for him," Astra quips.

"So, we've got a wealthy, well-connected family who made a habit out of covering for Tony's indiscretions," I say. "I wonder if his friends in high places ever looked the other way and didn't charge him for crimes he committed."

"Stands to reason," Astra says.

"Further adding to his belief that he's bulletproof."

This is all great information, but I need a closer look at him. I need to really get into his head and into his life. And there's only one way I know of to do that. I turn to Astra and give her a smile.

"What are you doing tonight?" I ask.

"You asking me out?"

"You know it."

THIRTY-THREE

Svboda Residence, Madrona District; Seattle, WA

"You sure know how to romance a girl," Astra says with a grin.

"Only the best for you, baby."

We share a quiet laugh as I get myself wired for sight and sound. I clip the pinhole camera to my collar, then hook the Bluetooth mic and speaker to my ear. I pull the black balaclava down to my forehead and zip up the black jacket I'm wearing. The night outside is dark. Thick clouds choke the sky, and thunder rumbles in the distance. Flashes of lightning light up the bank of clouds in spots, creating a beautiful strobe effect.

"You ready?" she asks.

I nod. "I am."

She looks down at the tablet in her lap, checking Svboda's location. The red dot that marks his car is stationary, showing him at a local bar. The trouble is the bar is only five minutes away. But we needed to get in tonight, so we're making the best of what we have. Lemons into lemonade and all that.

"Okay, we're good to go," she reports.

"Great. I'll see you soon."

"Keep your head on a swivel."

"Copy that."

I open the door and slide out of the SUV, then look around at the neighborhood. It's quiet. Most of the windows in the large houses are dark, and nobody seems to be out on the street. This neighborhood is affluent. Most of the houses are large and have multiple stories. No bars on the windows here. But I'm sure most of them are outfitted with state-of-the-art security systems. Which is why I had to bring in a little backup.

I hit the button on my Bluetooth bud to open the line. "Brody, are you there?" I whisper.

"Comin' to you live," he says.

"Hi, Blake!" Marcy screams in the background. "Make sure you tell her she owes me an exclusive!"

I laugh softly. "Tell Marcy it's hers as soon as I close this case out."

"Why didn't you have your own tech guru doing this?" Brody asks.

"Rick's already fulfilled his 'doing naughty things' quota for the day," I reply.

"It's because I'm just flat-out better, isn't it?" Brody questions.

"Rick isn't cut out for the black bag stuff, I'm afraid."

Brody laughs. "Yeah, it's okay. You don't have to say it. It's enough for me to know you're thinking it. I'm just better."

I'm smiling like an idiot and look through the SUV's windshield to see Astra, who's listening in, laughing.

"Okay, I'm heading across the street now," I say. "Are you set up, Brody?"

"Does a bear defecate in a sylvan environment?"

"Ummmm... yes?"

He chuckles. "We're ready to go," he confirms.

"Okay, great."

I dart across the street and up the long driveway, moving as quickly and quietly as I can. I veer off the driveway and head around to the side yard. I'm just about to scale the wrought-iron fence, but on a hunch, I turn the knob. It's unlocked. Stroke of luck, which just has me hoping it doesn't run out.

I slip inside, quietly closing the door behind me, then pull the balaclava down so only my eyes are showing.

"Okay, I'm on the side yard," I whisper.

There's a little space between the houses here, so I doubt anybody could overhear me if I spoke normally, but I'm not going to take the chance.

"You know, for being so wealthy, their security system is garbage. I'd have a tougher time hacking into somebody's Xbox," Brody cracks.

"I'll make sure he knows. Maybe I'll leave a note."

"You should do it as a kindness," Brody offers. "Less scrupulous types than me might take advantage of the situation."

I make my way to the back deck and pause for a moment to admire the pool and jacuzzi. They're both large and fashioned out of what's made to look like black volcanic stone. It's actually quite beautiful—all except for the beer bottles and cans floating on the surface of the pool. What a pig.

"Okay Blake, the alarm is disabled. The house is yours," Brody says in my ear.

I move over to the large French doors and grit my teeth as I turn the knob. It swings inward and no alarm sounds. I let out the breath I've been holding and smile.

"Nice work, Brody."

"Did you doubt me?"

"I won't next time."

"You said that last time."

"Yeah, but this time I really mean it," I tell him, and he laughs in my ear.

I slip a flashlight out of the pack on my waist and click it on, sweeping the blade of light across one side of the room and then the other. Moving silently, I leave the door open behind me just in case I need to make a quick exit.

I find myself in a great room that's tastefully furnished and decorated. It's clean. Spotless really. I make a circuit of the ground floor and don't find much of anything. The house is clean and well-ordered though, which tells me he still has a cleaning service. I just hope he doesn't have a live-in maid.

"Nothing on the ground floor," I announce. "Moving to the second. Astra, how are we doing?"

"Still stationary. We're good,"

I walk down a long hallway that ends in a door. I go inside and am immediately assaulted by the overpowering stench of stale body odor. The room is a disaster zone, with clothes and shoes strewn all over the place. The bed is unmade and the sheets are so dingy, I have to wonder when was the last time he changed them.

"What are you seeing, Wilder?"

"A pigsty," I croak. "This place is a mess, and it stinks."

"I guess money just can't buy you class," she comments.

"I say that about Paxton all the time," Brody chimes in.

I look through the drawers of Tony's dresser. Nothing. Same for his desk. I even peek into his closet and the steamer trunk at the foot of his bed. Other than the horrible mess, there's nothing interesting in this room so I back out of it and close the door. I turn around and see another door at the opposite end of the hallway. My guess is that it's his mother's room.

I move down the hall quickly and go inside, sweeping my

beam of light all over the room. What I see makes my mouth fall open. My eyes widen and a quiet gasp passes my lips.

"Holy crap," I whisper.

"Are you all right, Blake?"

"Yeah. Call up the pinhole camera feed," I tell her. "You have to see this."

Knowing she won't be able to see, I move over and flip the light on. This room has no windows facing the street, so we'll be okay. I turn around to show them what I mean. The dresser that was on that wall has been moved to the side. Clearly visible are the dark outlines and discoloration of paint that shows a large frame once hung on the wall. And in its place, there are dozens of articles about the three murders in Seattle— Emily Tompkins, Summer Kennedy, and Serena Monroe.

He'd cut out articles from newspapers as far away as Idaho so long as it dealt with the murders. He's obviously obsessed with them. Little wonder, since he did it. He obviously needs to relive the moment.

"That's a little disturbing," Astra mutters in my ear.

I turn around and freeze. Standing before me is the large four-poster bed I assume belongs to his mother. Like Tony's bed, it's unmade, and the sheets look just as dingy as his. But what catches my eye is what looks like a woman's nightgown half-lying on his pillow. It looks to me like Svboda has been... cuddling with it.

"I think he's been sleeping in here," I say. "In his mother's bed. I think he's been snuggling with her nightgown."

"Oh my God. Please tell me you're joking."

"I'm not."

"I'm officially completely creeped out," Astra replies. "And whatever you do, for the love of all things holy, please do not put that sheet under a blacklight. I'm begging you, Blake."

"You two have like... issues. Serious issues," Brody chimes in.

Trying to shake off the case of the creeps that suddenly crawled all over me, I move about the room, checking everything quickly but methodically. Again, I find nothing. No knife, nothing I can associate with the crimes. Nothing. And I know there's no way he was holding his victims either here or in his own bedroom. Their wounds would guarantee there would be blood in the primary crime scene. And it's not here.

"The basement," I say. "I need to check the basement."

"Uh Blake, you need to get out of there. Now," Astra says, a sense of urgency in her voice. "Svboda's on the move and he's coming home. Get out now."

A flash of adrenaline surges through me and my heart begins to race. Knowing I have a scant few minutes, I turn off the light and close the door behind me. I dash down the hallway and get to the head of the stairs when I hear Astra's voice.

"Two minutes," she says. "You need to move Blake."

I run down the stairs as quickly and safely as I can. The last thing I want is to turn an ankle and fall down the stairs. I'm pretty sure if Tony came home to find me on the foyer floor, it wouldn't go well for me. I make it back to the ground floor without incident, but as I move through the house, I bump into a table and send some of the figurines on top flying.

"Dammit!"

"One minute, Blake."

I bend down and pick up all the figurines I can and set them down on the table, then pick up the rest. Even if I had the time, I wouldn't know how to put them back correctly. I didn't see the table when I came in, so I don't know how they were ordered. All I can hope is that he's such a slob, he won't notice either.

"He's pulling into the driveway. Get out now, Blake!"

My heart is racing. I feel like fire is flowing through my veins as I dash out the back door, closing it behind me. I hear the rumble of the car's engine in the driveway and then it shuts off.

"Hit it, Brody," I gasp. "Turn the alarm back on."

"Alarm is now armed," he replies.

There's a long moment when I'm bathed in near silence, the only sound is my heart thundering in my ears. I move quickly along the side yard and make it back to the gate. I peer through the black iron bars and watch as Tony whistles to himself as he walks to the front door. I hunker down and wait for him to go inside.

"You're clear, Blake. Move, move, move," Astra calls.

I slip through the gate and take exaggerated care to close it again. Then I turn and run as fast as I ever have down the driveway, hoping I look like nothing more than another shadow. My feet slap the pavement hard, making me grimace at the sound. But I make it back to the SUV and dive in. Astra starts her up and pulls away from the curb, driving quickly down the street and to safety.

"Holy crap that was close," I gasp, still trying to catch my breath.

Astra is grinning wide at me. "You sure do know how to show a girl a good time."

"Like I said," Brody's voice sounds in our ears. "Issues, ladies. Y'all have some serious issues, and I encourage you to seek help."

Astra and I laugh hysterically as she drives, ferrying me to safety.

THIRTY-FOUR

Wilder Residence; The Emerald Pines Luxury Apartments, Downtown Seattle

WE DIDN'T GET what we needed with tonight's raid. Oh, I saw plenty that was suggestive. Put before a jury, I have no doubt they'd come back with the right verdict and send Tony Svboda away forever. The problem is that with what we have now, we won't ever see the inside of a courtroom. That famous old saying about a prosecutor being able to indict a ham sandwich doesn't apply here. What we have is more like a wish sandwich —two pieces of bread and we wish we had something between them.

The adrenaline that lit me up for most of the night has finally ebbed, leaving me feeling weak and shaky. I slump against the wall of the elevator car and when the doors open, I trudge slowly down the hallway to my door. My hands are shaking so badly, it takes me a minute to manage to get the key into the lock, but I finally get it. All I want right now is a hot shower and some sleep.

I close and lock the door behind me, and when I step into the dimly lit living room, I find Mark sitting on the couch, his face pinched and tight.

"Very moody. Atmospheric," I comment. "Sitting in the dark like this."

"Why are you dressed like a cat burglar?"

I shrug. "We had to do a little burgling tonight."

He stares at me with an expression on his face I can't interpret. It's obvious he's upset though, and there is nothing I want to do less tonight than argue about whatever the issue is.

"Listen, I can tell you're mad about something, but can we schedule our fight about whatever it is for tomorrow?" I ask. "I'm beat and—"

"I saw your room."

"I guess not," I mutter, letting out a heavy breath. "Fine. What room?"

"Your conspiracy room, I guess you'd call it."

That gets my attention and upsets me. The void inside of me left behind by the rush of adrenaline begins to fill again as a fresh flood of it washes in. I silently chastise myself for not getting the lock taken care of already.

"So, is that what we're doing now? Just snooping through all of my rooms?"

"I wasn't aware there were places I wasn't allowed to go."

"The door was closed. I closed it," I growl. "In most polite, civilized societies, a closed door means don't come in."

"Like I said, I didn't know there were places I wasn't allowed in here. Maybe we need to draw out a formal map and you can label the 'no entry' zones for me, so I don't see something I shouldn't see again," he snaps.

"I wasn't aware I was hiding it," I reply. "Because as best as I recall, I told you I wasn't giving up on the investigation. I seem to remember telling you that in very clear terms."

"Have you seen your board in there? It's conspiracy theory craziness," he fires back. "Are we going to need to start wearing paper robes and tin foil hats around here?"

I shake my head, feeling the anger swelling within me. "What are you so pissed off about, Mark? You knew I was looking into this. So, why are you acting so shocked and surprised right now?"

"Because I didn't realize how absolutely out there and nuts this all looks," he says. "So thank you for giving me a very well-illustrated demonstration of how crazy this conspiracy crap is."

I clench my jaw as I stare at him. "Did you read everything in my room? Do you know what a freaking violation of my privacy that is?"

"I had the time since you were out apparently robbing people or whatever you were doing tonight," he fires back. "I mean, do you really believe that somebody assassinated Supreme Court Justices?"

"I don't know what I believe right now," I shout at him. "That's why I'm investigating this. So I can separate what's real and what's not. So I can figure out what I believe and what I don't believe. Jesus, Mark, can you get off my back and let me do my thing?"

"I didn't realize doing your thing involved falling down a rabbit hole of absolute insanity."

I shrug. "Well, now you do."

We fall silent for a long moment, both of us just staring hard at one another. I can't believe he went through my things without my permission. What I can't believe even more is the fact that we're having this argument. Again. I thought we put this to bed the last time we fought. But apparently not.

"What is this really all about, Mark?" I ask. "Why are you freaking out so bad right now?"

"Other than the fact that what you're doing is nuts?"

"Yes, Mark. Other than that."

He opens his mouth to reply but closes it again without speaking. He stands up suddenly and starts to pace the room, more agitated than I've ever seen him before. It strikes me then that there is more going on here than he's saying. He can't be this upset about something he already knew I was doing. He knew I wasn't going to back off. No, I feel like there's something else at play here.

"What is really going on here, Mark?"

"I just think what you're doing is crazy."

"Yeah, I got that. But that's not news," I say. "So, what is the real issue here?"

He finally meets my gaze, and in his eyes, I see the fear and the worry. I see a man who is terrified of what could happen. Of what he fears might happen.

"Talk to me, Mark. What's really happening here?"

He looks at me and I see his eyes shimmering with tears that he's fighting hard to keep from falling.

"I'm just afraid, Blake. If you're right, and they can murder Supreme Court Justices, what's to stop them from getting to you?"

His words knock the wind out of me, and I find that I have no answer for him. So I do the only thing I can do and step forward. I pull him into a tight embrace and just hold him.

THIRTY-FIVE

I CHECK my watch and see that it's just after nine as Svboda exits his house. It's been a week and a half since our adventure into his house. After that night, we put him on round-the-clock surveillance. Mo, Astra, and I have all divided up the day, all of us pulling eight-hour shifts, watching him. Waiting for him to make his move.

I know the pressure is building up inside of him. The cooling-off period from Emily Tompkins, to Summer Kennedy, to Serena Monroe, had shortened considerably. And I know he has no other outlet, so his need to release has got to be growing stronger and stronger, day by day, hour by hour. It's only a matter of time before he tries to snatch another girl off the street and when he does, we're going to be right there.

I'm parked several houses down from his, camouflaged between a Range Rover and a Chevy Silverado. When I see his black Audi A4 pull out of his driveway, I start my engine and wait for Svboda to turn the corner before I pull my Suburban away from the curb and follow him at a distance. The tracker is still fixed to his car, so I'm able to keep a good gap between us.

I touch the button on my Bluetooth headset and wait until I hear the chime, connecting me to home base.

"Rick, are you there?" I ask.

"Here, boss."

"Svoboda is on the move," I tell him. "I'm about half a mile behind him. Keeping tabs on him with the tracker."

"Copy that," he replies. "Think tonight's the night?"

"God, I hope so. I'm ready to be done with this fool."

"That makes two of us," he replies. "Four of us, if you count Mo and Astra."

"Well, here's hoping we catch him in the act tonight."

"I'll be on comms," he says. "Happy hunting, boss."

I disconnect the call and glance over at the tablet fixed to the dashboard. Svoboda looks like he's heading for Belltown. Trendy and popular, Belltown is what people call a target-rich environment. There are more bars than Starbucks in Belltown, which is notable. The sidewalks are always crowded with people, and the party never seems to end. It's no wonder he likes hunting there.

I turn the corner onto Evergreen Avenue and see Svoboda about a hundred yards ahead of me. Evergreen is one of the less crowded streets in Belltown, but it's still pretty crowded. Svoboda is driving slowly down the street and I feel that charge of electricity fill my veins. He's on the hunt. This is it. Tonight is the night. He takes a right onto what looks like a dimly lit side street. Has he spotted somebody?

Suddenly, a group of college kids in pink button-up shirts, shorts, and boat shoes drunkenly waves their way across the street, forcing me to slam on the brakes, causing my tires to screech. I lay on the horn and earn fingers and a slew of curses from the group of kids. And with every second that passes, I feel Svoboda getting further away from me. Maybe I'm paranoid, but something doesn't feel right.

I glance at the tablet and see that his red dot is still sitting in the same spot and try to relax. He's probably running his usual routine on whichever girl he selected, which means I may have a minute or so before he slips that needle filled with ketamine into her.

"Come on!" I shout out the window. "Get the hell out of the way!"

Other groups of students, emboldened by the frat-boy crowd, began heedlessly walking across the street, holding up traffic going both ways. While I lay on the horn, they laugh and give me the finger in addition to hurling insults at me. My stomach is churning as I wait for these idiots to clear the road. The dot still hasn't moved, and the feeling of something being wrong grows even thicker inside of me.

The assholes finally clear the road and I jump on the accelerator. I take the right Svoboda did and race down the street as fast as I dare. The street ahead of me is empty. Svoboda's car is nowhere to be seen. But the red dot still has not moved. As I pull even with it, I slam on the brakes and jump out of my SUV. I turn in a circle, not understanding how the red tracking dot could still be on the screen when—

"Oh God," I groan.

On the sidewalk, I see a purse laying on the concrete. I run over and snatch it off the ground and open it up. There, nestled in with the girl's belongings, is the tracker.

"Dammit!" I shout.

I dig into the bag and find the girl's wallet. Her name is Scarlett Porter. She's blonde, thin, and beautiful. Just his type. Panic gripping me tightly, I key open my comm.

"Rick."

"Go ahead, boss."

"Svoboda knew. He knew we had a tracker on him," I say.

"He grabbed a girl, dumped the tracker, and took off. I lost him."

Rick groans. "Oh, God. How in the hell did he know?"

"I have no idea. Maybe his lifestyle makes him paranoid," I say. "Paranoid people are hypervigilant."

"What now?"

I turn in a circle, my hand on my head. My stomach is seething so hard, I feel like I'm going to be sick. I rack my brain, trying to figure out what to do next.

"Okay, here's what I'm going to do," I say as I move. "I'm going to drive. Try to find Svboda on the road. I need you to call Astra and Mo in. Get them on the road too. We need to find this guy, now."

"Copy that."

I drive the streets, searching for his Audi, but don't see anything. There are a thousand directions he could have gone. Driving around blindly feels like searching for a needle in a stack of needles. I'm feeling the tendrils of panic gripping and squeezing me so tightly, I can barely breathe.

Now that Svboda knows we're onto him, there's no telling what he'll do. There's no guarantee he'll stick to his usual pattern of keeping the girl for a night. If I were a betting woman, I'd say probably not. He'll be rushed. He'll be needing his release so badly that he may just do it to get it done.

But then, maybe his ritual is so important to him that he needs to accomplish it no matter what. Yeah, he's onto us, but part of me is hoping that since he found the tracker and got rid of it, he'll believe he's in control again. If he feels like he's got the upper hand on us, maybe he'll stick to his pattern and take his time with the girl he just snatched. And he does have the upper hand—we don't know where he is. But it may give us the time we need to figure this out.

I rack my brain, trying to come up with something. I turn

down his street and cruise by his house. The Audi's not there. I didn't think it would be, but I wanted to cover my bases. The last thing I'd want is to not go by his house and find out later that he'd killed the girl there.

"Where are you, Svboda? Where in the hell are you?"

Fear and dread have taken hold of me and it's keeping me from thinking clearly. I need to clear my head. I pull to a stop along the curb and close my eyes. I count to ten then let out a long breath. Then I do it again. And again. It takes me until I've counted to eighty before I'm even approaching rational thought once more.

"Okay, think," I mutter. "Think."

I remember something Paxton told me once that's stuck with me for a long time now. He said that when things are getting hairy and the world seems overly complicated, the best thing you can do is go back to basics. Do the most basic thing and build out from there. But the most important thing is to get that first block down, and to do that, you need to think and act in the simplest, most basic of terms.

For me, going back to basics is going back to my profile. Trusting my profile. I cycle through it all in my head a couple of times. I'm about to run through it again when the thought blindsides me. It is literally such a basic thought, I'm embarrassed I didn't have it before. I reach up and key my comm. For Svboda to do his work, he needs privacy. It was one of the first things we talked about.

"Rick, you there?"

"Go, boss."

"I need you to search property records. I need you to find a secondary property for Tony Svboda," I instruct him. "He's got to have a property someplace secluded. Somewhere private. That's where he's going."

"Copy that," Rick says. "Standby."

In the background, I can hear the clacking of his computer keys as his fingers fly across the board. I gnaw on my bottom lip, trying to stave off the panic that's still hovering like a malignant spirit waiting to descend upon me.

"There's nothing, boss," Rick sighs, sounding as dejected as I feel.

I shake it off and focus my mind again. "Okay. Try his father's name, and then his mother's," I say. "There's a property out there he's using as his kill site. I can feel it in my bones."

"Roger that."

I hear the clicking of the keyboard again and Rick muttering to himself in the background. And then the clacking stops and Rick gasps.

"Boss, you're a genius," he says excitedly. "There's a cabin in the name of Svoboda's father, out in the Olympic Forest."

"Great work, Rick. Shoot me the address."

"Already done," he tells me. "You've got a drive ahead of you. It's about three hours from where you are now."

"I'm on the road. Send Astra and Mo to my location. Also, I need you to liaise with the local LEOs. I want them on standby. But until we know for sure whether Svoboda is at that cabin or not, they don't leave their station. Make sure they understand we have jurisdiction and they're not to make a move without us."

"Roger that. I got it, boss," he replies. "Hit the road and good luck. And be careful."

"Thanks Rick."

I disconnect the call and pull the directions to the cabin up on the tablet. After that, I throw my bubble light up on the dashboard and stand on the accelerator. Svoboda has almost an hour lead on me, and I need to cut that time down. I need to get to that cabin before he has a chance to harm a single hair on Scarlett Porter's head.

"I'm coming for you, Tony."

THIRTY-SIX

Svboda Family Cabin, Olympic National Forest; Near Quinault, WA

"Talk to me, Rick," I say.

"There's a turnoff about half a mile ahead of you. The access road will lead you to the Svboda cabin about a quarter-mile in from the road," he reports.

"Where are Astra and Mo?"

"Still half an hour out," he replies. "I think this is the part where you let me liaise with the locals again and have them send everybody."

I pass the turnoff he mentioned and see the long, dark access road. I stop the car, pulling as far over onto the shoulder as I can, and turn on the hazard lights. The trees press close to the shoulder, and the interior of the forest beyond is nearly pitch black.

"Boss?" Rick asks.

"Yeah?"

"You're going to wait for the locals, right?"

My mind fills with images of the torture Scarlett could be enduring right this very minute. I picture Svboda putting his cigarettes out on her flesh. I can practically hear the sound of her screaming ringing in my ears. The bodies of Serena Monroe, Summer Kennedy, and Emily Tompkins flash through my mind. I see every slice, every stab wound, every bruise and broken bone. I see the deep purple bruises that ring their necks and see their wide-open eyes, glazed over, completely lifeless.

"Not sure Scarlett Porter has the time."

"If you go in there alone—"

"I'm not even sure he's there," I cut him off. "I'm playing a hunch."

"And your hunches are usually pretty well spot on."

"I don't want to call in the locals yet, just in case I am wrong. I don't want it blowing back on Rosie or the Field Office," I tell him.

"Fine. Get the lay of the land but seriously, please tell me you won't go in until help arrives," he tells me.

"Standby," I say, getting out of the car. I don't make promises like that when lives are on the line.

I hustle around to the trunk and pop it open. I pull out my Kevlar vest and strap it on, and secure my phone into one of the pockets on the chest. After that, I grab a couple more magazines from the lockbox and slip them into the pouch on my belt. Lastly, I grab the 20ga Mossberg shotgun and rack in the six rounds it holds.

"What's going on, boss?" Rick asks. "I hear something that sounds distinctly like you pumping a shotgun. But that can't be right, because you're waiting for backup, right?"

"There's no time. If Scarlett's in there, he could be cutting on her already," I say. "I need to get in there. She could be dead by the time backup arrives."

The decision made, I close the trunk and use the key fob remote to lock the car, then turn and head into the woods.

"Rick, can you use my phone to track me?"

"Of course, I can."

"Good. Do that," I order. "And guide me toward the cabin. It's blacker than pitch out here."

"Let me go on record to say this is a monumentally bad idea."

"Noted," I reply. "Now guide me."

Gripping the Mossberg tightly, I creep through the undergrowth, carefully but quickly picking my way, trying to avoid making noise as best I can. But even more, to avoid turning an ankle on an exposed root, a rock, or anything else that can snag me. As I move, I take note that there isn't another house around in eyesight. Maybe for miles, for all I know. Svboda's cabin might as well be on an island all its own. It's the perfect place for him to do what he's doing.

"Okay, turn about forty-five degrees to your right. That should put you right on line to the cabin," he says. "You should see the edge of the tree line in about two hundred yards or so."

"Copy that."

A cool wind rustles the branches above my head and stirs the undergrowth beneath my feet. The branches rub together with a dry, scratchy sound, groaning like spirits rising from the grave.

"Okay, I see the edge of the tree line just ahead," I report.

I creep to a screen of bushes just inside the tree line and peer through the thin, spidery branches. The cabin sits about fifty yards beyond, and another fifty yards beyond that is a vast lake. From my position, I can see the trees crowding close to the shore. Some of them are so massive, time has bowed their trunk, forcing their branches down into the water.

The moon slips out from behind the veil of clouds and

glimmers briefly off the surface of the water, turning it into a pool of radiant silver. But then the clouds reclaim the moon, and the light disappears, plunging us back into darkness.

I keep watching the cabin and my heart skips a beat when I see a shadow pass in front of a lighted window. The adrenaline starts as a trickle then begins to flow, quickly becoming a raging torrent.

"Suspect's vehicle, a black Audi A4 is parked in the drive," I say. "We have confirmation that Tony Svboda is here. Call in the locals, Rick. Tell them to send everybody."

"Good. Yes. Excellent idea," he says. "And you'll be waiting until they get there to go in, right?"

I open my mouth to reply, but a bloodcurdling scream shatters the air around me. Just the sound of it sends chills rushing through me, and I shudder.

"Jesus," Rick mutters. "What in the hell was that?"

"That was the sound of time beginning to run out for Scarlett Porter," I say. "Get on the phone with the locals and tell them to hurry."

I disconnect the call and pull the Bluetooth headset out of my ear, tucking it into a pocket. As I do, I hear another agonized wail that makes me grit my teeth. A man's voice echoes through the night. Even from out here, it's clearly audible. Svboda is screaming and shouting vulgarities at Scarlett. He's humiliating her. Degrading her. And I can only imagine that he's picturing his mother as he's doing it.

I get up from my position and cross the yard, freezing for a moment when the shadow passes across the drawn curtain in the window again. Moving low and fast, I make it to the side of the cabin. There's a gap in the curtain, so I press my eye to it and see Scarlett. She's stripped down to her bra and panties, her ankles and wrists bound to the chair by plastic cuffs. I see one eye is already swelling, and a thin rivulet of blood trickles from the corner of her mouth.

Angry welts line her arms and legs, and her shoulder is deeply cut, spilling blood down her chest. I keep looking, but I don't see Svboda anywhere, nor is he still yelling and screaming. My stomach roils and an ominous feeling descends that chills me to the very bone. I turn my gaze back to Scarlett. She's sobbing helplessly, her body shaking. The sight stokes the flames of my anger and sets the bar for my rage ever higher.

I feel his presence behind me a moment before I hear the crunch of the dirt and gravel driveway beneath his boot. Acting purely on instinct, I throw myself backward as hard as I can. A split second later, a thunderous roar splits the world around us, and I watch as a giant flame leaps from the barrel of his shotgun. Chips of wood go flying as his round tears into the siding of his cabin.

The moment I hit the ground, taking most of the blow on my backside, I bring my Mossberg to bear and squeeze off a shot that sends Svboda scrambling backward. The recoil of the shotgun is so powerful, it clacks my teeth together. I feel it reverberating through my entire body. The sound of my gun is still echoing as I jump to my feet and swing around, searching for him. But he's nowhere to be seen.

"FBI, Svboda," I call. "Give it up. It's over. Drop your weapon, get down on your knees, and put your hands in the air!"

The sound of him racking a shell in his shotgun puts a quiver in my heart. He's not going to go down easily. Knowing he's somewhere in the darkness in front of me, I back toward the house. And when I reach the door, I push my way inside and slam it shut, throwing both of the locks. Scarlett looks up at me with her one good eye opened wide.

"FBI," I tell her. "We're going to get you out of here, Scarlett."

"Please. Get me out of here," she cries. "I don't want to die. I want to go home."

"You're not going to die, Scarlett. We're going to get you home," I tell her with more confidence than I feel right now.

I move through the cabin and find the back door—the one he'd slipped out of to get around behind me. I shut and lock that one too. After all my bluster and bravado earlier, right now I'm totally content to hunker down and wait for the cavalry. Svboda seems right at home in the darkness of the woods, while I am most definitely not.

"You shouldn't have come out here."

The voice is deep and gruff, and somehow seems to be coming from everywhere at once. Somehow, the cabin is playing hell with acoustics, making it sound like Svboda is right there beside me when I know he's lurking somewhere in the shadows.

"I'm not going to let you hurt her," I shout back. "You're not going to hurt anybody anymore. You're done, Svboda!"

"We'll see," he replies ominously.

I slip the utility knife out of my boot and use it to slice through Scarlett's bonds. She looks at me with tears streaming down her face and a quavering but hopeful smile on her face.

"Get to one of the back bedrooms. Hide yourself and be very quiet," I whisper to her. "And don't come out until I tell you it's safe."

She gives me a nod and then, silent as a ghost, she disappears down the hall into one of the bedrooms, leaving me alone in the great room. I keep my shotgun at the ready and strain my ears, listening for the slightest hint of movement. But then the front door shatters inward. The sound of it crashing to the ground as loud as thunder fills the room. The shock of seeing

Svboda emerging through the cloud of dust and shattered wood roots me to my spot for a moment.

He raises his shotgun, glaring at me directly in the eye. My insides threaten to turn to mush, and my legs are shaking so horribly, I don't know how I'm managing to stay on my feet. He raises his shotgun, forcing me to dive to the side to avoid the blast that rips through the wall and the fireplace, spraying stone and chips of wood everywhere.

But he's not done. A growl of frustration crossing his lips, he swings around, leveling the barrel of his shotgun at me. I leap to the side once more, this time dropping my shotgun. The idea of going back for it is permanently dislodged from my mind when another blast from Svboda's gun fires again, this time tearing a hole through the floor as I'm reaching for it. I pull my hand back as quickly as if I'd been burned.

Svboda advances on me, keeping his shotgun trained on my face. He's apparently not going to miss for the third time. Just as he reaches me, I lash out with my feet. I score a direct hit, partially collapsing his leg. The knee buckles. He lets out an agonized roar as he falls to the ground with a hard thud.

I press my advantage and dart forward, kicking the shotgun from his grasp. The weapon spins and clatters, eventually ending up in the far corner and discharging. A spray of shrapnel nicks my leg, sending waves of pain like I've never known radiating through every square inch of my body. The pain is hard and blunt, and I feel for all the world like somebody just drove a sledgehammer into my calf. I howl in agony but manage to keep my feet, though I stagger away from him.

I barely have time to right myself before Svboda is back on his feet. Before I can bring the shotgun back up, he drives one of his meaty fists into my face. A sound like wet meat being slapped together fills my ears and my head is propelled backward, quickly slamming into the wall behind me. I'm literally seeing stars bursting behind my eyes, and I feel my blood, warm and viscous, spilling down my face and filling my mouth with its coppery taste.

My eyes are watering and I'm still having trouble seeing past the stars in my eyes. But I manage to see Svboda coming toward me again. He drives his fist into my midsection and the air is driven out of my body with a whoosh. I suddenly feel lightheaded and on the verge of passing out. I see Svboda reaching down for my dropped shotgun, and I have just enough of my wits left about me that I lash out with my foot, sending the shotgun skittering away from me.

Svboda lashes out and catches me with a vicious backhand that rocks my head to the side and I feel my energy leave me all at once. I collapse to my hands and knees, gasping for breath.

"I'm going to kill you," Svboda sneers.

I look up and see him snarling down at me. He's a large man that fills my entire field of vision. He's got wide, sloping shoulders, dark hair, and sapphire blue eyes. I hate to admit it but he's a handsome man, who's got a bit of that Ted Bundy look about him. I can see why he was able to charm these women he's been killing.

"You don't have to do this," I gasp.

"I do. This is who I am," he snarls. "This is who she made me to be."

"Who?"

"Enough talk. I must kill you quickly," he says. "Then I need to find the one you set free. I have plans for her. I cannot deviate from the plan. I have to kill mommy."

"I've seen how your plans play out. Just leave her be, Svboda," I say. "Kill me, if you absolutely have to kill. But leave her alone."

"Shut up! Just shut up!" he screams so loud, it feels like the floor is quaking underneath me.

Svboda snatches up the shotgun and stalks back toward me with it. As he gets in range and starts to bring the barrel up, I shoulder roll toward him, close the gap between us, and drive the bottom of my foot into his knee with all the force I can muster. I feel something give beneath my foot and he howls in sheer agony. Pressing my advantage, I spin around and use my arm to sweep his feet out from under him.

He falls backward, a look of shock on his face. The shotgun hits the wooden floor with a loud bang and goes off, blowing a hole in the wall across from us. Svboda hits the ground hard, and he grunts as the wind is driven from his lungs. Without thinking and heedless of the danger, I throw myself on top of him, straddling his chest, and wildly start to drive my fist into his face.

As I punch him, I feel his nose give way, then his jaw, and watch his face turn to a bloody pulp. I feel an electric thrill run through me.

I hear myself laughing. It's exhilarating.

The feeling pushes me onward, compelling me to keep punching him until my arm grows tired. All I can see is red and I'm unaware of time, completely lost in the moment. I feel like I'm outside of my body, watching this strange animal battering the unconscious man.

The next thing I know, two sets of hands are hauling me off him. I struggle and thrash in their grasp, trying to break free, desperate to finish my destruction. But they hold me fast and I'm unable to slip them. And all the while, I keep hearing a name. My name. They're calling me over and over, and slowly, I start to come back to myself. I open my eyes and look to my left and to my right. And for a moment, I don't recognize either person holding me.

But then all at once, I feel like I've been slammed back into my body with incredible force. I gasp and draw a lungful of air as if I've been holding my breath forever.

"Astra, Mo," I wheeze. "Oh good, you made it."

They both laugh like it's the funniest thing they've ever heard. I'm not thinking very clearly at the moment and don't know what they find so funny. I'm about to ask them to clarify when Astra speaks.

"Yeah, we made it," she says. "But it looks like we already missed one hell of a party."

That sets them both off again, and as they giggle with each other, I'm able to break free of their grasp. Uniformed police are swarming into the cabin, the night beyond lit up by red and blue strobing lights. I stand and stare at the cabin's large, empty great room for a minute as I try to recall where I am and how I got here. My head is spinning, and I feel sick to my stomach. But then I remember what brought me here in the first place.

"The girl," I say as my memories come roaring back. "Where is she? Is she all right?"

"She's fine," Astra tells me. "In fact—"

She never finishes her statement because the girl—Scarlett is her name—wrapped in a blanket, throws herself into me. She squeezes me tightly and sobs.

"Thank you," she gasps. "Thank you, thank you, thank you."

The EMTs have to pry her off me, and I watch numbly as they walk her out of the cabin and to one of the ambulances waiting outside. Astra takes me by one arm and Mo takes the other, and they start walking me toward the door as well.

"What are you doing?" I ask.

"You're going to the hospital," Astra says.

I shake my head and grimace at the shockwave of pain that races through me. "I'm fine. The shot just grazed me. I don't need to go to the hospital."

"Yeah, you do, Supergirl," Mo says.

"They're right. You really do," adds an EMT who takes over for them in guiding me toward an ambulance.

"Svboda," I gasp, suddenly remembering him. "Where is he? What happened to him?"

"Well, the unfortunate thing is, he's going to be all right," Astra says.

"The fortunate thing is that you rearranged his face pretty well, and he's going to be eating through a straw for months."

"Definitely months. Remind me to never get on your bad side," says the EMT with a chuckle.

They load me into one of the ambulances and lay me down on a gurney. Astra is sitting beside me, my hand in hers. She squeezes it gently and offers me a smile.

"We did it, huh? We won?" I ask.

She nods and I see her eyes shimmering with tears. "Yeah. We did it. We won."

I nod to myself. "Good. I'm glad."

THIRTY-SEVEN

Black Tie Burgers, Capitol Hill District; Seattle, WA

I SLIP INTO THE BOOTH, a small grimace touching my lips. It's been a couple of weeks since the ordeal at the cabin, and I'm still healing up. Fortunately, the shrapnel really was just a graze; I'll be limping for a couple more weeks but there's no major damage. Most of the bruises have faded and the swelling in my face has finally gone down. I no longer feel like a balloon in the Macy's Thanksgiving Parade, so I'm counting that as a win. But I will have to wear a soft cast on my right hand for a while yet. It seems as if I fractured a bone in my hand on Tony Svboda's face.

And speaking of Svboda, he really will be eating through a straw for months. He'll also be spending that time in the prison infirmary. Though part of me wants to feel bad for my savagery, I just don't. Sucker had it coming. There was a brief review at the Field Office, but I was found to have acted in self-defense and in the defense of others, and the case was closed—though I did get an unofficial talking to about not letting myself get that

.

out of control again. Rosie told me to blow it off though and said that I did good.

The girl, Scarlett Porter, stopped by my hospital room to check on me every day I was there. She made a game of smuggling in food and other treats for me and couldn't stop thanking me for saving her life. She's a sweet kid who is now apparently thinking about changing her major to criminal justice and applying to go to the academy at Quantico. I gave her my card and told her to call me if she had any questions. I'm sure I'll be hearing from her, which is just fine with me. I'm happy to help in any way I can.

"You're looking better."

I look up from my reverie to see Aunt Annie slipping into the booth across from me. I give her a smile as she takes my hand and gives it a squeeze.

"How are you feeling?" she asks.

"Better," I reply. "I'll be good as new in no time flat."

Annie looks closely at me, and though they're healing, you can still see the bruises. They make her wince.

"I worry about you," she sighs.

"I know you do. But I'm good, Annie. I survived. Beat the bad guy."

"You did," she says softly. "And I'm so very proud of you, Blake."

I look up so suddenly, I nearly give myself whiplash. The look on my face must be comical, because she breaks into laughter. In my whole life, that is the first time Annie has ever said she was proud of me—at least when referencing my career. In all the time I've been with the Bureau, she's either ignored it, or has offered only scathing commentary about my career choice. Hearing her say she's proud of me hits me like a freight train.

"I know I don't say that enough—or really, at all, I suppose," Annie admits. "But it's not that I didn't feel it."

"Thank you, Annie. That means the world to me."

"Your job—it scares me. I don't want to lose you like I lost your mother," she goes on. "But I want you to know that I know the work you do is important. The work you do is good. You save lives, Blake. That girl owes you her life."

I shake my head. "She doesn't owe me anything. That's my job."

Annie offers me a smile and I can see her eyes shimmer with tears. When Annie called me earlier today and asked to get together for dinner, I'd been surprised. And I secretly dreaded it. After the way our last dinner went, I wasn't looking forward to a repeat performance. The last thing I want to do is pick up where we left off and continue arguing with each other.

But Annie is somehow different this time. She seems a little bit lighter of spirit and doesn't seem quite so gloom and doom as she did. It's a remarkable change, because the gloom and doom Annie is the one I grew up with. It's the only one I really know. I'm not really sure who this seemingly lighter and freer Annie is.

"Are you all right, Annie?"

She nods. "I am. I'm—well—a lot has happened since we last spoke. And I wanted to apologize for the way I stormed out on you."

"There's nothing to apologize for. Things were heated, and I think we both said some things," I tell her. "I have just as much to apologize for."

"You don't, Blake. You simply held up a mirror and I didn't like what I saw," she says. "You were right. I have been holding Maisey back and putting my baggage onto her. I've been smothering her with my own fears and insecurities."

I don't know what to say to that, so I fall silent. She gives me a gentle smile.

"Maisey and I had a long heart-to-heart talk, and we both got a lot of things out in the open. Things that have been festering for a long time," she tells me. "It was a painful but ultimately good talk. I truly feel like we are closer than we've ever been."

"Annie, that's wonderful. I am so happy to hear that."

"She told me about Marco. And that it was you who encouraged them to see each other," she smiles

I swallow hard and give her an abashed smile. "I'm sorry I went behind your back like that, Annie. I feel bad that I kept it from you—"

"You were right to do so at the time. I'm sure if you had told me, I would have found some way to screw it up for Maisey. And that's a resentment she would have held onto, driving the wedge further between us," she interrupts. "So yes, even though it did hurt at first, finding out that you had kept it from me, I do understand why you did it and know it was for the best."

This change in Annie is stunning to me. I honestly never expected to hear the things she's saying. It makes me feel bad for all the things I've said and thought about her. It makes me feel even worse that I've spent so much time dodging her and never making an effort to spend time with her.

If I had known she had this inside of her, maybe I would have spent more time with her. But I've never seen this from her before, so how was I supposed to know? I don't know how it's come to pass, but she's an entirely different person than the woman who stormed out of the restaurant on me just a few weeks ago.

"I'm hoping that all three of us—you, me, and Maisey—can all start with a fresh slate. That we can all learn from all these things and grow together, rather than drift apart," Annie continues. "I want us to be a family. A real family, Blake."

"I want that too. More than you know."

"It makes me happy to hear you say that. I can't promise that I won't mess up or fall back into old habits from time to time. But I want you and Maisey to call me out on it rather than stuff it away and let it fester," she says. "I want all of us to be able to communicate with one another. Real honest, open communication."

"I think that would be fantastic. I really do."

"So do I."

We lapse into silence for a moment, and I ponder these changes in her. It's amazing to me to see how hard she's trying to be different. To be better. I think it's a lesson I can stand to learn too. If Annie can learn from her past and her mistakes and strive to be a better person, I can too.

I give her a smile. "So, is this burger place part of your image makeover?"

"Why yes. Yes, it is," she says. "I've spent too many years denying myself the things that sound amazing to me. I haven't had an honest-to-goodness cheeseburger in more years than I can remember. So I thought, what better way to honor this fresh start we're all giving ourselves by indulging in something I've denied myself for too long?"

"I think that's an amazing idea."

The waitress comes to the table to take our order and I give my aunt a smile. Things really are looking up. They're getting better, and I feel like I'm finally getting the family I've been missing. The family I've long desired. And we'll do it one cheeseburger at a time.

THIRTY-EIGHT

Criminal Data Analysis Unit; Seattle Field Office

"OKAY, OKAY, OKAY," I call out as I dance my way into the shop. "It's payday, people."

My team looks up as I step to the front of the bullpen, a smile on my face so wide it feels like it's going to split my cheeks wide open.

"Back from the fiery depths of Hell, huh?" Astra asks.

"I sure am."

"And how is the newest resident demon?" Mo asks.

"Evil as hell," I reply. "He fits right in with the rest of the degenerates."

I spent the last two days at the King County Correctional Facility. That's where they're holding Tony Svboda before trial, so I figured I'd take advantage of the opportunity to interview him. There's value in picking the brains of people like Svboda. There's always a chance to expand our understanding of the human mind. And talking to serial and mass murderers helps me to understand them. Understand their motivations. It helps me to understand why they are the way they are and figure out what went wrong in their lives that led them to the path they found themselves on.

Some people think talking to killers is an exercise in academic masturbation. They think it's a waste of time, and that nothing of value can be achieved from it. I disagree entirely. Understanding the deviant mind can help us single out and identify the risk factors better. And if we can really understand the risk factors, we can better help some people. And if we can identify people who are at risk, it might even be possible to get to some of these people before they make a decision that will destroy not just their life, but the lives of everybody they touch.

If we can learn about the way these people think—what leads them to kill in the first place—we might be able to help stop some of these murders before they happen. If nothing else, learning about their minds teaches me more about my field. And I think it ultimately makes me better at my job. I may not be able to stop every single murderer out there, but maybe I can stop a murderer before he takes more lives.

"So, I do believe that you two need to pay up," I say.

"Pay up?" Astra asks.

"I do recall that a wager was made."

"I remember that," Rick calls out. "I was here for that. I heard it."

"Nobody asked you, new boy," Astra shoots back.

"You and Mo both challenged my profile, if you remember," I say, still grinning wide. "You both believed it was a girl-friend or a fiancée who was Svboda's stressor. It was I who declared the stressor would be a relative—specifically his mother. And I do believe the wager was for one crisp C-note."

Mo and Astra both groan as the memory comes back to

them. Seeing the realization that I won our bet—and they lost—made me laugh out loud. That reaction from them is almost better than the money.

"I'm bringing it to you in pennies," Astra quips.

"And if you further remember, I even went so far as to say he and his mother engaged in a sexual relationship," I add, earning more boos and groans of disgust from my team.

"You can stop right there," Mo calls out. "Nobody wants to hear that!"

"According to Svoboda, his mother was extremely abusive from the time he was young. He detailed dozens of trips to the ER with a host of different injuries, including broken bones, concussions, and one time, a lacerated kidney," I say. "And, yes, cigarette burns."

"Jesus," Astra mutters low.

Everybody shifts in their seats, looking uncomfortable as I run down the laundry list of injuries Svoboda suffered in his life. Given that sort of upbringing, it's not surprising he became a monster filled with nothing but hate and rage.

"The abuse continued for most of his life. He said it only stopped when she became too weak and frail to beat him anymore," I tell them.

"I don't want to feel pity for this guy, but wow," Mo said. "In that sort of toxic environment, is anybody surprised he turned out like he did?"

Nobody said anything. There really wasn't anything that could be said.

"Anyway, according to Svoboda, from the age of thirteen until the day she died, Helen sexually abused him," I say. "And the reason he put his own victims in bodies of water is because his mother tried to drown him in the lake when he was seven years old. That same lake right outside his cabin door, if you're interested. That's why it's significant to him. He almost died in a lake, so others are going to suffer as he did. Symbolically, of course."

More moans and cries of revulsion issue from Mo, Astra, and Rick, which only makes me cackle louder. I let them sit with that for a minute just to torment them. A moment later, the doors to the shop open and the waiters bring in the lunch I ordered to celebrate closing a big case. The smell of roasting meat fills the air as I direct them to just set up in the back of the bullpen.

"Carnitas, chicken, and steak," I tell them. "Tacos, burritos, tostadas... whatever floats your boat. Eat as much as you want. Take plates home. Eat it all if you can."

"You didn't happen to have some beer brought in, did you?" Astra asks.

A Hispanic man carries an ice chest over to one of the tables and sets it down. He flips it open with a smile and gestures for everybody to take a look.

"*Cerveza,*" he tells us.

"I'll have to tell you all to exercise restraint with the beer, though. Seriously, we can't have sloppy drunks wandering the halls."

"Restraint is good advice."

We all spin around to see Rosie standing behind us, her hands on her hips and her eyebrow arched. She's staring straight at me.

"Beer? At the office?" she asks.

"I'm just congratulating my team on another job well done," I say.

The sizzling of the meat on the grill of the taco cart echoes around the room and the air grows thick with the aroma of authentic Mexican spices.

"What brings you down to our totally far and well out of your way basement, Rosie?" I ask, swallowing hard.

"I actually wanted to come down and congratulate you all for cracking that case and doing a stellar job," she says, then pauses. "But now, I suppose I'll be staying for lunch and a beer."

That brought out the cheers and hoots from everybody in the room. I grab a beer from the cooler, pop the top, and hand it to Rosie, then grab one of my own. I tap my bottle against hers and smile.

"Thanks for not busting us. I just wanted to show my team some appreciation."

"I think it's great that you do. That's what leaders do, Blake," she tells me. "Next time, just clear it with me first."

"You got it," I say and tap my bottle against hers again.

"You and your team are doing some great work, Blake. The brass couldn't be prouder," she says. "You can tell how happy they are with you by the number of people falling all over themselves to take credit."

"Yeah well, we know the credit belongs to you," I say. "You're the one who had the faith in me."

"And I always will," she replies. "You produce and you make me look good. How can I not support that whole-heartedly?"

I laugh, knowing it's more than that, but the servers in the back are signaling to me that the food's ready to go. I walk to the front of the bullpen and call for everybody's attention. The room falls silent, and all eyes turn to me. I raise my bottle to them.

"I just wanted to take a minute to say something to you guys," I start. "When we started this team, I honestly had no idea how it was going to work. I had no idea if it would work.

But you have wildly exceeded my expectations. You've wildly exceeded my hopes and dreams for what this team would be.

"I'm proud of each and every one of you. As individuals, you are all amazing, fantastic people. As individuals, you are all incredible FBI agents—and tech gurus too. As individuals, you're great. And as a team, we are amazing together."

That brings applause from our small but mighty team. I give them a moment to bask in it before I start to speak again.

"So anyway, I wanted to say thank you. Astra, Mo, Rick... you are truly the best team a person could ever have. I am proud of each and every one of you," I tell them. "And also, we need to give a big thank you to Rosie for always having our backs. Without her, this team would not exist. So, thank you guys. All of you."

They cheer again and Rosie raises her bottle with a big smile on her face. Rick puts on some music overhead, and for only five people in the shop, the conversation is loud and boisterous. As I watch my team, feeling a powerful sense of satisfaction, I feel my phone buzz in my pocket. I pull it out and see that it's Detective Lee.

I retreat to my office and close the door, then connect the call and press the phone to my ear.

"Hey," I say. "Detective Lee, how are you?"

"We have a problem, Blake," he replies brusquely. "Or rather, you have a problem."

"I've got quite a few. Can you be more specific?"

"Gina Aoki was found dead today," he says.

Time seems to slow down around me. My heart falls into my stomach and a queasy feeling washes over me. I look through my office windows, out to the bullpen, and watched Rosie and my team talking, laughing, and joking with one another. Everybody is eating, drinking, and having a good time. But with six words, Detective Lee brought my whole world crashing down around me. I suddenly feel as if I'm standing among the smoking, charred wreckage of my day.

"Wh—what did you say?"

She was found in her office," Lee says. "Her throat was cut, Blake."

"Jesus."

"Yeah, it was bad. Be glad you weren't at the scene."

Waves of disbelief batter me. They threaten to pull me under and swamp me. But there's something wrong. I can tell. My first clue is that Lee is calling to tell me somebody is dead. Why would he do that? Unless...

"What is it, Detective Lee?" I ask.

"Your card was found on her, Blake," he explains. "And according to her calendar, you are the last person she saw before she died."

"Yeah, we met up to discuss a few things."

"What did you discuss?"

"It was personal," I say.

"Yeah, you may not have much of a choice but to talk about it."

"And why do you say that?"

I hear Lee sigh on the other end of the line. "Torres is gunning for you, Blake. He's using your card and the calendar as proof that you're mixed up in this somehow. He's coming for you."

"Let him come. I have nothing to hide," I say. "I had nothing to do with Gina's death."

"I believe that, but Torres is pushing hard for an investigation into you."

I sigh and feel the bright, happy shine I'd carried around all day dim and then gutter out. The day had been so good too. But I did nothing wrong, and I sure as hell didn't kill Gina. All Torres is doing is trying to either intimidate or sideline me. His dream would be to either get me fired or force me to quit. But I'm not the one in the wrong. I did nothing, no matter what Torres tries to implicate me in.

"Did you hear me, Blake? Torres is coming for you."

"I appreciate you giving me the heads up, Detective Lee."

"What are you going to do?"

"I've done nothing wrong, so let him come."

EPILOGUE

Olympic Sculpture Park; Seattle WA

WITH THE THICK, black clouds overhead, the darkness was nearly absolute. Thunder rumbled in the distance, adding an ominous note to the already somber atmosphere. A gust of wind buffeted him, making Mark shiver and pull his coat around himself even tighter as he grumbled under his breath. His eyes darted everywhere, searching the shadows for the man he was meeting, but as far as he could see, the park was empty, save for him.

Mark paced back and forth in front of the giant stone head in the sculpture park. He had his hands buried deep in his coat pockets and his scarf wound up tight, so it covered the bottom half of his face completely. Beads of sweat rolled down his back, making his shirt stick to his skin uncomfortably. His stomach churned hard. It wasn't that Mark was afraid of Potter. He just found the man deeply unsettling.

It was never good when Potter called. It was even worse when Potter asked for a meet. The man was reclusive, only sticking his head out of his hidey-hole when some bit of terrible business had to be done. And Mark had gotten both the call and the request for a meet both in one day, which set his nerves on edge. His body trembled with nervous energy. He wanted to get this over with, one way or the other, sooner rather than later.

As he paced, he felt the weight of his 9mm in the holster at the small of his back and the cold steel of the .25 in the palm of his hand. He was relatively certain he was faster than Potter and could get the drop on him if push came to shove. It was a worst-case scenario and one he hoped wouldn't come to pass. If things with Potter went sideways, he would be spending the rest of his life—not that he expected there to be much of his life left—on the run, constantly looking over his shoulder.

His employers were not the forgiving sort, and if he failed them, they would come for him and they would come hard. If this meeting went to pot, he fully expected that he wouldn't live to see the end of the week.

"Good evening, Mr. Bahn."

A hot shot of adrenaline flooding through his veins, Mark spun around, his heart racing, ready to pull his hand from his pocket and fire. He relaxed when he saw Potter standing there, but silently chastised himself for not hearing him walk up. That was one of the things that unsettled him the most about Potter. The man seemed to float rather than walk. He always just turned up places. One minute you were alone and the next he was just there. As if he'd materialized out of thin air somehow.

Potter stood there looking at him, an amused smirk flickering across his thin lips. His hands were in the pockets of his dark blue overcoat, he had a red scarf around his neck, and a newsboy cap atop a head of hair that had gone mostly iron gray. Beneath the overcoat, Mark knew Potter would be wearing a natty three-piece suit, complete with a pocket square and a pocket chain attached to a gold pocket watch. The man was a walking anachronism, but even Mark had to admit he had a certain stylishness.

"Oh, I'm sorry. It's Walton this time around, isn't it? Dr. Mark Walton?" Potter said, his voice colored by a faint British accent. "Forgive me, Mr. Bahn. I have no wish to compromise your cover. It's just so difficult to keep up sometimes."

Mark knew Potter had no difficulty keeping up with anything. The use of his real name, as well as his cover name, was a subtle reminder of just who he worked for and what his job was. Mark was no fool and Potter was too smart to make a mistake like that accidentally. Potter knew full well, the value and power of words. Dr. Mark Walton was his cover identity. His real name was Levi Bahn—though he would not speak that name again until this op was completed. Potter knew this every bit as well as he did.

"What can I do for you, Potter?" Mark asked. "Why the meet?"

Potter let out a breath as though emotionally pained to even have to be there and began to pace. He stopped in front of the giant head sculpture, looking at it for a long minute. Then he turned and looked around at some of the other pieces that fill the sculpture park and frowned.

"You Americans have horrendous taste in art," he said. "I don't even understand what half of these things are supposed to be."

Mark shrugged. He couldn't argue that point. Most of what filled the sculpture park he found to be repulsive. But hey, he wasn't an art critic or expert, so what did he know?

"It's cold, Potter. Can we get to the point of this meet?"

The older man smiled softly at him. "That's another thing about you Americans. You're always in such a rush. As they say, stop and smell the roses now and then, lad."

"My nose is so cold right now I couldn't stop and smell anything even if I wanted to," Mark snapped. "So please, tell me what this is about."

"Our employers are... concerned."

"Concerned?"

Potter nodded. "Very much so. They believe you've gotten too close to the girl. They fear your emotional connection to her is clouding your judgment," he continued. "Further, they fear that if you are not in fact, able to control her as you were ordered to do, that you would hesitate to eliminate her. That your feelings are such that they fear you would not only not eliminate her, but that you would betray them as well."

Mark shuddered as he thought about her war room. Thought about all the connections she was starting to make, and how close to the truth she was getting. It worried him like little else did right now. But Potter was right. He did care about her. And despite everything that happened between them, he still felt compelled to protect her.

"That's crap," Mark spat. "I have been loyal to them for more than a decade now."

"This is true," Potter said, his shoes making a hollow thump on the concrete as he paced. "But prior to now, you've never pleaded for the life of one of your marks. You've never intervened on their behalf. If your emotional state regarding this woman is clear, why intercede on her behalf when it became necessary to eliminate her?"

"Because it wasn't necessary. I had the situation well in hand."

"Our employers don't agree. In fact, some believe the situation has passed the point of no return and that you've lost all operational control already," Potter replied, his voice smooth.

"Think about it, Potter. If I eliminate a freaking FBI agent, one who is very well thought of and respected in her field, do you even understand what a can of worms it will open?" Mark almost shouted. "Do our employers know what an avalanche of crap that will unleash?"

A faint smile touched his lips. "I believe they might understand it a little better than you do, Mr. Walton. They have been at this grand game for a long, long time. I dare say your comprehension of the dynamics of this situation pales in comparison to theirs."

"I have it under control and—"

"Do you?" Potter cut him off. "Have it under control?"

The question hung in the air between them, more a challenge than anything. Mark stared him down, his jaw clenched and the anger within him rising like a deep, dark tide.

"Yes. It's under control. It's fine," he growled.

"Then why was she almost allowed to meet with Corden?"

"I took care of that, didn't I?" Mark spat. "The meeting never went off, did it?"

"That was a rather messy affair. As you can imagine, our employers were not well pleased by it."

"The bottom line is that it was handled."

Potter cocked his head and look at him for a long moment. Mark shifted on his feet, feeling uncomfortable beneath the man's gaze.

"If your feelings for her are not conflicted, why do you insist on keeping her alive?" he asked as if he genuinely didn't understand.

"Because there's no reason to kill her. She's a good woman who does a lot of good in this world. To be honest, there are things about her I admire," Mark said. "Killing her would be a waste. Not to mention the fact that, as I said before, the Bureau would bring everything crashing down on me. You. Even the Thirteen."

Potter sighed. "You said you would dissuade her from

looking into the murder of her parents. And yet, she continues doing so. Why have you not put a stop to this already? We understand she found Gina Aoki?"

"She's... difficult. She's determined," he replied. "But I have it in hand. I handled Aoki and the crack in the dam has been plugged. Permanently. That is now a dead end for Blake. She's got nothing and nowhere else to go."

"I do seem to recall you saying that to me before and yet, here we are," Potter pointed out.

"It's handled."

Potter stared into Mark's eyes for a long moment, as if weighing and measuring him. Or perhaps he was just deciding whether to kill him on the spot or not. Mark wasn't sure. He really thought it could really go either way at that moment. But then Potter spoke, breaking the silence.

"I like you, Mr. Bah—Mr. Walton. I believe you are a valuable asset to the group," he said. "But don't think for a moment that if you fail us, or if you betray us, I will put two bullets in you faster than you can blink."

"Understood."

"Make sure to keep her in line."

"I will."

Without another word, Potter turned and walked off. And as Mark watched him go, he thought about how complicated this op had gotten. His job had been simple—watch the girl. Keep tabs on her. Make sure she wasn't making connections regarding her parent's death. And above all, derail her investigation. Keep her from learning the truth.

What had complicated everything was that he'd developed feelings for her. She'd started as a mark, but the more he got to know her, the more he found something different in her. Something special. Something that really clicked with him. It made him feel more than a little conflicted. Especially when it came to eliminating her if the need arose.

No. As he thought about it, Mark knew there was no conflict in his mind. He would not kill her. Period. If the order came down, he would disobey it. He would find some way to get her out from under the kill order. Out from under The Thirteen. Somehow. Someway. The simplest way to keep that order from coming down was to derail her investigation into her parents' death—permanently. And that, he had no idea how to go about doing.

But he needed to figure it out. And fast. Otherwise, they both very well might end up dead.

THE END

NOTE FROM ELLE GRAY

I hope you enjoyed *The Chosen Girls*, book 4 in the *Blake Wilder FBI Mystery Thriller series*.

My intention is to give you a thrilling adventure and an entertaining escape with each and every book.

However, I need your help to continue writing and bring you more books!

Being a new indie writer is tough.

I don't have a large budget, huge following, or any of the cutting edge marketing techniques.

So, all I kindly ask is that if you enjoyed this book, please take a moment of your time and leave me a review and maybe recommend the book to a fellow book lover or two.

This way I can continue to write all day and night and bring you more books in the *Blake Wilder* series.

By the way, if you find any typos or want to reach out to me, feel free to email me at egray@ellegraybooks.com

Your writer friend,
Elle Gray

ALSO BY ELLE GRAY

.

Made in United States
Orlando, FL
02 March 2025

59079763R00164